TWISTED VOWS

BIANCA COLE

Edited by: Liana Valerian

CONTENTS

AUTHOR'S NOTE

Hello reader,

This is a warning: this is a **DARK** mafia romance, much like many of my other books, which means there are very sensitive subject matters and dark, triggering content. If you have any triggers, proceed with caution and read the warning below.

As well as a possessive, dominant anti-hero who doesn't take **no** for an answer and a lot of spicy scenes, this book also addresses sensitive subjects. A list of these can be found on my website: www.biancacoleauthor.com

If you have any triggers, then it's best to read the warnings and not proceed. However, if none of these are an issue for you, read on and enjoy this dark romance.

1

CARMELA

I pull my car into the circular driveway of the Bianchi estate, gravel crunching under the tires. The imposing stone mansion looms ahead, all sharp angles and old money. This place hasn't felt like home since our parents died, but Gio still insists on living here, keeping up appearances and tradition.

"Twice in one week, must be my lucky day," I call out as I spot my brother waiting at the entrance, his tall frame rigid against the ornate doorway.

Gio's face breaks into a smile. "Maybe I just missed my little sister."

"Bullshit." I kiss his cheek. "You never invite me over without a reason."

"Can't a man want to see his sister?"

I follow him through the marbled foyer into his study. The room smells of leather and cigars—Dad's smell. Gio has done everything possible to become our father's ghost, right down to sitting in the same chair behind the massive mahogany desk.

"You look tired," I say, pouring myself a drink from the

crystal decanter without asking. "Business keeping you up?"

"Business always keeps me up." He loosens his tie, watching me. "How's that gallery job going?"

"Boring as hell. Rich people buying art they don't understand to impress people they don't like." I perch on the edge of his desk. "Cut the small talk, Gio. Why am I here?"

He laughs, but it doesn't reach his eyes. "Still impatient as ever. Remember when you were six and couldn't wait for Christmas? You unwrapped all your presents two weeks early."

"And you rewrapped them all so Mom wouldn't find out." I smile at the memory. "But you're stalling."

Gio sighs, leaning back in his chair. His playful expression melts away, replaced by something I rarely see—uncertainty. His shoulders tense as he drums his fingers on the armrest, jaw clenched tight.

My stomach knots. I've seen this look before, right before he told me Dad's rivals had put a price on my head last year.

"Gio?" My voice sounds smaller than I intend. "What's wrong?"

The silence stretches between us, heavy with unspoken words. Whatever he's about to say, I already know I won't like it.

"Carmela." Gio's voice drops, all business now. "I've made an arrangement with another family. For you."

I freeze, glass halfway to my lips. "What kind of arrangement?"

He meets my eyes, unflinching. "A marriage arrangement."

The crystal tumbler slams onto his desk, whiskey sloshing over my hand. "You've done what?"

"It's a good match. Strategic. The paperwork is already—"

"Paperwork?" I laugh, but it sounds more like a growl. "Are you fucking kidding me? You sold me off like I'm property and you're sitting there talking about paperwork?"

Gio rises, palms flat on the desk. "I didn't sell you, Carmela. This is an alliance—"

"An alliance?" I'm shouting now, heart hammering against my ribs. "This isn't the nineteenth century, Gio! Women aren't traded like baseball cards anymore!"

"You know how this works. You've always known—"

"Known what? That my brother would betray me? That I'd be shipped off to some stranger's bed because it's convenient for business?"

His jaw tightens. "Our family needs this. We need the protection, the strength this alliance brings. You've always understood what our name means, what it requires."

"Don't you dare." I step closer, jabbing my finger into his chest. "Don't pretend this is about family duty. This is about power. Your power."

"Three families have moved against us in the last month alone. We're vulnerable, and everyone knows it."

I cross my arms, trying to contain the trembling rage. "So, I'm the sacrificial lamb? Your little sister for your seat at the table?"

Gio's eyes soften. "I wouldn't do this if there was another way. You know that."

"Who is he?" My voice cracks despite my best efforts.

"A good man. Powerful. Respected."

"His name, Gio."

He hesitates. "You'll meet him soon enough. The arrangements—"

"Fuck your arrangements!" I snatch my purse from the chair. "And fuck you for making them without me."

I storm toward the door, tears burning behind my eyes that I refuse to let fall.

"Carmela, please—"

"Don't." I whirl around one last time. "You're not my brother today. You're just another mobster who thinks he owns me."

The heavy door slams behind me with a satisfying bang that echoes through the marble halls of our family tomb.

I storm out of the mansion, heels clicking angrily against the marble steps. The midday sun hits my face, but I barely register its warmth against my flushed skin. My hands shake as I fumble with my car keys, dropping them twice before managing to unlock my Mercedes.

"Fuck!" I slam my palm against the steering wheel once I'm inside, the leather cool against my burning skin. My breath comes in short, angry bursts as I start the engine. The tires squeal against the gravel as I peel out of the driveway, barely missing one of Gio's pretentious garden statues.

Traded away. Like property. Like I'm nothing but a bargaining chip in his power games.

My vision blurs, and I pull over a few blocks from the estate, unable to drive through the rage clouding my mind. I need to get out, I need to do something before I explode. My fingers find my phone and dial the only person who might understand.

Sophia answers on the third ring. "Well, if it isn't my favorite troublemaker. What's up, babe?"

"I need a night out." My voice comes out steadier than I

feel. "Something wild enough to make me forget this whole fucking day."

"Whoa, sounds serious. Are you okay?" Concern colors her tone.

I bite my lip, the urge to spill everything almost overwhelming. But no—I can't talk about it yet, can't make it real by saying it aloud.

"Just family bullshit. Nothing new." I force a lightness I don't feel. "You in or what?"

"Always in. Where are we going?"

A bitter laugh escapes me. "Ironically, I'm thinking of Gio's club. Free drinks and the best DJ in the city. Might as well take advantage of the Bianchi name for something fun."

"Perfect. I've got that new dress I've been saving for something special."

"Wear it. We're not holding back tonight." I check my makeup in the rearview mirror, noticing the fire in my own eyes. "Meet me there at ten?"

"You got it. And Carmela? Whatever happened, we'll fix it."

If only it were that simple. "See you at ten."

2

CARMELA

The pulsing beat of music reverberates through me as I weave through my brother's crowded club. Sophia is close behind me, her hand clasped in mine so we won't get separated in the throng of sweaty, gyrating bodies.

"I need a drink!" I shout over the music, tilting my head toward the bar. Sophia nods in agreement, her dark curls bouncing. We push our way through, finally emerging at the long, polished bar.

I flag down the bartender, a cute guy with a sleeve of colorful tattoos. "Two vodka sodas, please!"

As I wait for our drinks, I let my eyes wander over the club, taking in the flashing lights and the sea of faces. I need to get laid tonight. As of tomorrow, I'll be fucking engaged to some Mafia jerk. Sophia is unaware, since I didn't want to ruin tonight.

My eyes snag on a possible target. Tall, with broad shoulders stretching the fabric of his black shirt. His arms are covered in intricate tattoos, the designs snaking up to disappear beneath his sleeves.

I'm so busy ogling this gorgeous stranger that I don't notice the bartender sliding our drinks across the bartop.

"Your drinks are ready," the bartender says, pulling my attention away from tall, tattooed, and gorgeous. I reach for them just as the mystery man steps up to the bar. As I turn back around, I manage to knock my drink right into him and spill it all down his front.

"What the hell?" he snaps, glaring at me. Up close, he is even more devastatingly handsome, with chiseled features and piercing blue eyes.

"Oh my god, I'm so sorry!" I grab a handful of napkins, pressing them against his damp shirt. He catches my wrist, his fingers easily encircling it.

"I got it," he says gruffly, taking the napkins from me.

"Let me buy you a drink," I offer, feeling my cheeks heat. "It's the least I can do."

He studies me for a long moment, his gaze intense. Finally, he gives a curt nod. "Whiskey, neat."

I signal the bartender and place the order as well as ordering another vodka for myself, sneaking a glance at the man from beneath my lashes. He is still watching me, his expression unreadable.

"I'm Carmela, by the way," I say, offering my hand. "Carmela Bianchi."

Something flickers in his eyes at my last name, there and gone too quickly for me to decipher, as if he recognizes it. Odd. He takes my hand in a firm grip. "Silvo."

I can't help but smile at Silvo's grumpy demeanor. There is something about his brooding intensity that I find irresistible. Not to mention, he's gorgeous. His face is all sharp angles—high cheekbones, a strong jawline covered in dark stubble. His eyes are a piercing blue, framed by thick, dark lashes. He has this intense way of looking at me, as if he can see right through me.

"So, Silvo," I say, leaning against the bar. "What brings you out tonight?"

He takes a sip of his whiskey, his gaze never leaving mine. "Just needed to blow off some steam."

"Rough day?" I ask, my fingers playing with the stem of my glass.

He shrugs, the motion pulling his shirt taut across his muscular chest. "You could say that."

I bite my lip, trying to think of a way to keep the conversation going since he doesn't seem like much of a talker. "Well, you've come to the right place. Nothing like loud music and overpriced drinks to take your mind off things, right?"

He huffs out a laugh, the sound sending a shiver down my spine. "I guess."

I take a sip of my drink, the vodka burning pleasantly as it slides down my throat. "So, what do you do, Silvo? When you're not brooding in clubs, that is."

His jaw clenches, and for a moment I think he isn't going to answer. "I work in the family business," he says finally, his tone making it clear that is all he is going to say on the matter.

I raise an eyebrow, intrigued. "Sounds mysterious. I like a man with secrets."

He leans in closer, his breath hot against my ear. "Trust me. My secrets are the kind you don't want to know."

A thrill runs through me at his proximity and the danger that radiates off him in waves. I know I should heed his warning, walk away before I get in too deep. But I have never been good at doing what I should.

"Maybe I like a little danger," I whisper, holding his gaze.

His hand comes up to brush a strand of hair from my face. "You don't know what you're asking for."

"So show me," I challenge, my heart hammering in my chest.

For a long moment, he stares at me, his expression unreadable. Then, he downs the rest of his whiskey in one swallow and sets the glass down on the bar with a clink, as if he's made a decision.

"Let's get out of here," he suggests.

I don't hesitate, downing my drink and grabbing my purse. Sophia's eyes are on me as I follow Silvo toward the exit, and I glance back at her. She hesitates, then gives me a reluctant thumbs up like she knows she won't stop me.

I smile before following the God of a man out of my brother's club. No one stops me—no one ever does at Gio's club. This is reckless. Exactly what I need.

The moment we slide into the back of the taxi, I can feel the sexual tension crackling between us like a live wire. Silvo's large frame takes up most of the space, his muscular thigh pressing against mine. I try to ignore the heat that rushes through me at the contact.

He gives the driver an address, no doubt his place. As the car pulls away from the curb, I turn to Silvo with a bright smile. "So, where are you from? I detect a bit of an accent."

He grunts, his stare fixed out the window. "Italy. Originally."

"Really? My family is Italian too! What part are you from?" I ask, determined to draw him out of his shell.

"Sicily," he says, clearly not in the mood for small talk.

I refuse to be deterred by his grumpiness. "I've always

wanted to visit Sicily. I hear it's beautiful. The food, the history, the architecture..."

"It's a place like any other," he interrupts, his tone brusque. "Nothing special."

I frown, taken aback by his dismissiveness. "Well, I think it sounds magical. Maybe you could show me around sometime, give me a local's perspective."

He finally turns to look at me, his blue eyes intense. "I don't do tours, sweetheart."

The endearment, spoken in his deep, gravelly voice, does things to me I can't explain. I lick my suddenly dry lips, watching as his gaze drops to follow the movement.

"That's a shame," I say, leaning in closer. "I bet you'd be an excellent guide."

His expression darkens, his hand coming to rest on my thigh. "I can think of better things to do with you than sightsee." His fingers trace patterns on my skin through the thin fabric of my dress.

My breath catches in my throat, desire pooling hot and heavy in my belly. "Is that so?" I manage.

He leans in, his lips brushing the shell of my ear. "Yes, I'd definitely make it worth your while."

A shiver runs down my spine, my eyes fluttering closed as his hand slides higher, skimming the sensitive skin of my inner thigh. "Silvo..."

Just then, the taxi pulls to a stop outside the Ritz Hotel. Either he's visiting, or he prefers hotels to home for hookups. Silvo pulls back, the sudden loss of his touch leaving me aching and wanting. He smirks, clearly aware of the effect he has on me.

"This is our stop," he says. "Coming?"

He pays the driver, and we step out onto the sidewalk. The night air is cool against my flushed skin as he takes my hand, leading me into the opulent lobby. My heart races with anticipation. I barely know this man, and yet here I am, following him to his hotel room like some kind of wanton hussy.

But I can't help myself. There is something about him, a magnetic pull that I'm helpless to resist. As we step into the elevator, Silvo pulls me against him, his strong arms encircling my waist.

"You sure about this, Carmela?" he asks, his lips brushing my temple. "Last chance to back out."

I tilt my head back to meet his gaze, my hands sliding up his muscular chest. "I'm not going anywhere," I reply, rising up on my toes to brush my lips against his.

He groans, his grip on my hips tightening as he deepens the kiss. I melt against him, my fingers tangling in his dark hair as his tongue sweeps into my mouth. By the time the elevator dings and the doors slide open, I'm breathless and weak in the knees.

Silvo leads me down the hall to his room, his hand never leaving the small of my back. He swipes the key card and pushes open the door, ushering me inside. The room is spacious and elegantly appointed, but I barely have a chance to take it in before Silvo is on me.

He walks me backward until my legs hit the bed, and I fall back onto the plush comforter, pulling him down with me. His body is hard and heavy above me, his hands roaming my curves as he kisses me deeply.

I arch into him, my own hands exploring the planes of his back, the coiled strength of his muscles. I want him with a desperation that frightens me, a need that consumes me.

"Silvo." I take a sharp inhale as his lips trail down my neck, his teeth grazing my pulse point. "Please..."

He lifts his head to look at me, his blue eyes dark with

desire. "Please what, sweetheart?" he asks, his voice a low rumble that I feel all the way to my core.

I swallow hard, my fingers digging into his shoulders. "I want you," I whisper, holding his gaze. "All of you."

He stares at me for a long moment, his expression unreadable. Then, with a growl, he claims my mouth once more, his hands making quick work of my dress, dragging it up and off. I surrender, losing myself in the fervor of his kiss, the heat of his skin against mine.

I gasp as Silvo's hands roam my body, leaving trails of fire in their wake. For a moment, I feel a flicker of self-consciousness, but it is quickly extinguished by the hunger in his gaze as he drinks me in.

"God, you're beautiful." His touch skims up my sides to cup my breasts. I arch into him, a moan escaping my lips as his thumbs brush over my nipples.

He lowers his head, trailing kisses down my neck and chest until he reaches my breasts. He takes one nipple into his mouth, sucking and nipping until I am writhing beneath him, my fingers tangled in his hair.

"Silvo, please," I beg, my hips rocking against his. "I need you."

He lifts his head, his gaze dark with desire. "Patience," he says, his hands sliding down my body to grip my thighs and slowly peel my panties off. "I'm going to take my time with you."

And he does. His mouth and hands explore every inch of my skin, leaving me trembling and desperate for more. When he finally settles between my thighs, his breath hot against my most sensitive flesh, I think I might combust from the anticipation.

But then his mouth is on my pussy, his tongue delving into my folds, and I lose all coherent thought. I cry out, my back arching off the bed as he licks and sucks, his fingers joining the assault until I am teetering on the edge of oblivion.

"That's it, baby," he breathes against my skin. "Let go for me."

And I do, shattering apart with a cry of his name, my body shuddering with the force of my release. Silvo pushes me through it, his touch gentling as I slowly come down from the high.

He crawls back up my body, his lips finding mine in a searing kiss. I can taste myself on his tongue, and it only reignites my desire. I reach for him, desperate to feel his skin against mine, but he catches my wrists, pinning them above my head.

"Not so fast," Silvo rumbles, his grip on my wrists tight but not painful. "I'm not done with you yet."

I shiver at the promise in his voice, anticipation coiling low in my belly. "What are you going to do to me?" I whisper.

He gives me a wolfish grin, his eyes glinting dangerously in the low light. "Everything you've ever imagined, and then some."

He releases my wrists and quickly strips off his shirt, shedding the rest of his clothes. A sharp inhale catches in my throat when I see his cock. Thick, veined, and dripping with precum.

He climbs back onto the bed and lifts my hips, spreading my legs wide. I flush under the intensity of his gaze because I'm exposed, vulnerable, but also incredibly turned on. "Such a pretty pussy," he mutters.

With one powerful thrust, he is inside me, filling me up in the most delicious way. I cry out, arching up to meet him as he begins to move.

His pace is unhurried but forceful, each roll of his hips stoking the pleasure inside me higher and higher. My hands roam the hard planes of his chest, nails digging into the inked skin as I urge him on wordlessly.

"That's it, sweetheart," he growls, his own hands gripping my hips hard enough to bruise. "Take it."

I wrap my legs around his waist, changing the angle so he hits that spot deep inside that makes me see stars. My climax is building fast, my body tensing as the pleasure mounts.

"Silvo," I gasp, teetering on the edge. "I'm close..."

His pace increases, his powerful body working mine relentlessly towards ecstasy. "Come for me, Carmela," he commands. "Now."

That is all it takes to send me flying over the precipice with a sharp cry. My vision whites out, distantly aware of Silvo following me over with a low groan.

As I slowly float back down to earth, I become aware of Silvo's weight still pressing me into the mattress. His breath is hot against my neck, his heart thundering against my chest. I stroke his sweat-slicked back lazily, utterly spent and satisfied.

After a long moment, he lifts his head to look down at me, a satisfied smirk playing about his lips. "Told you I'd make it worth your while."

I laugh breathlessly, swatting his shoulder. "Don't get cocky. I'm not that easy to impress."

His grin widens, turning wolfish once more. "Is that a challenge?"

Before I can respond, he rolls us over so I am straddling his waist. His hands come up to grip my hips possessively as he regards me with smoldering eyes.

"Round two?" he suggests, one brow arched.

I bite my lip, feeling him already stirring back to life inside me. I grind my hips against him experimentally, drawing a hiss from his lips.

"Bring it on," I purr, leaning down to kiss him. If one round with Silvo is mind-blowing, I can't wait to see what he will do with an encore.

As his hands slide up to cup my breasts, kneading insistently, I have a feeling I am in for a long night. But I find I don't mind one bit. In fact, I hope it never ends. Reality sucks, and I'll spend as long as possible ignoring it wrapped up in a fantasy with one of the most gorgeous men I've ever met.

3

SILVO

Last night haunts me as I fumble with the last button of my shirt.

Carmela was an inferno in my bed, all passion and desire, but I know she'll be pissed as hell when she finds out I am the man she is to marry. I can't blame her. It was a shitty move on my part, but I wanted her from the moment I saw her across the crowded club.

Grabbing my jacket, I head out, the bright California sun making me squint. Gio has arranged for us to meet at some fancy-ass restaurant downtown.

I merge into traffic, my mind still reeling from the bombshell my father dropped on me last week. Marry a girl from another family? What the fuck is this, the Middle Ages? I've been pissed as hell, ready to tell the old man to shove it where the sun doesn't shine.

But then I saw her at the club last night. Carmela Bianchi. Long dark hair, green eyes that sparkle with mischief, and a body that won't quit. I knew exactly who she was, but she had no clue who I was. I couldn't resist the temptation to approach her, to see if she is as fiery as she looks.

And damn, she was. I smirk to myself as I picture her reaction when she finds out who I really am. She'll be furious, no doubt. But that just makes it all the more exciting. I can't wait to see her passionate anger directed at me.

Maybe this arranged marriage thing won't be so bad after all. Carmela is a wildcat in bed, and I have a feeling life with her will never be boring. I'll have to play my cards right, though. Can't let her know I am actually looking forward to this now.

I pull up to the restaurant and hand my keys to the valet. Time to face the music and officially meet my future bride. I school my features into a mask of indifference, but inside, anticipation hums through my veins.

The restaurant is crowded, the clinking of glasses and cutlery nearly drowning out the smooth jazz playing in the background.

The maître d' leads me to a private room where Gio is already waiting, a glass of scotch in his hand. He stands when I enter, a grin spreading across his face. "Silvo! Good to see you."

"Gio," I greet, shaking his hand firmly before taking a seat across from him, accepting the drink he offers. "So, where's the lovely Carmela?" I ask, trying to keep my tone casual.

Gio chuckles. "She'll be here soon. Probably still getting all dolled up. You know how women are."

I force a smile, my stomach doing a little flip. Yeah, I know exactly how, and I have a feeling she is going to make my life a living hell once she realizes who I am.

The door opens, and Carmela walks in, looking stunning in a form-fitting red dress. Her eyes widen when she sees me, and I can practically feel the anger radiating off her. Oh yeah, I'm in for it now.

Gio stands up, oblivious to the tension in the room. "Carmela! Come meet your future husband, Silvo De Luca."

Carmela's eyes narrow as she stares at me, her jaw clenched tight. I meet her gaze head-on, a slight smirk playing at the corners of my mouth.

I stand up, buttoning my suit jacket as I walk over to her. "It's a pleasure to officially meet you," I say, extending my hand.

She glares at me, ignoring my outstretched hand. "Wish I could say the same," she hisses under her breath so only I can hear.

I chuckle, amused by her sharp-tongued attitude.

Gio claps me on the shoulder, oblivious to the tension between us. "Why don't we all sit down and enjoy this lovely meal?"

We take our seats, Carmela purposefully choosing the chair furthest from me. The waiter brings out a bottle of expensive red wine and begins pouring it into our glasses.

"So, Silvo," Gio says, swirling the wine in his glass. "I trust you'll take good care of my little sister."

I nod, my eyes never leaving Carmela's face. "Of course. She'll want for nothing as my wife."

Carmela scoffs, taking a large gulp of her wine. "Except maybe happiness and freedom," she mutters.

I lean forward, my elbows resting on the table. "Now, now, Carmela. Let's not start off on the wrong foot. I think you'll find that being married to me has its perks." I let my gaze travel slowly down her body, appreciating the way the red dress hugs her curves.

She slams her glass down, the wine sloshing over the

rim. "I'm not some prize to be won, Silvo. And I certainly don't appreciate being lied to and manipulated."

Gio frowns, looking between us. "What's this all about?"

I sit back in my chair. "It seems your sister and I already had the pleasure of meeting. Last night, in fact."

Carmela's cheeks flush red with anger and embarrassment.

Gio's eyes widen in surprise before he lets out a hearty laugh. "And she didn't know who you were!"

I chuckle, reaching for my wine glass. "Clearly not. But I look forward to getting to know Carmela better." I raise my glass in a toast, my eyes locked with hers. "To our future together, Miss Bianchi."

Carmela glares at me, her grip tightening on her own glass. I can tell this is going to be a bumpy ride, but I do love a challenge. And Carmela Bianchi is shaping up to be the biggest challenge of my life.

After a tense meal, Gio receives a call and swears. "Sorry. I've got to take this." He glances between Carmela and me. "Hopefully, you can handle yourselves for a bit without killing each other."

Carmela glares at me as her brother leaves the room. The tension crackles between us like a live wire.

"You knew," she accuses, jumping to her feet. "You knew who I was last night and you still..."

I lean back in my chair. "So what if I did?" I shrug, my eyes boring into her. "We're going to be married anyway. Might as well see if we're compatible in bed."

She scoffs. "Compatible? Is that what you call manipulating me into sleeping with you?"

I huff a laugh. "Don't act like you didn't enjoy it,

Carmela. The way you moaned my name, begged me for more..."

Her cheeks flush bright red at my words. "That's not the point," she snaps. "You lied to me. You took advantage of me."

I stand up. "I didn't lie. I just didn't tell you everything. You wanted it just as much as I did." I move closer. "In fact, I remember you coming on pretty strong, telling me you wanted to learn my secrets."

I see the anger flash in her eyes at my words, but something else too. That spark of desire she is trying so hard to hide.

"I didn't know who you were," she bites out, rising to her feet to face me. "And I certainly didn't beg. You're delusional if you think—"

"Didn't you?" I cut in, stepping closer, invading her personal space. "Maybe you're not as innocent in this as you think."

Her breath quickens, her chest rising and falling in that damn dress that shows off her curves. "As if you'd let anyone take advantage of you," she scoffs, eyes flicking over me with a hint of challenge. "Mr. Brooding Mafioso. Too tough for anyone, right?"

I'm enjoying this volatile side of her. "You think you know me, Carmela? You have no idea." I lower my voice. "But you will. Soon enough."

She narrows her eyes, the spark turning into a burning flame. "Is that a threat, Silvo? Because let me tell you, I'm not some frightened little mouse you can push around."

"Threat?" I laugh, taking a step closer, so our bodies are nearly touching. "Carmela, if anything, it's a promise. A promise that you're going to enjoy being my wife a hell of a lot more than you think."

Her cheeks flush, and damn if my body doesn't react to the flash of desire in her eyes. She wants to deny it; I can see the war going on within her, but the attraction remains, whether she likes it or not.

She lowers her voice, her face inches from mine. "You wish."

Neither of us backs down. I let my gaze drop to her lips, remembering the feel of them against mine. "We both know it's not just my wish, baby."

She inhales sharply, her chest rising, our lips inches apart.

The door to the private room swings open, the moment shattering as Gio reappears, saving us or interrupting—I'm not sure which. We step apart quickly, our gazes locking once more, a silent challenge passing between us.

Carmela smooths her dress, regaining her composure, but I know she feels the same electricity buzzing between us. It is a game of cat and mouse, and I have a feeling I've met my match.

Gio raises an eyebrow at us, his lips twisting in amusement. "Well, well. Seems like you two have already gotten well acquainted. Excellent." He claps me on the shoulder, his eyes gleaming with satisfaction. "Let's get down to business then, shall we?"

Let's get down to business indeed. After not being keen on this marriage, I can't wait to make Carmela Bianchi my wife.

4

CARMELA

"I can't believe this!" I yell, slamming my purse down on the kitchen counter.

Sophia jumps, nearly spilling her glass of wine. "Whoa, what's got you so worked up?"

I pace back and forth, fuming. "My idiot brother Giovani, that's what! He arranged for me to marry some mafia guy from a rival family. Without even asking me!"

"What?" Sophia gasps. "He can't do that! Can he?"

"Apparently, he can," I say bitterly. "It's to *unite the families* or some crap like that. Never mind what I want."

I collapse onto the sofa, holding my head in my hands. Sophia sits down next to me, rubbing my back soothingly.

"That's so messed up," she says. "You deserve to be with someone you actually love, not some random guy."

I look up, my eyes blazing. "Oh, it gets even better. I've already met the guy Giovani wants me to marry."

Sophia's eyes widen. "You have? When?"

"Last night at the club," I say. "Tall, muscular, tattoos everywhere. We bumped into each other at the bar and ended up flirting. And then..." I trail off, my cheeks flushing at the memory of what happened next.

Sophia gasps again. "Wait—the guy you left with last night?"

I bite my lip sheepishly. "Yeah. We couldn't keep our hands off each other. It was so intense and passionate."

Despite my anger, I can't help but smile a little, remembering Silvo's kisses, his hands on my body.

Sophia fans herself dramatically. "Wow, sounds steamy. So the guy you left with last night—you had no idea who he was?"

"None," I say, my smile fading. "But then today, Gio introduced me to him. I walk into the restaurant and find the man I fucked last night sitting at the table, smirking." I groan, dropping my head into my hands. "Of all the guys in that club, I had to hook up with my future husband. The one I'm being forced to marry against my will!"

"Oof, awkward," Sophia grimaces.

"It's so unfair!" I cry. "Silvo is incredible in bed, but I don't even know him. And now I'm expected to just marry him, no questions asked?" I jump to my feet, resuming my angry pacing. "That's not even the worst part," I continue. "Get this. I'm going to be forced to move all the way to Philly with him!"

Sophia's eyes widen in shock. "What? Philly? But that's so far from LA!"

I throw my hands up in exasperation. "I know! Giovani calmly informed me that Silvo is from Philadelphia, so I'll be expected to relocate there after the wedding."

I collapse onto the sofa again, utterly defeated.

Sophia looks stricken. "But... but Carmela, your whole life is here!" she cries. "Your family, your friends, everything you know is in LA!"

I bury my face in my hands. "Tell me about it," I moan. "I'll be completely isolated in a strange city, married to a virtual stranger. It's like a nightmare."

Sophia wraps her arms around me tightly. "That evil brother of yours!" she says vehemently. "How could he do this to you?"

I shake my head wordlessly. We sit in silence for a minute, contemplating the mess I'm in.

"Maybe I should run away," I muse. "Disappear somewhere Giovani would never find me."

Sophia looks thoughtful. "You know, that's not a terrible idea. I have an aunt in Seattle who would take you in, no questions asked."

I consider it briefly, but then shake my head again. "He'd hunt me down in no time. When it comes to family matters, there's no one more ruthless than Gio."

Sophia sighs. "Yeah, you're probably right." She gives me a sympathetic pat on the back.

I wipe at my eyes, which are starting to fill with angry tears. "I just feel so powerless, like I have no say in my own future."

Sophia hugs me again. "We'll figure something out," she promises. "I'm here for you, no matter what."

I manage a small, grateful smile. At least I have my best friend on my side. But the rest of my life is spiraling rapidly out of control.

Sophia gets up and heads to the kitchen, returning a moment later with a generous glass of red wine.

"Here, drink this," Sophia says, pressing the glass into my hand. "I'm ordering us pizza too. Pizza makes everything better."

I take a long sip, letting the rich wine slide down my

throat. "Thank you, Soph," I say. "I don't know what I'd do without you right now."

She waves her hand dismissively. "Oh stop, you know I'm always here for you." She picks up her phone to call our favorite pizza place.

While she orders, I nurse my wine, feeling some of the tension start to ease from my shoulders. Sophia is right—between the wine and the cheesy deliciousness on its way, I am already feeling a little less stressed.

My best friend just gets me, always knowing how to make me feel better. She never judges, never pushes me to open up before I'm ready. With everything going on, I need that unconditional support more than ever.

Sophia hangs up the phone. "Alright, pizza will be here soon. In the meantime..." She tops up both of our wine glasses.

I smile, some of my spark coming back. "Well in that case, cheers!" We clink glasses and I take another sip. Having Sophia here reminds me that I'm not alone, that she has my back no matter what.

"Thank you, seriously," I say. "Just having you here, being able to vent and cry and curse out Giovani—it helps more than you know."

"Of course, what are best friends for? Now drink up, pizza will be here any minute!"

I laugh and take another big gulp of wine, feeling bolstered by my best friend. With Sophia's support, I know I can handle whatever curveball my brother decides to throw at me next. The problem is, once I'm married I won't have her support. I'll be on the other side of the country, thousands of miles away.

5

SILVO

I adjust my tie in the mirror, making sure everything is perfect. It's not the grand wedding I had always imagined, but given the circumstances, an intimate affair is probably for the best. Since the tense meeting with her brother last week, I haven't seen Carmela. According to him, she's still pretty pissed about the whole arranged marriage thing. Can't say I blame her.

My nerves are on edge. I'm not usually the type to get anxious, but something about Carmela gets under my skin. Maybe it's the way she challenges me, unafraid to speak her mind. Or maybe it's the memory of our passionate night together, the way her body felt against mine...

I shake my head, pushing those thoughts aside. Today is about business, about solidifying the alliance between our families and expanding into California. I can't let my personal feelings get in the way.

A knock at the door interrupts my train of thought. "Come in," I call out, turning away from the mirror.

My brother, Federico, enters looking dapper in his charcoal suit that matches mine. "Ready, bro?" he asks with a grin.

I nod. "As I'll ever be."

We head out to the waiting car, the driver holding the door open for us. As we slide into the backseat, I can't help but wonder what Carmela is feeling right now. Is she as nervous as I am? Is she angry, or has she resigned herself to her fate?

I guess I'll find out soon enough. For better or worse, we're about to become husband and wife. And despite the unconventional circumstances, a part of me can't help but feel a thrill of excitement at the prospect of spending my life with such a stunning and passionate woman.

The car ride to the church drags on forever, even though it's only a few minutes. I fidget with my cufflinks, trying to distract myself from the churning in my stomach.

Fed notices my restlessness and nudges me. "Relax. It's not like you're marrying a complete stranger. You've already had a taste of the goods, if you know what I mean." He waggles his eyebrows.

I shoot him a glare. "Shut up, Fed. This isn't about that."

"Oh, so you're telling me you're not looking forward to the wedding night?" He smirks, enjoying my discomfort.

I can't help but let out a chuckle. "You're an ass, you know that?"

"Hey, trying to lighten the mood." He holds up his hands. "But seriously, Silvo, you got this. Carmela's a lucky girl."

I nod, appreciating his support even if he shows it in his own obnoxious way. "Thanks, little brother."

The car pulls up to the church and we climb out, straightening our suits. I take a deep breath, as we make our way inside.

White flowers and candles decorate the altar, creating a soft and romantic atmosphere.

I take my place at the front, Fed standing beside me as my best man.

As we wait for the ceremony to begin, I can't help but let my mind wander to Carmela. What will she be wearing? How will she look walking down the aisle toward me?

Federico leans in. "Ten bucks says she trips on her way up here."

I elbow him in the ribs. "Have some respect, jackass."

He just shrugs, unrepentant. "What? It would make for a memorable story."

I shake my head, but I'm grateful for his presence. Having him here helps ease some of the tension I'm feeling.

The music starts up, signaling the beginning of the ceremony. I square my shoulders as I prepare to face my future wife.

The music swells and the church doors swing open, revealing Carmela in all her breathtaking glory. A sharp inhale catches in my throat. She's wearing a form-fitting white gown that hugs her curves in *all* the right places, the delicate lace bodice showcasing her smooth, olive skin. Her dark hair is swept up in an elegant updo, a few loose tendrils framing her face.

But it's her eyes that captivate me. Those piercing green eyes that had first drawn me to her that night in the club. They lock onto mine as she begins her slow march down the aisle, her gaze unwavering.

In that moment, any lingering anxiety I had about this arranged marriage fade away. Seeing Carmela walking toward me, looking like a fucking goddess, I've never felt surer about anything in my life.

She reaches the altar and hands her bouquet to her

maid of honor, Sophia. As she turns to face me, I can see the mix of emotions playing out on her face. Nervousness, excitement, and a hint of that addicting defiance that I admire.

I reach out and take her hands in mine, marveling at how perfectly they fit together. "You look incredible," I murmur.

A faint blush colors her cheeks, but she lifts her chin defiantly. "Let's get this over with," she mutters, her tone clipped.

Even on our wedding day, she's determined to fight.

The priest begins the ceremony, but I barely hear his words. I'm too focused on the stunning woman before me, aware of the way her hand trembles in mine.

When it comes time for the vows, I repeat the traditional words without hesitation. "I, Silvo De Luca, take you, Carmela Bianchi, to be my lawfully wedded wife..."

But when it's her turn, Carmela falters. She clears her throat, her gaze darting away from mine. "I, Carmela Bianchi, take you...Silvo De Luca...to be my husband." Her voice is barely above a whisper, the words forced out through gritted teeth.

She may not like it, but this marriage is happening whether she wants it or not.

The priest pronounces us husband and wife, and I don't waste a second. I pull Carmela into my arms, my lips claiming hers, sealing our vows.

She stiffens against me, her hands coming up to push at my chest. But I don't let her go. I deepen the kiss, my tongue delving into her mouth, tasting her like I've been fucking starving. In all honesty, I have been starving without her.

After a long moment, she relents, her body melting into

mine. I can feel her surrender, feel the way she yields to my dominance.

When I finally release her, she's breathless and flushed, her lips swollen from my kiss. I can't help but feel a sense of satisfaction at the dazed look in her eyes.

"You're mine now," I murmur, my hand cupping her cheek. "And I always take care of what's mine."

She jerks away from my touch, her eyes flashing with anger. "I don't belong to anyone," she hisses. "Least of all you."

"We'll see about that, *cara mia*. We'll see."

With that, I take her hand and lead her back down the aisle, ignoring the murmurs and whispers of the guests. Let them talk. As far as I'm concerned, Carmela is the only one who matters now.

She may not have chosen this marriage, but I have no doubt that in time, she'll come to accept her place by my side. And until then? Well, I've always enjoyed a challenge.

6

CARMELA

I glare out the window as the car speeds toward the reception venue, my blood boiling with barely contained rage. How dare Gio do this? How dare my own flesh and blood sell me off like some prized cow to the highest bidder?

I didn't ask for this. I didn't want any of it. And yet here I am, trapped in a loveless marriage to a man I barely know, all because my bastard brother decided it was good for *business*.

My hands clench into fists, nails digging into my palms. The pain is a welcome distraction from the suffocating reality closing in around me. I can still feel Silvo's lips on mine, claiming me in front of everyone as if I'm now his property. The memory makes me want to scrub my mouth raw.

Beside me, the devil in question reaches over to place his hand on my thigh and I flinch away from his touch. "Don't," I hiss through gritted teeth, not even bothering to look at him.

"Carmela..." He starts, but I cut him off with a sharp shake of my head.

"I said don't." My voice is pure venom, each word dripping with barely restrained fury. "You don't get to touch me. Not now, not ever."

Silvo sighs and withdraws his hand. "This wasn't my choice either, you know. I'm trying to make the best of a difficult situation."

A harsh bark of laughter escapes my throat. "Well congratu-fucking-lations, you must be so proud of yourself." I finally turn to face him, my eyes blazing. "Meanwhile, I'm being ripped away from everything and everyone I've ever known and loved. My home, my family, my friends... all gone. And for what? So you and your family can get a bit more power?"

Silvo at least has the decency to look somewhat ashamed. Good. He should be. They all should be.

I turn away again, blinking back the angry tears that threaten to spill down my cheeks. I refuse to let him see me cry. I refuse to let any one witness how much this hurts.

But god, it hurts so fucking much. The thought of leaving Los Angeles, of leaving Sophia and the only life I've ever known... it's unbearable. This is my home. These are my people. And now I'm being forced to abandon it all and start over somewhere else with a stranger.

I can feel Silvo's eyes boring into me, but I refuse to meet his gaze. The tension in the car is thick enough to cut with a knife.

"Carmela," he says, his voice softer than I've ever heard it. "I understand that you're upset. But this bratty behavior ends now."

My head snaps toward him, eyes narrowing into slits. "Excuse me?"

"You heard me." He leans in closer, invading my personal space. "I won't tolerate tantrums or disrespect. Like it or not, we're married now. That means you will show me the proper respect as your husband."

I let out an incredulous laugh. "Respect? You want me to respect the man who helped rip me away from my entire life? Fat fucking chance."

Silvo's jaw clenches, but he doesn't rise to the bait. "I know this isn't ideal for either of us. But I'm trying to make this transition as smooth as possible for you. Fighting me every step of the way will only make it harder."

"Oh, well, thank you so much for your consideration," I bite out sarcastically. "How very noble of you."

He sighs, pinching the bridge of his nose. "Carmela, please. Can we just... start over? I promise I'll do everything in my power to help you adjust to your new life in Philadelphia. It won't be easy, but we can make this work if we try."

I cross my arms over my chest. "And what if I don't want to try? What if I refuse to play along with this farce of a marriage?"

Silvo's expression hardens. "Then you'll leave me no choice but to take a firmer hand. I don't want it to come to that, but I will if necessary. Don't test me on this."

I swallow hard; the thinly veiled threat makes my stomach churn. This man is dangerous; that much is clear. He may put on a charming front, but beneath that polished exterior lies a ruthless criminal who always gets what he wants.

And right now, what he wants is my obedience. My submission. He expects me to just shut up and play the dutiful wife, no matter how much it kills me inside.

Well, screw that. Screw him. I didn't survive growing up

in a mafia family by rolling over and letting men walk all over me. I have a mind of my own, and I'll be damned if I let Silvo De Luca crush my spirit.

I meet his steely gaze head-on, lifting my chin in defiance. "Do your worst then. But know this, you can force me to marry you, but you can't force me to respect you. Or desire you. You'll never have my heart or my willing participation in this sham. I'll fight you every step of the way."

Silvo's eyes flash with a dark and primal spark. "Willing participation? Oh, I think you'll find I can make you very willing."

His large hand suddenly grips my thigh hard, and I gasp at the contact, my heart hammering against my ribs. I try to jerk away, but his fingers only tighten, digging into my flesh through the fabric of my dress.

"I was trying to be a gentleman. Attempting to ease you into all of this." His voice is a low rumble that resonates through my body. "But if it's a fight you want, then it's a fight you'll get. Just remember, I have no qualms about conquering and claiming what's mine. By any means necessary."

Silvo's hot and hungry gaze lingers on my heaving chest and parted lips. I feel stripped bare before him, completely at his mercy. A thrilling concoction of fear and anticipation unfurls deep in my core.

"You may not like it now, but I guarantee you'll be screaming my name in pleasure before long," he promises. "I'll have you begging me for more. Just wait."

With that, he releases my thigh and exits the car, leaving me shaken and breathless in his wake. I have no doubt Silvo intends to make good on his word.

I just pray I'm strong enough to resist him when he does.

7

SILVO

I take a deep breath, watching Carmela glare at me from across the private jet. The tension in the air is palpable as she stubbornly refuses to acknowledge my presence, arms crossed over her chest.

"You can't ignore me forever," I say, my voice low and even. I reach out, grasping her arm and pulling her toward me. She resists at first, but I'm stronger, and soon she finds herself perched precariously on my lap.

"Let go of me!" She hisses, her body tense and vibrating with fury. I can see the pulse throbbing in her neck, betraying the arousal I know she's trying to conceal.

"Not until you stop acting like a petulant child," I murmur, my hand sliding around her waist to hold her in place. "We're in this together, whether you like it or not."

Carmela's eyes flash with defiance. "I never asked for this," she spits. "You and your family forced this on me. How dare you act like I should just accept it?"

"Accept it?" I force her closer until our faces are mere inches apart. "I think you're forgetting that I didn't have a choice in this either. But I'm done fighting it." My hand slides up her thigh, eliciting a shiver that she tries in vain to hide. "And I have a feeling you are too."

Carmela's breath catches, her lips parting as she searches my gaze. The fire in her eyes has been replaced by a smoldering heat. "I'll never accept this," she whispers.

"We'll see about that," I capture her lips in a kiss.

They yield under mine, her resistance crumbling as a soft moan escapes her throat. The sound sends a thrill of satisfaction through me, knowing that despite her defiance, she can't resist the attraction between us.

My tongue delves into her mouth to claim her more fully. Carmela's fingers slide into my hair, gripping the strands as she presses herself against me. I can feel the curves of her body molding to mine, igniting a hunger that threatens to consume me.

Breaking the kiss, I trail my lips along her jaw, nipping at the sensitive skin below her ear. "Is this bringing back memories, Carmela?" I murmur. "Are you thinking about me fucking you? The way you felt writhing beneath me, the way I made you come undone?"

Carmela shudders, her nails digging into my shoulders. "Silvo..." she breathes, and the sound of my name on her lips is nearly my undoing.

When our lips meet again, the kiss turns desperate. My hands roam her body, exploring her curves and seeking out the most sensitive spots. Carmela arches into my touch, her hips rolling in a way that makes me groan.

"Tell me you want me," I growl against her lips. "Tell me you need me as much as I need you."

Carmela hesitates, a flicker of uncertainty in her eyes. But then she's kissing me again, her tongue tangling with mine in a dance of surrender.

I smirk against her mouth as Carmela breaks away from

our heated kiss, her chest heaving and eyes flashing with a mix of desire and anger.

"You're an asshole," she hisses, shoving at my chest. But I don't let her go, my hands gripping her hips.

A low chuckle rumbles in my throat. "An asshole you can't resist," I murmur, trailing my fingers up her thigh.

Carmela shivers even as she glares at me. "Don't flatter yourself," she snaps. "I'm not some swooning damsel ready to fall into your arms."

"No, you're not," I agree, my voice dropping to a husky whisper. "You're a fiery little minx who likes to play hard to get. But we both know the truth, don't we?"

I lean in, my lips brushing the shell of her ear. "You want me, Carmela. You crave my touch, my kiss, the way I make you feel. Denying it only makes you want it more."

Carmela sucks in a sharp breath, her fingers curling into my shirt. "You're delusional," she says, but her voice wavers.

"Am I?" I pull back to meet her gaze, my eyes boring into hers. "Then tell me to stop. Push me away."

For a long moment, we stare at each other, the tension crackling between us. I can see the war raging in Carmela's eyes, the battle between her pride and her desire.

Then, with a muttered curse, she grabs my face and crashes her lips against mine again. I growl in satisfaction, my arms wrapping around her waist to pull her flush against me.

I match her passion, my hands roaming under her shirt to feel the soft skin beneath.

"Fuck, Carmela," I groan as she grinds against me. "You drive me crazy."

She laughs breathlessly, nipping at my bottom lip. "Good. Someone needs to keep you on your toes."

I grin, my hands gripping her ass to pull her harder against my aching cock. "Oh, I think we'll be keeping each other on our toes for a long time to come, Mrs. De Luca."

Carmela's eyes darken at the use of her new title, a shiver running through her. "We'll see about that, Mr. De Luca," she whispers, before pushing herself off my lap and returning to the seat opposite, pinning me with a defiant glare.

This is going to be one hell of a ride, and I can't fucking wait.

8

CARMELA

My eyes widen as I step out of the car, taking in the sight before me. Silvo's home is a sprawling mansion, all elegant lines and stately grandeur. The immaculate landscaping and towering white columns make it look like something out of a fairytale. I glance over at Silvo uncertainly as he comes around to my side, offering his arm.

"Shall we, Mrs. De Luca?" His voice is tinged with amusement.

I scowl but take his arm, letting him lead me up the front steps. The massive wooden doors swing open, and suddenly we're engulfed in a whirlwind of activity.

An older couple rushes forward, the woman embracing Silvo tightly. "Oh my boy, welcome home!" She pulls back, her eyes falling on me. "And this must be your bride! Carmela, yes? We've heard so much about you."

I paste a smile on my face, trying to mask my discomfort as she pulls me into a hug. Over her shoulder, I see Silvo smirking. Bastard. He's enjoying this.

"Mother, Father, may I present my wife, Carmela?" Silvo takes my hand, tucking it into the crook of his elbow.

Mr. De Luca steps forward, taking my hand and placing a kiss on my knuckles. "Welcome to the family, my dear. We're so pleased to have you. I'm Antonio, and my wife is Giulia." He gestures to an older woman who smiles warmly at me.

"Thank you," I murmur. "You have a lovely home."

"Ah, and here comes my baby brother now," Silvo says, his tone teasing. "Late as usual."

I turn to see the younger version of Silvo striding toward us, the same man who'd stood by his side at the wedding and I spoke with briefly at the reception. "I prefer to think of it as making an entrance," he says, punching Silvo in the shoulder. He turns to me, his blue eyes twinkling. "It's good to see you again so soon. How are you feeling after marrying this loser? I almost forgot how beautiful you are. Silvio is a lucky man indeed."

Federico was the only family member of Silvo's who attended the wedding. I watch the two brothers banter back and forth, Silvo rolling his eyes at Federico's quips.

"Watch it, little brother. That's my wife you're talking to," Silvo growls, pulling me closer to his side.

Fed throws his hands up in mock surrender. "My apologies, oh great one. I forgot how protective you are of your things."

"Carmela is not a thing," Silvo says, his voice taking on a hard edge. "She's my wife, and you'll treat her with respect."

I glance up at him, surprised by the vehemence in his tone. Maybe there's more to this man than I thought.

Fed is unfazed, grinning conspiratorially at me. "Don't let him fool you, Carmela. Underneath that tough exterior beats the heart of a hopeless romantic. Did he tell you about the time he tried to serenade a girl from outside her window?"

"Fed!" Silvo barks, his cheeks reddening.

I can't help but giggle at the image of Silvo, the big bad mafioso, crooning love songs in the moonlight. He shoots me a betrayed look, and I quickly school my features.

"Sounds like there's a lot I don't know about my husband," I say, arching a brow at him. "Perhaps you'd be willing to fill me in, Fed?"

The younger De Luca brother grins, slinging an arm around my shoulders. "It would be my pleasure, sister. Did Silvo ever tell you about the summer we spent at Lake Como? There was this girl..."

"Alright, that's enough," Silvo interrupts, steering me away from his brother's grasp. "Carmela doesn't need to hear any more of your tall tales."

Fed pouts, but there's a mischievous glint in his eye. "Spoilsport. Fine, I'll behave. For now." He winks at me before sauntering off, whistling a tune.

Silvo sighs, pinching the bridge of his nose. "I apologize for my brother. He's always been a bit...much."

"I like him," I say honestly. "He seems fun. Unlike some people I know."

Silvo gives me a stern look. "Careful, wife. Keep talking like that and I might start to think you prefer my brother's company to mine."

"Well, he does have better stories," I tease, feeling a thrill at the way his eyes darken.

"Stick with me, baby. I'll show you a real good time." His voice is a low rumble that sends shivers down my spine.

As Silvo leads me further into the house, I spot a beautiful dark-haired woman descending the grand staircase. She has the same striking blue eyes as Silvo and Fed.

"Isabella," Silvo greets her warmly, placing a kiss on her cheek. "I'd like you to meet my wife, Carmela."

Isabella turns to me. "It's a pleasure to meet you, Carmela. Welcome to the family."

Her voice is soft and melodic, a stark contrast to Fed's boisterous energy. I find myself instantly drawn to her calm presence.

"Thank you. It's wonderful to meet you as well." I return her smile, feeling a bit more at ease.

"I hope my brothers haven't been too overwhelming," she says, shooting Silvo a look. "They can be a bit... enthusiastic at times."

Silvo scoffs, but I can see the affection in his eyes. "We're excited to have a new member of the family, that's all."

Isabella rolls her eyes good-naturedly. "Of course you are." She turns back to me, her expression softening. "I know this must be a lot to take in. If you ever need someone to talk to, I'm here."

I feel a lump form in my throat at her kindness. "Thank you, Isabella. That means a lot."

She nods, giving my hand a gentle squeeze. "You're one of us now. We take care of our own."

I glance at Silvo, seeing the pride shining in his eyes as he watches our exchange. Maybe being a part of this family won't be so bad after all.

As we settle into our seats at the lavishly set dining table, I can't help but feel a bit overwhelmed. The De Lucas spare no expense, from the glittering chandeliers overhead to the fine china and crystal glasses before me. Silvo pulls out my chair, ever the gentleman, and I sit down gingerly, smoothing my dress over my lap.

The first course is served, a delicate soup that I can barely pronounce. I take a tentative sip, my eyes widening at the explosion of flavors on my tongue. Beside me, Silvo chuckles at my reaction.

"Good, isn't it?" he murmurs, leaning in close. "Our chef is world-renowned."

I nod, taking another spoonful. Across the table, Fed regales us with tales of his latest conquest, a model he met at a party in Milan. Giulia tuts disapprovingly, but I can see the amusement dancing in her eyes.

"Federico, please. We have a guest," she chides.

Fed grins, unabashed. "Apologies, Mother. I forgot how delicate your sensibilities are."

Silvo snorts into his wine glass, earning a glare from his mother. I hide my own smile behind my napkin, feeling a sense of camaraderie with these people I barely know.

As the meal progresses, I start to notice the little quirks and eccentricities of the De Luca family. Antonio has a habit of tapping his fingers on the table in a specific pattern, as if sending a secret message. Isabella barely touches her food, instead pushing it around her plate and sipping delicately at her wine. And Fed, well, he seems to have a story for every occasion, each one more outrageous than the last.

But it's Silvo who intrigues me the most. He's quiet, observing his family with a watchful eye. Every now and then, he'll lean over and whisper something in my ear, his breath hot against my skin. It sends a shiver down my spine, reminding me of the night we shared.

As the plates are cleared away and dessert is served, Giulia turns to me with a warm smile. "So, Carmela, tell us about yourself. What do you like to do for fun?"

I blink, caught off guard by the question. "Oh, um, I enjoy reading and painting," I say, feeling a bit self-conscious. "And I love to dance."

Silvo's hand finds mine under the table, giving it a reassuring squeeze. "Carmela is a woman of many talents," he says. "I'm a lucky man."

I glance at him, surprised by the sincerity in his tone.

As the meal comes to an end, I find myself feeling more relaxed than I have in days. The wine has left me pleasantly buzzed and the conversation has been surprisingly enjoyable. Even Silvo seems to have let his guard down a bit, his hand resting casually on my thigh.

Giulia rises gracefully, setting her napkin beside her plate. "Before we move to the sitting room, I should mention that Antonio and I are leaving for Sicily in two weeks time."

"We've had this trip planned for months," Antonio adds. "Six weeks visiting family in Palermo, then some time at the villa in Taormina. We're leaving two weeks from tomorrow—gives Silvo time to handle the business transition properly."

"Father with everything happening—" Silvo starts, but his father waves him off.

"You're a married man, running the family business. You don't need us hovering over your shoulder." Antonio's gaze shifts to me. "And you two need time to build your life together without us interfering."

Giulia comes around the table, taking both my hands in hers. "Carmela, *cara*, this is your home now. You can't truly become the mistress of this house with me running everything."

Her smile is warm but knowing. "Besides, we've been

looking forward to this trip for so long. Antonio needs the rest, and I want to see my sister."

"Six weeks is a long time," I say, unsure if I'm relieved or terrified at the prospect of being alone with Silvo in this massive estate. Well, not entirely alone, Federico and Isabella live here too.

"You'll barely notice we're gone," Giulia assures me with a laugh. "And Isabella and Federico are always around if you need anything." She pats my cheek affectionately. "By the time we return, you'll have found your rhythm here."

"The household staff will take care of everything," Antonio adds. "And Silvo knows how to reach me if there's any real emergency with the business."

Silvo's hand finds mine under the table again, squeezing. I can't read his expression—is he pleased about this privacy, or does he feel the same uncertainty I do?

"Why don't we retire to the sitting room for coffee and digestifs?" Giulia suggests, her tone making it clear this topic is closed. "We should enjoy our time together over the next two weeks."

We all follow suit, Silvo offering me his arm as we make our way to the cozy room filled with plush sofas and armchairs. A fire crackles in the hearth, casting a warm glow over everything.

I settle onto a loveseat, Silvo taking the spot beside me. His arm drapes over my shoulders, pulling me into his side. It feels strange, being so close to him in front of his family. Intimate.

Isabella perches on the arm of Fed's chair, sipping delicately at a small glass of limoncello. She catches my eye and gives me a subtle wink, as if we share a secret joke.

Antonio leans back in his armchair, swirling a snifter of brandy. "So, Silvo," he says, fixing his son with a pointed look. "Now that you're a married man, it's time to start thinking about the future. The family business."

I feel Silvo tense beside me, his fingers tightening on my shoulder. "Father, I don't think now is the time—"

"Nonsense," Antonio cuts him off with a wave of his hand. "Carmela is a part of this family now. She deserves to know what she's gotten herself into."

"Carmela doesn't need to be involved in any of that," Silvo says, his voice tight. "I'll handle the business, like always."

"And what about when you have children?" Giulia asks, her eyes flickering to me. "Will you keep them in the dark as well?"

Children.

The word lands like a sucker punch. I hadn't even considered the possibility, too caught up in my own drama to think about the future.

Silvo must sense my discomfort because he takes my hand, lacing our fingers together. "We'll cross that bridge when we come to it," he says firmly. "For now, let's enjoy the evening. It's not every day a man gets to introduce his beautiful wife to his family."

I force a smile, trying to push down the rising panic in my chest. What have I gotten myself into?

9

SILVO

The night air is cool against my skin as I step out onto the terrace, a glass of scotch in hand. My gaze falls upon Carmela, her green eyes sparkling with laughter as she converses with Fed. The way she handles his antics with grace and wit impresses me. Despite the rocky start to our union, she carries herself with a confidence that pulls me in like a magnet.

Fed leans in, no doubt cracking another one of his outrageous jokes. Carmela throws her head back, laughing freely. The sound is infectious, and I find myself smiling in response. Her cheeks flush with amusement, and I can't help but admire her beauty. She's angelic.

As our eyes meet across the terrace, a charge of electricity passes between us. Carmela's laughter fades, replaced by a look of curiosity and desire, perhaps? I take a sip of my drink, never breaking our heated gaze.

"Aw, come on, Carmela," Fed whines, trying to regain her attention. "That one was a classic!"

Carmela tears her eyes away from mine, offering my

brother an apologetic smile. "Sorry, Fed. You had me going for a minute there."

He shakes his head. "You wound me, sister-in-law."

The term *sister-in-law* rolls off his tongue so casually, yet it sends a shiver down my spine. The reminder of our newfound bond only serves to heighten the tension between Carmela and me.

I make my way over to them, unable to resist the pull any longer. Federico notices my approach and raises an eyebrow, a mischievous grin playing on his lips.

"Well, well, if it isn't the elusive groom," he teases. "Don't mind me, I was entertaining your lovely wife with some of my finest material."

Carmela shoots him a playful glare. "More like torturing me with your terrible jokes."

I chuckle at their playful banter, feeling a strange sense of contentment wash over me. "Now, now, you two. Play nice."

Fed shoots me a wolfish grin. "I'm always nice, brother. Can't say the same for you, though." He winks exaggeratedly at Carmela. "This one's got her hands full with you."

Heat rushes to my face at his insinuation. I open my mouth to retort, but Carmela beats me to it.

"Don't I know it," she says dryly, rolling her eyes. Despite her nonchalant tone, I catch the way her gaze flicks over me, a hint of that same smoldering desire from earlier.

My brother barks out a laugh. "That's my girl! Give as good as you get." He claps her on the shoulder affectionately.

An unexpected flare of jealousy twists in my gut at their easy camaraderie. I want—no, I need that connection with her. More than anything.

Sensing the shift in my mood, Federico's grin widens

infuriatingly. "Well, I'll leave you two lovebirds to it." He winks again before strolling into the house.

I turn my full attention to Carmela, my voice low. "Alone at last."

She meets my intense stare head-on, refusing to be cowed. "So it would seem."

We stand there in silence, the air crackling with unspoken tension. I take a step closer, unable to resist.

Carmela's breath hitches almost imperceptibly, but I catch it. My lips quirk up in a satisfied smirk.

"Something on your mind, wife?" I ask silkily, purposely using the term to get a rise out of her.

Her eyes narrow at the bait, but she doesn't take it. Instead, she closes the remaining distance between us in one fluid motion.

The scent of her perfume—rich and intoxicating—envelops me as she leans in close.

"You tell me, husband," she purrs. "Seems you can't take your eyes off me."

A delicious shiver runs through me at her bold words. This woman is fire personified, and I'm utterly entranced by her flames.

"Can you blame me?" I murmur, allowing my gaze to roam shamelessly over her curves. "You're a vision."

She arches an eyebrow, unimpressed by my attempt at flattery. "Is that the best you've got? Sweet talk won't work on me."

I step even closer, crowding into her personal space until our bodies are a hairsbreadth apart.

"Who said anything about sweet talk?" I growl, letting my eyes blaze with undisguised want.

Carmela's confident facade slips for just a moment. Good. Let her see that I'm not playing games anymore.

I reach out and trail a finger along the delicate line of her jaw, relishing the way she trembles at my touch.

"You think you've got me all figured out, don't you?" I murmur, leaning in until my lips graze the shell of her ear. "But the truth is you've got no idea what you've gotten yourself into, *piccina*."

I pull back enough to meet her wide, captivated eyes.

"The question is..." I continue. "Are you brave enough to find out?"

Carmela swallows hard, her gaze locked with mine. The air between us thrums with an intensity I've never felt before. For a long, heated moment, neither of us moves.

Then, slowly... defiantly... she licks her lips.

"Try me," she breathes.

White-hot desire lances through me like a lightning bolt. With a low growl, I fist a hand in her hair and pull her against me.

I crush Carmela's soft curves against me as our kiss ignites every nerve ending in my body. She melts into my embrace, her fingers tangling in my hair with a desperation that matches my own. Months of simmering tension finally boils over between us.

Our mouths move together in a frenzied duel, tongues stroking and teeth nipping. Carmela whimpers into the kiss, the needy sound sending white-hot lust spiking through my veins. I angle her head for deeper access, plundering her mouth with a ravenous hunger.

Desire rages like an inferno, consuming every rational thought. All I can focus on is the intoxicating taste of her, the velvet heat of her body pressed flush against mine. I need more—so much more.

Breaking the kiss, I trail open-mouthed kisses along the column of her throat. Carmela arches into me with a breathy moan, begging for more. The scent of her arousal surrounds me, thick and heady.

"Silvo..." she gasps out my name like a prayer as my teeth graze that sensitive spot below her ear.

Hearing her desperate plea only inflames me further. With a low growl, I lift her against me, pinning her between my body and the cool stone of the terrace wall. Carmela locks her legs around my waist as I grind against her center.

"You want this," I rasp against the fevered skin of her neck. "Don't try to deny it."

She keens in response, rolling her hips in a way that makes us both shudder with need. "Yes..." Carmela breathes. "I want you, Silvo. God help me, I want you so much."

A feral growl rumbles from deep within my chest at her admission. I capture her lips again in a scorching kiss, reveling in her utter surrender.

One of my hands runs along the silken length of her thigh, bunching the fabric of her dress around her hips. Carmela moans into my mouth as my calloused palm cups the lace-clad heat between her legs. She's drenched for me, her arousal seeping through the flimsy barrier.

"You're so wet, *piccina*," I growl in approval against her lips. "Is this what you want?" I apply pressure with the heel of my hand, massaging her through the damp lace.

Carmela throws her head back with a cry of pleasure. "Yes! Don't stop, please don't stop..."

The sound of her impassioned pleas is like a siren's call, luring me deeper under her intoxicating spell. I increase the rhythm, drinking in every breathless moan and whimper that spills from her lips.

This is what I've craved—to have Carmela at my mercy, uninhibited and writhing in ecstasy.

I'll never get enough of this… of her. My wife, my Carmela. Mine.

Someone clearing their throat behind us startles us apart.

I turn to see who has interrupted us. Federico stands there, an insufferable grin plastered across his face.

"Don't mind me," he says, holding his hands up. "Just came to grab my jacket. Please, continue what you were doing. I'll wait."

I scowl, knowing he's enjoying this far too much. Carmela avoids my gaze, her cheeks burning crimson. She hurriedly smooths her dress back into place.

Fed saunters over to grab his discarded jacket off a chair, whistling cheerfully all the while. I fold my arms across my chest and glare daggers at him.

"You always did have impeccable timing, brother," I deadpan.

He shrugs, grinning like the cat who caught the canary. "What can I say? It's a gift."

I resist the urge to roll my eyes. Barely.

Federico glances between Carmela and me, looking positively tickled by the whole situation. "Don't worry, I won't breathe a word of this little tryst to Mama and Papa. Your secret rendezvous is safe with me." He mimes zipping his lips.

"How gracious of you," I grumble. I can only imagine how mortified Carmela must feel right now. As much as I want to continue what we started, the mood has been effectively ruined.

Fed seems to sense this as well and, for once, has the decency to wipe the smug look off his face.

"Right, well… I'll leave you two." He offers Carmela a conciliatory smile. "My apologies for the interruption. I'll try to be more careful about walking onto our balcony in future."

An awkward silence descends in his wake. I sigh and run a hand through my hair. So much for the passionate night I had envisioned with Carmela.

I watch as Carmela pulls away from me, her eyes hardening. The passion that had consumed us mere moments ago dissipates, replaced by an icy chill.

"I'm tired," she says, refusing to meet my gaze. "It's been a long day."

I reach out to touch her arm, but she flinches away as if burned.

"Carmela..." I begin, but she cuts me off with a sharp shake of her head.

"Don't. Just... don't." Her voice is strained. "This doesn't change anything, Silvo. I didn't ask for this marriage, and I certainly didn't ask for you."

Her words are like a slap to the face. I clench my jaw, trying to rein in my temper.

"You think I had a choice in the matter?" I growl, my frustration getting the better of me. "I'm as trapped in this arrangement as you are."

Carmela scoffs, finally meeting my gaze with a defiant glare. "Spare me the self-pity. You hardly have to adjust much to our situation. You still live in your home, in your city! And you are enjoying this far more than me."

I narrow my eyes at her. "And what's that supposed to mean?"

She throws her hands up in exasperation. "Oh, please! You've been all over me since the moment we met. Don't try to pretend like you're not enjoying this on some level."

I take a step closer. "You weren't protesting a few

minutes ago," I remind her. "In fact, if I recall correctly, you were begging me not to stop."

Carmela's cheeks flush with a mixture of anger and embarrassment. She jabs a finger into my chest, her eyes blazing. "That was a mistake. One I won't be making again."

I catch her wrist in a firm grip, holding her in place. "Keep telling yourself that, *piccina*. But we both know the truth."

She wrenches her arm free, taking a step back. "The truth is that I want nothing to do with you or this sham of a marriage. Now, if you'll excuse me, I'm going to bed. Alone."

With that, Carmela turns on her heel and stalks off toward the house, leaving me seething in her wake. I watch her retreating form until she disappears inside, my hands clenched into fists at my sides.

This woman will be the death of me. But even as the thought crosses my mind, I know I'll never stop chasing her. She's a flame I'm drawn to like a moth.

One way or another, I'll make Carmela mine. Body, heart, and soul.

10

CARMELA

I wake up alone in the sprawling, opulent bedroom, sunlight streaming through the gauzy curtains. Silvo is nowhere to be seen. Typical.

I slide out of the plush bed, my bare feet sinking into the thick carpet as I pad over to the closet. I select a simple sundress and slip it on, running my fingers through my sleep-tousled hair.

Restless and curious, I decide to explore the lavish De Luca estate. I wander down the hallway, trailing my fingertips along the smooth wood paneling. Portraits of stern-faced De Luca ancestors line the walls, their eyes seeming to follow me.

I come to a set of heavy double doors and push them open. My breath catches. It's a library, with soaring ceilings and rows upon rows of leather-bound books. Mahogany shelves reach up to the ceiling, rolling ladders allowing access to the upper levels. Plush armchairs and reading nooks are scattered throughout.

I walk along the shelves, running my fingers over the spines, breathing in the scent of old paper and leather.

Classics, first editions, rare volumes—it's a book lover's paradise. At least there's one bright spot in this suffocating arrangement of a marriage.

I select a book at random and sink into an armchair by the window. As I begin to read, I finally feel a small measure of peace. At least here, among the pages, I can escape the reality of my unwanted marriage, if only for a little while.

I'm so engrossed in my book that I don't even hear Silvo enter the library. It's only when his shadow falls across the pages that I startle, looking up to see him looming over me.

"Carmela," he says. "I've been looking for you."

I snap the book shut, setting it aside. "Well, you found me. Congratulations."

Silvo sighs, running a hand through his dark hair. "I wanted to apologize. For last night. I was out of line."

I stand, closing the distance between us. "You think?" I scoff. "Silvo, you can't just decide how far things go whenever you feel like it. That shouldn't have happened. I'm your wife, not your property."

He takes a step closer, his eyes intense. "I know that. But you're also a De Luca now. You have to understand the expectations that come with that."

I laugh humorlessly. "Expectations? Like being a good little wife? Popping out babies on command?" I shake my head. "That's not me, and it never will be."

Silvo's jaw clenches. "I'm not asking you to change who you are. But there are certain things that are expected of us. Certain roles we have to play."

I step forward, poking him in the chest. "Well, I didn't sign up for this role. In case you forgot, I didn't have a choice in this marriage."

His eyes flash with anger. "Neither did I," he growls.

"You think I wanted to be saddled with a wife I barely know? A wife who clearly despises me?"

I flinch at his words, but I refuse to back down. "Can you blame me? You keep trying to control everything between us since the moment we met."

Silvo takes a deep breath, trying to calm himself. "I'm not trying to control everything. The world we live in... it's dangerous. I wish to protect you."

I feel a flicker of fear at his words, but I push it down. "I don't need your protection. I can take care of myself. If you forgot, I'm from this world too—even if I've spent most of my life trying to stay on the edges of it."

He reaches out, cupping my cheek in his hand. I hate myself for leaning into his touch, even for a second.

"Let me take care of you," he murmurs. "Let me show you that this marriage doesn't have to be a prison sentence."

I pull away, my skin burning from his touch. "I'll never be the wife you want me to be. You might as well accept that now."

I turn away from him, my heart racing. Part of me wants to believe this marriage could be more than a business arrangement. But I can't let myself hope.

"I need some air," I mutter, brushing past him before I say something I can't take back.

I flee the library, my sundress swishing around my legs as I hurry down the hallway. I can hear Silvo calling after me, but I don't stop. I can't face him right now.

I burst out of the house, the warm sun hitting my face. I take a deep breath, trying to calm my nerves. The De Luca estate is sprawling, with manicured gardens and bubbling fountains. It's like something out of a fairy tale. But I know the truth. This is no fairy tale.

I wander through the gardens, lost in thought. I know I should try to make the best of this situation. Silvo is my husband now, for better or worse. But every fiber of my being rebels against the idea of being a mafia wife.

I find a secluded bench and sink down onto it, burying my face in my hands. Tears prick at my eyes, but I blink them back. I won't cry. I won't give them the satisfaction.

"Carmela?"

I look up to see Federico standing a few feet away, concern etched on his handsome face.

"Are you alright?" he asks, taking a step closer.

I force a smile. "I'm fine, Federico. Just needed some fresh air."

He sits down next to me, his shoulder brushing against mine. "I know this must be difficult for you. But Silvo... he's a good man. He'll take care of you."

I let out a humorless laugh. "I don't need anyone to take care of me, Federico. I can take care of myself."

He nods, a small smile playing on his lips. "I don't doubt that. But it's okay to lean on others sometimes. That's what family is for."

I look at him, surprised. "Family? You barely know me."

Federico shrugs. "You're a De Luca now. That makes you family." He stands up, offering me his hand. "Come on. Let's go back inside."

I hesitate for a moment before taking his hand and allowing him to pull me to my feet. As we walk back toward the house, I can't help but wonder what the future holds. But one thing is certain. I won't let this marriage break me. I'll find a way to survive, no matter what it takes.

11

SILVO

I pour two glasses of Scotch from the crystal decanter and hand one to Marco. He takes a sip, his eyes scanning the opulent dining room he's been in countless times before.

"Is marriage treating you well?"

I grunt, not particularly eager to discuss my arranged union with Carmela. Before I can respond, she enters the room, her emerald dress hugging every curve. Marco''s appreciation is obvious.

"You must be Carmela," he says, taking her hand and brushing his lips across her knuckles. "Marco Rossi. Silvo's told me all about you."

Carmela raises an eyebrow at me. "Has he? Funny—he's never mentioned you."

Marco laughs. "Can't have that. We'll have to remedy it over dinner."

I watch him work his charm, that easy smile and quick wit that's always served him well. When Carmela actually laughs at something he says, jealousy twists in my gut. It's irrational—Marco's my best friend—but I can't help it.

The staff enters with dinner—risotto ai funghi and osso buco. The rich aroma of slow-cooked veal fills the room.

"This looks amazing," Marco says, picking up his fork.

Carmela closes her eyes briefly as she tastes the risotto. "It really is."

I cut into the tender meat, the marrow melting on my tongue. "We have the best cook in the city," I say, taking a sip of the robust Barolo.

"I can see why you locked this one down so fast," Marco says with a wink at Carmela. "Beautiful *and* appreciates good food? Lucky bastard."

Carmela's smile doesn't quite reach her eyes. "Yes, well. So many blessings to count."

The bitterness in her voice cuts through me. I reach over and take her hand, feeling her tense under my touch. She still doesn't want this—doesn't want me—not really.

"We're both lucky," I say, holding her gaze. "I plan to make sure she knows it."

Marco clears his throat. "So, Carmela—what do you do for fun? Besides tolerating my friend here."

As she tells him about her love of painting and horseback riding, I lean back and sip my wine. Marco's right about one thing—I'm a lucky bastard. Now I just need to convince my wife that I can make her happy. Winning over my fiery bride won't be easy, though.

I take another drink, watching Carmela. She's laughing again, her eyes bright with genuine amusement, and something possessive stirs in my chest. She gives him that warmth so freely, while I have to fight for every smile.

"Marco," I interrupt. "Tell Carmela about your latest case. I'm sure she'd love to hear about corporate law."

Marco's smirk tells me he knows exactly what I'm

doing. "Sure. Nothing more exciting than contract negotiations and intellectual property disputes."

"Actually, I find the law interesting," Carmela says, leaning forward. "Go ahead."

As Marco explains his current case, I watch the candlelight play across her face, highlighting those sharp cheekbones and full lips. She's stunning, and legally mine.

But is she really? Our marriage might be legitimate on paper, but her heart's another matter entirely. She wants me physically, that much was obvious the night we met, but she keeps a wall around everything else. Every time I try to get closer, she pulls back.

When Marco finally wraps up, he leans back with that insufferable grin. "Enough about boring legal work. What I want to know is—why aren't you two off on some exotic honeymoon?"

I notice Carmela stiffen beside me. "Honeymoons are usually for people who choose to get married and have time to plan for one."

"Come on, Silvo. You've never been one to waste an opportunity. Surely you could turn a honeymoon to your advantage."

"I have responsibilities. I can't just disappear."

"Ah yes, the weight of being a mafia boss." Marco's sarcasm is thick. "How could I forget?"

I lean forward, my voice dropping. "Careful, Marco. Friend or not, there are lines you don't cross."

He raises his hands. "Easy. I'm just saying—a little time away might do you both good."

"I think I know what's best for my own marriage."

Carmela sets down her fork. "Are you two finished with the pissing contest? Because I'd love to enjoy the rest of this meal in peace."

Marco laughs and raises his glass to her. "Touché. I see why Silvo's so taken with you."

She rolls her eyes. "Flattery won't work on me, Mr. Rossi."

"Noted. I'll have to try harder."

I drain my wine and set the glass down harder than necessary. "That's my wife you're flirting with."

"Just keeping you on your toes."

I shake my head, but I can't quite suppress my grin. "You're impossible."

"Part of my charm." Marco shrugs. "Besides, someone needs to keep you humble now that you're a married man."

"My wife handles that just fine on her own."

Carmela gives me a dry look, but there's something softer in her eyes now. "I do what I can."

Marco laughs and raises his glass to her. "And doing a stellar job. I've never seen Silvo whipped."

"Watch it," I say, though I'm fighting a smile. Because it's true. I'm besotted with my wife, even if she hates my guts. "Married or not, I can still kick your ass."

"Easy, big guy. Just having some fun." Marco's expression softens. "You know I'm happy for you, right?"

I nod, the truth of it settling over me. "I know. Even if you're a pain in the ass."

He clutches his chest. "And here I thought we were friends."

"Don't push it."

He grins and takes another sip. "I wouldn't dream of it."

I glance at Carmela, who's watching our exchange with clear amusement. The wariness has faded from her eyes, replaced by something gentler. I reach for her hand. "Sorry about him. He doesn't come with an off switch."

She squeezes my fingers, a genuine smile touching her

lips. "It's nice, actually. That you have someone like him. Even if he's a troublemaker."

That smile does something to my chest—makes it tight in a way that has nothing to do with the Scotch. Maybe there's hope for us after all.

"I prefer *charming rogue*, thank you very much," Marco says.

I snort. "More like incorrigible bastard."

"Now *that* I'll drink to," Marco replies.

We all laugh, and for a moment, the weight lifts. The arrangement that brought Carmela and me together, the responsibilities waiting outside this room, the fact that my wife still looks at me with caution more often than affection—all of it fades. Right now, it's just three people sharing good food, decent wine, and better company.

I watch Carmela laugh at another one of Marco's jokes, and something shifts inside me. This marriage started as an obligation, but maybe—just maybe—it could become something more. I've conquered territories, eliminated rivals, and built an empire. Surely I can win my own wife's heart.

For tonight, that's enough. Tomorrow, I'll start working on forever.

12

CARMELA

Silvo guides me through the bustling streets of Philadelphia. The city's energy pulses around us, and despite myself, I'm starting to relax. Maybe I've been holding onto my resentment too tightly.

"Over there, you'll see the Liberty Bell," Silvo points out. "Symbol of American independence and freedom."

I can't help the small laugh that escapes. "Freedom. That's rich, coming from the man who married me through an arrangement, effectively imprisoning me."

Silvo glances at me, his brow furrowing. "I know this isn't how either of us imagined marriage. But I'm trying here. Can you give me a chance?"

I meet his gaze, softening slightly. "I wanted you that night at the club. You know I did." I bite my lip. "But finding out the next day that you were the man I was being forced to marry... it felt like the universe was playing a cruel joke."

He sighs, running a hand through his hair. "I should have told you who I was that night. I knew who you were, and I didn't say anything. That was wrong."

I shake my head. "You knew I was going to be your wife

and you seduced me anyway. Got into my panties pretty damn fast without bothering to mention that little detail."

Silvo's eyes widen, then a hint of guilt crosses his face. "I won't apologize for wanting you. But I am sorry I wasn't honest. Can we try to move forward?"

I consider his words. My anger isn't really about that night—it's about losing control of my life, being traded like property between families. But Silvo didn't make that choice any more than I did.

"Fine," I concede, my voice softening. "But I'm still angry about being forced into this marriage. Just... not necessarily at you."

A small smile tugs at his mouth. "I'll take it, *tesoro*."

As we continue our tour, Silvo points out hidden gems tucked away in the city's winding streets. He takes me to a quaint little bookshop, and I can't help but feel warmth bloom in my chest at the thoughtful gesture.

As we step into the cozy bookshop, the scent of old pages and leather bindings envelops me. It's a comforting smell, one that instantly puts me at ease. Silvo watches me with a soft smile as I run my fingers along the spines of the books, marveling at the sheer variety of titles.

"See anything you like?" he asks, his voice low and warm.

I nod, pulling out a well-worn copy of "Pride and Prejudice." "I've always loved this one," I confess, flipping through the pages. "There's something about the way Austen writes that just speaks to me."

Silvo takes the book from my hands, examining the cover. "A classic," he muses. "I can see why you're drawn to it."

I reach for the book, but he pulls it away, a playful glint in his eye. "Let me buy it for you," he insists.

I shake my head, frowning. "Silvo, I can pay for my own books."

He chuckles, tucking the book under his arm. "I know you can, *tesoro*. But let me do this for you. Consider it a peace offering."

I hesitate for a moment, torn between my desire for independence and the genuine warmth in his gaze. Finally, I sigh, relenting. "Fine. But just this once."

Silvo grins, victorious, and heads to the counter to pay for the book. As I watch him, I can't help but feel a flutter of something in my chest. It's not quite affection, but it's not entirely animosity either. Maybe, just maybe, there's a chance for us to find some common ground after all.

When he returns, he hands me the book, his fingers brushing against mine. "For you," he murmurs, his voice soft.

I take the book, clutching it to my chest. "Thank you," I whisper, feeling a blush creep up my cheeks.

Silvo nods, his eyes never leaving mine. "Shall we continue our tour?" he asks, offering me his arm. "I'm quite hungry and we're not far from the best Italian restaurant in the city."

I take Silvo's arm, allowing him to lead me out of the bookshop and onto the bustling streets of Philadelphia once more. The sun is starting to set, casting a warm glow over the city, and I can't help but feel a sense of contentment wash over me. Despite my initial reservations, spending the day with Silvo has been surprisingly enjoyable.

Before long, we arrive at the restaurant Silvo mentioned. It's a quaint little place, tucked away on a side street, with a red awning and twinkling fairy lights strung across the entrance. The aroma of garlic and tomato sauce wafts out from the open door, making my mouth water.

My husband holds the door open for me, ushering me inside with a gentle hand on the small of my back. The interior of the restaurant is cozy and inviting, with checkered tablecloths and candles flickering on each table.

We're seated at a table near the back, and Silvo orders a bottle of red wine without even glancing at the menu. When the waiter returns with the wine and two glasses, Silvo pours each of us a generous serving.

"To new beginnings," he toasts, raising his glass.

I hesitate for a moment before raising my own glass to meet his. "To new beginnings," I echo, taking a sip of the rich, full-bodied wine.

As we peruse the menu, Silvo points out his favorite dishes, describing each one in mouthwatering detail. I find myself drawn to the pasta carbonara, and when our food arrives, I'm not disappointed.

The pasta is cooked to perfection, with a creamy sauce and crispy pancetta. I close my eyes, savoring each bite. When I open them again, I find Silvo watching me with a soft smile on his face.

"Good?" he asks, his eyes twinkling.

I nod, swallowing my mouthful of pasta. "Incredible," I admit. "You were right about this place."

Silvo grins, looking pleased with himself. "I'm glad you like it, *tesoro*."

We eat in comfortable silence for a few minutes, the only sounds the clink of our forks against the plates and the soft murmur of conversation from the other diners.

As he finishes his meal, Silvo leans back in his chair, his eyes fixed on me with an intensity that sends shivers down my spine. "You know, Carmela," he says, his voice low, "I've been thinking about that night at the club."

I feel my cheeks flush, remembering exactly how good it had been between us. "Have you?"

"How responsive you were. How you said my name." His gaze darkens. "How perfect we were together."

The heat in his words makes my stomach flip, but I refuse to make this easy for him. "That was before I knew you'd kept the truth from me."

Silvo leans forward. "Would it have changed anything? If I'd told you that night who I was, would you have walked away?"

I open my mouth to say yes, but the word won't come. The truth is, I probably wouldn't have. The chemistry between us was so strong and completely instant.

"That's not the point," I reply.

"Isn't it?" His eyes hold mine. "You wanted me then. You want me now. The only difference is now you're angry about circumstances neither of us controlled."

"I have a right to be angry."

"You do," he agrees, surprising me. "But not at me for wanting my own wife. Not when you want me just as much."

I grip my fork tighter. "You're awfully confident."

"I know what I felt that night, *piccina*. And I know what I see in your eyes right now." He reaches across the table, his fingers brushing mine. "We can keep fighting this, or we can try to build something real."

The sincerity in his voice catches me off guard. I look down at our hands, at the way his thumb is gently stroking my knuckles.

"I'm not ready to just forgive and forget," I say quietly.

"I'm not asking you to." His voice is surprisingly gentle. "I'm asking you to try. With me. For us."

I meet his gaze and see something there beyond desire or possession—genuine hope. Maybe he's right. Maybe we can build something from this mess our families created.

"Okay," I whisper. "We can try."

His smile is slow and warm, and it does dangerous things to my heart.

13

SILVO

I pace across the room, my mind racing. After our dinner last week, things have been... better between Carmela and me. She's stopped treating me like the enemy, at least. But there's still a wall between us—one I'm determined to break down.

An idea strikes me, and I grab my phone, quickly typing out a message.

> Carmela, I'm heading to a poker game with some friends tonight. I'd like you to join me.

I hit send before I can second-guess myself. Maybe a night out together, showing her more of my world, will help bridge the remaining distance between us.

The click of her footsteps approaching signals she's read my message. As she enters the room, I look up to see her green eyes holding curiosity rather than the suspicion I'm used to seeing. "A poker game? With your business associates?"

I nod. "High stakes. I thought you might enjoy a night out. See more of my world."

She tilts her head, considering. "And why would I enjoy that?"

I step closer to her, feeling the warmth radiating from her body. "Because you're my wife. And I want to include you in my life. All of it."

Her breath catches, and I see something flicker in her eyes—interest, maybe even excitement.

"Fine," she says, and this time there's no edge to her voice. "I'll go. But don't expect me to just sit there and look pretty."

I smirk. "I wouldn't dream of it, *bella*. Now go get ready. Wear something... memorable."

She rolls her eyes, but I catch a genuine smile playing at the corner of her mouth as she turns to leave. I watch her go, my blood thrumming with anticipation. Tonight feels different—like we're finally moving forward instead of constantly circling each other.

I pour myself a scotch and settle in to wait, my mind already conjuring images of her commanding attention at the poker table.

Anticipation builds as I hear the click of heels on the marble floor. I turn and nearly drop my glass.

Carmela stands before me, a vision in a slinky black dress that hugs every curve. The neckline plunges dangerously low, revealing the swell of her breasts. A slit runs up her thigh, teasing a glimpse of smooth, tanned skin.

My mouth goes dry as I rake my gaze over her. She's breathtaking. Stunning. I've never wanted a woman more.

I set my glass down and move toward her, my eyes locked on hers. "You look... incredible," I murmur.

She lifts her chin, that familiar defiance still there but softened somehow. "I know."

I chuckle. "Confident. I like that." I reach out and trail a finger along her collarbone, feeling her shiver beneath my touch.

"This dress, baby... it's sinful. You're going to be the death of me." I lean in, my lips brushing her ear. "Every man in that room is going to want you. But you're mine."

She sucks in a sharp breath, and I feel a thrill of satisfaction. I pull back, my eyes roaming her body appreciatively.

"Maybe I should take you upstairs and peel this dress off you. Slowly." My voice is low and suggestive. "Worship every inch of your skin until you're begging for more."

Carmela swallows hard, her eyes darkening. But she steps back, a playful smile on her lips now rather than the angry retreat I'm used to.

"We have a poker game to get to, remember?" She asks.

I smirk, enjoying this new dynamic between us. "For now. But later... I make no promises about keeping my hands to myself."

Her eyes sparkle with anticipation. "What makes you think I'd want you to?"

The shift in her response catches me off guard—in the best way. I step closer, invading her space until I can feel the heat radiating off her body. "You see, Carmela, I know you. I know the fire that burns inside you, the passion that consumes you. And I know that deep down, you crave the same thing I do."

I reach out and run my fingers along her bare arm, feeling her tremble at my touch. "You want to be consumed by desire, to lose yourself in pleasure so intense it borders on pain. And I'm the only man who can give that to you."

This time, she doesn't scoff. Instead, she leans in slightly, her voice dropping. "You're awfully sure of yourself."

"With good reason," I murmur, my lips a hairsbreadth

from hers. "I've seen the way you look at me. Not with anger anymore—with hunger. You can deny it all you want, but we both know the truth."

I pull back slightly, my eyes locked on hers. "So go ahead and make me work for it, *piccina*. I enjoy the chase. But we both know where this night is heading. Now, shall we? We have a poker game to attend, and I'm eager to show off my beautiful wife."

I offer her my arm. She doesn't hesitate this time, sliding her hand into the crook of my elbow.

As we make our way out to the car, I can't help but feel a thrill. Tonight is going to be a turning point. And by the end of it, I'm determined to have Carmela in my bed—not simply sleeping beside me, but finally giving herself to me completely.

Once we arrive, I guide Carmela into the dimly lit room, the scent of cigars and whiskey hanging heavy in the air. The poker table is surrounded by some of the most powerful men in the city—my inner circle, the ones I trust with my life.

Marco catches my eye from across the room and raises his glass in a silent toast. I nod in acknowledgment, my hand resting possessively on Carmela's waist.

"Gentlemen," I say, my voice carrying over the low murmur of conversation. "I'd like to introduce you to my wife, Carmela."

All eyes turn to her, and I feel a surge of possessive pride. She's a vision in that dress, her beauty outshining every other woman in the room.

I lead her around the table, introducing her to each man in turn. They greet her with polite nods and appreciative glances, but I can see the calculation in their eyes. They're trying to figure out how she fits into the power dynamics at play.

As we reach Marco, he stands and takes Carmela's hand, brushing a kiss across her knuckles. "A pleasure to see you again, Mrs. De Luca."

A flare of possessiveness at the familiarity in his tone ignites, but I keep it in check. Marco is my closest friend and ally—I trust him with my life. But something about the way he looks at Carmela still sets my teeth on edge.

I guide her to a seat beside me as the game begins and order her a glass of wine, expecting her to sit back and observe. But to my surprise, she leans forward and taps the table.

"Deal me in," she commands.

The table goes silent for a moment before erupting into surprised laughter. I stare at her, my eyebrows raised.

"Are you sure, *bella*?" I ask. "This is a high stakes game."

She meets my gaze, her eyes flashing with challenge. "I'm certain."

I hesitate for a moment before nodding to the dealer. He slides a stack of chips toward Carmela and begins dealing the cards.

As I watch her pick up her hand, I feel a mix of pride and excitement. This boldness, this fearlessness—it's exactly what drew me to her in the first place.

I lean back in my chair, my eyes never leaving her face as the game begins.

The cards are dealt, and the game begins. I watch Carmela intently, trying to read her expression as she studies her hand. Her face is a mask of calm concentration, giving nothing away.

"So, Mrs. De Luca," one of the men says, a smirk playing

at the corner of his mouth. "You think you've got what it takes to play with the big boys?"

Carmela looks up, her eyes narrowing slightly. "I guess we'll find out, won't we?"

The man chuckles, shaking his head. "I like a woman with spirit. But this isn't exactly a ladies' game, sweetheart."

Carmela leans forward. "I'm no lady," she says. "And I'm not your sweetheart. I'm here to play, just like everyone else."

The table goes silent for a moment before Marco lets out a low whistle. "Damn, Silvo. You've got yourself a fire-cracker there."

I shoot him a warning look, but pride swells in my chest.

The game continues, the banter flying fast and furious. The men seem to have accepted Carmela's presence, but they can't resist making the occasional joke at her expense.

As the night wears on, I watch with growing admiration as Carmela outplays one man after another, even as she grows tipsy from the wine. Her quick wit and sharp instincts serve her well at the poker table, and I can see the begrudging respect in the eyes of my associates.

The jokes and jabs at her expense slowly taper off as she accumulates a sizable stack of chips in front of her. Even Marco, usually so quick with a quip or a barb, falls silent as he watches her play.

I lean back in my chair, sipping my whiskey and studying her face. There's a fierce determination in her eyes, a refusal to back down or be intimidated. It's the same fire I saw in her the night we met, the same spark that drew me to her like a moth to a flame.

As the final hand is dealt, it comes down to Carmela

and Hernandez, one of the most ruthless men in the room. I watch as they stare each other down, the tension thick enough to cut with a knife.

Hernandez pushes his remaining chips into the center of the table, a smug grin on his face. "All in," he says, his voice dripping with confidence.

Carmela doesn't hesitate. She matches his bet, her eyes never leaving his face.

The cards are flipped, and a collective gasp goes around the table. Carmela has a straight flush, beating Hernandez's full house.

She reaches forward and scoops the chips toward her, a small smile playing at the corner of her mouth.

His face turns red with anger, and he opens his mouth to say something, but I cut him off with a sharp look.

"Well played," I say, raising my glass to Carmela.

She meets my gaze, her eyes sparkling with triumph. "Thank you," she says, her voice soft but firm.

As the men begin to disperse, muttering to themselves about the unexpected turn of events, I stand and offer Carmela my arm.

"Shall we?" I ask, gesturing toward the door.

She takes my arm without hesitation, her skin warm against mine. As we walk out into the cool night air, I can't help but feel a sense of pride and desire coursing through me. My wife, the woman I was forced to marry, has just proven herself to be a force to be reckoned with—and I've never wanted her more.

Tonight, I'm determined to show her exactly how much.

14

CARMELA

Silvo guides me out of the smoky room, the effects of the wine making my head swim. He steadies me with a firm hand on my elbow, and I find myself leaning into his touch. Maybe it's the alcohol, but I'm starting to see him in a different light.

"You know, you weren't half bad in there," I say, gesturing vaguely behind us. "I mean, for a mafia man."

Silvo chuckles, his dark eyes glinting with amusement. "And you, my dear wife, were absolutely brilliant. I don't think Hernandez knew what hit him."

I can't help but grin at the compliment, feeling a flush of pride. "Well, what can I say? I'm full of surprises."

As we walk, I stumble again, and Silvo tightens his grip on my arm. "Easy there, tiger. I think you've had a bit too much to drink."

I wave him off, giggling. "Nonsense! I'm perfectly fine. I could drink you under the table any day."

Silvo raises an eyebrow, a smirk playing on his lips. "Is that a challenge, Mrs. De Luca?"

The sound of my new last name sends a shiver down

my spine, and I find myself leaning closer to him. "Maybe it is, Mr. De Luca. What are you going to do about it?"

There's a charged moment between us, the air thick with tension. Silvo's gaze drops to my lips, and I feel my breath catch in my throat.

"I think," he murmurs, his voice low and rough, "that it's time I take my wife home."

My heart races at the implication. "Lead the way, husband."

As we make our way to the car, I can't help but wonder if maybe, just maybe, this arranged marriage might not be so bad after all. Or maybe that's just the wine talking.

Silvo opens the door to the sleek black car waiting at the curb, and I slide into the plush leather seat, sighing as the cool interior envelops me.

He slips in beside me, thigh brushing against mine. I find myself hyper-aware of his proximity, the heat of his body seeping into my skin.

"You know," I muse, "you're not so bad, Silvo De Luca. I mean, for a husband I didn't choose."

Silvo chuckles. "And you, Carmela, are not so bad for a wife I didn't choose."

I giggle, the sound foreign to my own ears. "Look at us, bonding over our shared misery. How romantic."

Silvo's hand finds mine, his fingers lacing through my own. "Perhaps it's not all misery, hmm? We could make the best of it."

I turn to look at him, my vision slightly blurred. "And how do you propose we do that?"

His eyes darken, and he leans in closer. "I have a few ideas."

My breath hitches, and I find myself leaning in too, drawn to him like a moth to a flame. "Oh?"

Silvo's free hand comes up to cup my cheek, his thumb brushing over my bottom lip. "For starters, I could kiss you."

My heart pounds in my chest, and I nod slowly. "I think I'd like that."

He closes the distance between us, his lips capturing mine in a searing kiss. I melt into him, my free hand coming up to tangle in his hair.

When we finally break apart, we're both breathing heavily. Silvo rests his forehead against mine, his eyes closed.

"Carmela," he murmurs, his voice rough with desire.

"Silvo," I whisper back, my own voice sounding foreign to my ears.

As Silvo's lips claim mine again, I feel a fire ignite deep within me. His kisses are demanding, possessive, just like they were that first night at the club. And god help me, I love it.

His hands roam my body, gripping my hips and pulling me flush against him. I gasp into his mouth, my fingers digging into his shoulders. He growls in response, the sound sending shivers down my spine.

"Carmela," he rasps, his voice rough with need. "I want you. Now."

I nod frantically, beyond words. He captures my mouth again, his tongue delving deep, claiming me. I moan, melting into him, surrendering to the delicious sensations he's evoking in me.

Silvo's hands slide under my dress, his fingers skimming up my thighs. I tremble at his touch, my body aching for more. He reaches the lace of my panties and hooks his fingers into the waistband.

With a quick tug, he rips them away, tossing the scraps

of fabric aside. I gasp at the sudden cool air on my heated flesh, but it's quickly replaced by the warmth of Silvo's hand as he cups me intimately.

"So wet for me already," he growls, his fingers sliding through my slick folds. "You want this as much as I do, don't you, baby?"

"Yes," I whimper, my hips bucking into his touch. "Please, Silvo..."

He chuckles darkly, his fingers circling my clit. "Please what, Carmela? Tell me what you want."

I'm lost in a haze of pleasure, my mind clouded with desire. "I want you," I manage to gasp out. "I need you inside me. Now."

Silvo groans, his control snapping. He yanks me onto his lap, his hard length pressing against my core. I grind down on him, desperate for friction.

"Fuck, baby," he hisses, his hands gripping my hips hard enough to bruise. "You're going to be the death of me."

I grin, loving the power I have over him in this moment. "But what a way to go, right?"

He laughs, the sound dark and seductive. "You're playing with fire."

"Then burn me," I challenge, my eyes locking with his. "Make me yours."

Silvo's eyes flash with hunger, and he crushes his mouth to mine in a bruising kiss. I know in that moment that I'm lost, completely and utterly under his spell.

I gasp as Silvo frees himself from the confines of his pants, his hard length springing free. My pussy throbs with need at the sight of him, and I can't wait a moment longer.

Throwing caution to the wind, I hike up my dress and straddle his lap, positioning myself over his rigid shaft.

Silvo's hands grip my hips, his eyes dark with desire as he gazes up at me.

"Carmela," he groans, his voice strained. "Ride my cock," he demands.

In answer, I sink down onto him, taking him deep inside. We both moan at the sensation, lost in pleasure.

I start to move, rolling my hips in a slow, sensual rhythm. Silvo's fingers dig into my skin as he guides my movements, urging me to take him deeper, harder.

The world falls away as we lose ourselves in each other, our bodies moving in perfect sync. The car fills with the sounds of our passion—breathy moans, needy whimpers, the slick slide of skin on skin.

Silvo's hand slips between us, his fingers finding my clit. I cry out, my head falling back as he strokes me in time with our movements.

"That's it, baby," he rasps, his eyes burning into mine. "Let go for me. Come on my cock."

His words are my undoing. I shatter in his arms, my body convulsing around him as wave after wave of ecstasy crashes over me. Silvo follows me over the edge, his own release pulsing deep inside me as he groans my name.

I collapse against his chest, my body spent and sated. Silvo's arms wrap around me, holding me close as we both struggle to catch our breath.

In that moment, the reality hits me. I just had sex with my husband in the back of a car. But somehow, it doesn't feel reckless or wrong—it feels inevitable. Like this is exactly where we were always meant to end up.

Silvo presses a tender kiss to my temple, murmuring words of praise and affection. I can't bring myself to regret it.

As I slowly extract myself from Silvo's embrace, I can't

help the satisfied grin that spreads across my face. He watches me with hooded eyes, looking utterly debauched and thoroughly satisfied.

I straighten my dress, suddenly self-conscious under his intense gaze. "What?" I demand, arching a brow.

Silvo shakes his head slowly, a lazy smirk curving his lips. "Nothing, *querida*. Just admiring the view."

I scoff, rolling my eyes. But I can't deny the thrill that shoots through me at his words. "You're ridiculous," I mutter, even as my cheeks flush.

"Maybe," he allows, his eyes dancing with mirth. "But you love it."

I open my mouth to protest, but he silences me with a scorching kiss, leaving me breathless and dazed.

"Shall we go home, wife?" he purrs, his voice a low rumble that sends shivers down my spine.

I swallow hard, my body still thrumming with desire. "Whatever you say, husband."

As the car glides through the city streets, I find myself pressed against Silvo's side, my head pillowed on his broad shoulder. His arm is a solid and reassuring weight around me.

Despite the lingering ache between my thighs, I've never felt more content. Silvo presses a kiss to my temple, and I can't help but snuggle closer, basking in his warmth.

In this moment, it's easy to forget the circumstances that brought us together. The bitterness and resentment have melted away, replaced by a connection so raw and visceral that it steals my breath.

I know this fragile peace can't last forever. The reality of our situation will inevitably come crashing back down around us. But for now, I allow myself to get lost in Silvo's embrace, savoring the sweetness of our twisted passion.

As the city lights blur past the tinted windows, I tilt my head up and capture Silvo's lips in a slow, languid kiss. He responds eagerly, his fingers tangling in my hair.

When we finally break apart, he rests his forehead against mine, his eyes burning with an intensity that sends my heart racing.

"You're mine, *mi alma*," he murmurs. "Mine, Carmela. No one else's."

I shiver at the possessive promise in his voice. But instead of fear, I feel only a bone-deep sense of rightness.

As Silvo presses a tender kiss to my temple, murmuring words of praise and affection, I can't bring myself to regret it. Maybe this arranged marriage won't be so bad after all.

15

CARMELA

I wake with a groan, my head throbbing and a delicious ache between my thighs. Memories of last night flood back—the poker game, the wine, the frenzied passion in the back of the car. Heat rushes through me at the memories.

I sit up gingerly, the silk sheets pooling around my waist. The bed beside me is empty, and I can't decide if I'm relieved or disappointed by Silvo's absence. Part of me wants to see him, to gauge his reaction to what happened between us. But another part of me needs time to process these confusing feelings.

I drag myself out of bed, wincing at the soreness in my muscles. Evidence of our tryst is written all over my body—love bites on my neck, finger-shaped bruises on my hips. I feel marked, claimed in a way that makes my stomach twist.

I stumble into the bathroom, catching my reflection in the mirror. My hair is wild, my lips swollen, my skin flushed. I look thoroughly ravished, and despite my confusion about where we're heading, I can't deny the satisfaction curling through me.

I turn on the shower, cranking the heat up until the room fills with steam.

As I step under the scalding spray, I let the water cascade over me. But no matter how hot the water runs, I can't wash away the memory of Silvo's touch, the way he made me feel alive in a way I never have before.

I brace my hands against the cool tile, trying to sort through my tangled emotions. What the hell is happening to me? A month ago, I was furious about this arranged marriage. Now I'm craving his touch, anticipating his return, caring about his safety.

The walls I built are crumbling, and I'm not sure whether to rebuild them or let them fall completely.

I think back to the progression—our hostile first meeting after the club, the tense wedding, our dinner where we started to understand each other. Each moment has brought us closer, breaking down my resistance piece by piece.

And last night... last night was different. Not just lust or chemistry, but a deeper connection. The way he looked at me with pride when I won that hand. The possessiveness mixed with tenderness in his touch.

Maybe I'm not falling into his arms like some lovesick fool. Maybe I'm choosing to walk toward him, eyes open, knowing exactly what I'm doing.

I wrap the plush towel around my body, taking a moment to gather my thoughts. My reflection in the foggy mirror shows a woman changed—not broken, but transformed.

Steeling my resolve, I step out of the bathroom and into the opulent bedroom. I dress quickly, slipping into a flowy sundress that does little to conceal the marks Silvo left on my body. The dull ache between my thighs reminds me of last night with every step—not as a source of shame, but as evidence of passion freely given.

With a deep breath, I venture out of the bedroom and make my way downstairs. The scent of freshly brewed coffee and sizzling bacon greets me as I enter the kitchen. Federico is there, looking far too chipper considering it's before noon.

"Well, well, look who finally decided to grace us with her presence," he teases, flashing me that infuriatingly charming grin of his.

I open my mouth to retort, but the words catch in my throat as his gaze drops to my neck. His eyes linger on the purplish bruises marring my skin, and I feel a flush creep up my cheeks.

"Rough night?" he asks.

I bristle slightly, but more from embarrassment than anger. "It's none of your business," I say, wrapping my arms around myself.

Federico holds up his hands in surrender, though the mischievous glint remains in his eyes. "Hey, no judgment here. I'm glad to see you and my brother finally stopped circling each other like angry cats."

I can't help the small smile that tugs at my lips. "We're... figuring things out."

"I can see that," he says, glancing at my neck.

"I'm sorry for snapping," I murmur, tucking a strand of hair behind my ear. "I'm just... this is all still new to me."

Federico nods in understanding. "It's okay, Carmela. I get it—this whole situation is intense." He leans back against the counter. "But for what it's worth, I think you're handling it really well. And Silvo… I haven't seen him this happy in years."

I feel something soften in my chest at his words. "Really?"

"Really." Federico's expression turns more serious. "My brother doesn't let people in easily. But you've gotten under his skin in the best way possible."

I don't know what to say to that, so I just nod, feeling touched by his honesty.

Federico chuckles, that rich, warm sound that's quickly becoming familiar to me. "Although those love bites are a bit of a giveaway about how your night went."

I self-consciously tug at the collar of my dress. "Shut up," I mutter, though there's no real heat behind my words.

"Good morning."

Silvo's deep voice cuts through the air, my heart stuttering in my chest. He strolls into the kitchen. My gaze is immediately drawn to the way his shirt stretches across his broad shoulders, the sleeves straining against the swell of his biceps.

Before I can respond, he's closing the distance between us, his intoxicating scent of sandalwood and whiskey enveloping me. I suck in a sharp breath as his hand curves around my waist, pulling me flush against him. His lips brush my cheekbone in a lingering kiss, the rough scratch of his beard setting my skin ablaze.

"Sleep well?" he murmurs, his voice a low, gravelly purr that sends a shiver down my spine.

I can only nod mutely, suddenly robbed of the ability to form coherent thoughts. My body melts into his solid frame as if it were made to fit against his.

Silvo's dark gaze holds mine for a heated moment before he finally tears it away, shifting his attention to

Federico. "You behaving yourself over there?" he asks, his tone light but laced with an underlying warning.

Federico shoots me a conspiratorial wink, as if he can sense the tumultuous effect his brother's presence is having on me. "Always," he quips easily. "Although your wife here was getting a bit defensive about those love bites."

I can't tear my gaze away from Silvo as he moves around the kitchen with that effortless grace of his. The way his muscles ripple beneath his shirt with every subtle movement is utterly mesmerizing, and I find myself shamelessly following the contours of his body.

"Eyes up here, baby," Silvo rumbles, his lips curving into a smirk as he catches me staring.

I feel my cheeks flush hot with embarrassment at being caught ogling him so blatantly. Silvo's blue eyes glitter with amusement, and I have to resist the urge to stick my tongue out at him like a petulant child.

"Don't flatter yourself," I retort, lifting my chin defiantly. "I was just trying to figure out how someone so brutish managed to dress themselves this morning."

Federico snorts out a laugh, clearly enjoying our back-and-forth banter. Silvo, however, merely arches an eyebrow at me, completely unfazed by my jab.

"Is that so?" he murmurs, taking a slow sip from his coffee mug. His gaze drops pointedly to the marks littering my skin, and I feel my face grow even hotter under his heated appraisal.

"Well, if it's brutish you're into, I can definitely be that for you," he adds, his voice a low, dangerous purr that sends a shiver of anticipation down my spine.

I open my mouth to deliver a scathing retort, but the words die on my tongue as Silvo closes the distance between us once more. He reaches past me to grab a second cup from the cabinet, his body pressing against mine in a way that's entirely too intimate.

I suck in a sharp breath as his solid frame molds against my back, the hard planes of his chest brushing against me with every subtle movement. His scent—that intoxicating blend of sandalwood, whiskey, and something purely masculine—surrounds me, making my head spin.

"Coffee?" he murmurs, his lips brushing against the shell of my ear. The simple word sends a delicious shiver racing down my spine.

I can only nod mutely. Silvo chuckles low in his throat, the rich sound vibrating against my back in a way that makes my knees go weak.

He takes his time preparing my coffee, his movements slow and deliberate as he adds cream and sugar—just the way I like it. All the while, his body remains pressed against mine in a delicious tease, stoking the simmering embers of desire that never seem to fully extinguish between us.

Finally, he hands me the steaming cup, his fingers brushing against mine in a lingering caress. Our gazes lock, the air between us crackling with an electric tension that's becoming all too familiar.

"Thanks," I manage to murmur, my voice coming out breathier than I intended.

Silvo's lips curve into a slow, predatory smile that makes my pulse kick up a notch. "My pleasure, baby," he rumbles, his gaze drifting over me in a way that leaves me feeling utterly exposed.

With a wink and a final brush of his hand against the small of my back, he moves away, leaving me flustered and aching in a way that has become far too common in his presence.

As Silvo and Federico delve into a discussion about

business, I watch the subtle movements of Silvo's lips as he speaks, remembering what they felt like against my skin last night—warm, insistent, relentless.

It frustrates me that I can't shake these feelings of desire for my husband. But maybe I don't want to avoid them anymore. Maybe I want to lean into them, see where they lead.

Even as I allow myself that thought, my gaze remains fixed on him. His eyes glint with an unreadable mix of emotions, and I realize with a start that he's aware of my scrutiny. A lazy smile curves his lips, and I feel my cheeks flush.

As if sensing my turmoil, Federico chooses that moment to interject. "You two lovebirds heading out today?" he asks.

Silvo's eyes flick to me, a silent question in their depths. I feel a moment of uncertainty as I search for the right answer, one that won't give away the fact that we haven't discussed our plans.

Before I can respond, Silvo speaks. "Actually, I have some business to take care of this afternoon."

His words hit me with unexpected force. Of course, he has business to attend to—illegal, dangerous business that could get him killed or thrown in prison. The realization cuts through my haze of contentment, reminding me that our world is still dangerous, still unpredictable.

"Be careful," I blurt out, the words rushed and unguarded.

Silvo's eyebrows shoot up, clearly surprised by my concern. His gaze softens as he studies me. "I will," he murmurs, reaching out to tuck a stray lock of hair behind my ear. His thumb lingers on my cheek, his touch sending a rush of heat through my body.

I swallow hard, my pulse pounding in my ears. When did his safety become so important to me? When did I start worrying about whether he'd come home?

"Carmela..." he breathes.

His lips descend on mine—the kiss is slow and intoxicating—ending a rush of desire coursing through my veins. I feel myself melt against him, my hands reaching up to tangle in his hair as the kiss deepens.

Finally, he pulls away, his eyes dark with desire. He leans close, his lips brushing my ear as he whispers, "That's just a taste of what's to come tonight, baby."

I shiver as his words send a bolt of anticipation straight to my core. My eyes flick to Federico, who watches us with an amused glint in his eye. I can feel the heat creeping up my neck, knowing he's witnessed the entire exchange.

Silvo grins. "I'll see you later, baby," he murmurs, placing one last lingering kiss on my lips before turning to leave.

As I watch him walk away, I realize I'm no longer torn between desire and fear—I'm simply wanting him back already. Being with Silvo De Luca is like playing with fire, and I've stopped trying to resist the flames.

16

SILVO

I stride down the hallway, my footsteps echoing off the marble floors. My mind is consumed with thoughts of the Moretti situation. Strategies forming and discarding themselves with each passing moment. So focused am I on my own thoughts that I nearly collide with Carmela as she rounds the corner.

"Whoa, easy there," I say, my hands instinctively reaching out to steady her.

Her green eyes flash with surprise, then soften when they land on me. After last night and this morning, there's a new ease between us—fragile, but real.

"Silvo," she says, her lips curving into a small smile. "Everything okay? You look tense."

I realize my jaw is clenched tight, my shoulders rigid. "Just came from a meeting with my father. Nothing for you to worry about."

Her smile fades, replaced by concern. "The Morettis?"

I'm surprised she's picked up on the family dynamics so quickly. "You're observant."

"I pay attention." She reaches up, smoothing the furrow

between my brows with her thumb. The gentle gesture catches me off guard. "What did he say?"

I hesitate, the instinct to shield her from the darker aspects of my world warring with a newfound desire to include her. "He's handing over full control of operations to me. The Morettis have been pushing boundaries, and he wants me to handle it."

Carmela's hand drops to my chest, resting over my heart. "That's a lot of responsibility."

"It's what I was born for." But saying it out loud, with her looking at me like that, makes the weight feel heavier somehow.

"Still," she says softly, "it's okay to admit it's overwhelming."

Her understanding, her willingness to see beyond the role I'm expected to play, loosens something in my chest. I pull her closer, not caring that we're standing in the middle of the hallway where anyone could see.

"Last night," I murmur, my lips brushing her temple, "this morning—that's what I need. You. Us. It's the only thing that makes sense anymore."

She tilts her head up, her green eyes searching mine. "I'm scared, Silvo."

"Of me?"

"Of how much I'm starting to need this. Need you." The confession seems to cost her something, vulnerability shining in her gaze.

I cup her face in my hands. "Then don't fight it anymore. I'm done fighting it."

"What if I lose myself?"

"You won't," I promise, my voice fierce. "I'll never let that happen. Your fire, your independence, your strength—

those are the things I'm falling for, Carmela. I don't want to change you. I want all of you, exactly as you are."

Her breath catches, and for a moment, we just stand there, the weight of what's building between us heavy in the air.

"I don't want to lose myself to this marriage," she finally says, her voice barely above a whisper. "There's more to me than just being Mrs. De Luca, your wife."

Her words pierce through me, and I understand completely. I take a step back, giving her space to breathe.

"You're right," I say, meaning it. "Being my wife will never eclipse who you are, Carmela."

She blinks, surprise flickering across her features as if she hadn't expected me to understand.

"You're a force of nature," I continue. "Fierce, passionate, uncompromising. Those are the qualities that drew me to you from the moment we met. I don't want you to lose that fire, that essence that makes you who you are."

Her gaze holds mine, searching for any hint of deception, but finding only sincerity. Slowly, the tension in her body begins to dissipate, and she offers me the faintest of smiles.

"Thank you, Silvo," she says softly. "I needed to hear that."

I nod, brushing a stray strand of hair from her face. "I can promise you I will never try to change who you are at your core. Your independence, your strength, your passions... they're what make you, you. And I want nothing more than for you to embrace them fully."

Carmela's eyes shine with understanding, and in that moment, I feel a shift between us. A barrier has been broken, a wall of mistrust and fear chipped away, allowing a glimmer of real connection to shine through.

"Alright then," she says, squeezing my hand. "I'm holding you to that, Mr. De Luca."

I chuckle, pulling her into an embrace and relishing the feeling of her body against mine, the warmth and vitality that seems to radiate from her very being.

"Wouldn't have it any other way, Mrs. De Luca."

I pull back slightly, studying her face. "Come with me to my office. I want to show you something."

Curiosity flickers in her eyes. "What is it?"

"You'll see."

I take her hand and lead her to my private study. Once inside, I unlock a drawer in my desk and pull out a thick folder.

"What's this?" she asks as I hand it to her.

"Everything about the Moretti family. Their operations, their weaknesses, their history with us." I lean against the desk. "If you're going to be my wife in this world, you should understand the players."

Carmela opens the folder, her eyes scanning the documents. "You're trusting me with this?"

"You proved yourself at that poker table. You're smart, observant, strategic." I cross my arms. "And you're right—you're more than just my wife. You could be an asset to this family if you choose to be."

She looks up at me, something shifting in her expression. "You really mean that."

"I do." I move closer. "I told you I wouldn't change who you are. But I also won't waste your talents by keeping you in the dark."

A slow smile spreads across her face. "Teach me, then. Everything."

The trust implicit in those words hits me harder than any bullet. This is what I've been hoping for—Carmela choosing to be my partner, not just accepting her role but embracing it.

"It starts with the Morettis," I say, opening the folder to the first page. "And why does my father want them eliminated?"

As we bend over the documents together, our shoulders touching, I realize this is the real turning point. Not the sex, not the passion, but this—the moment she chooses to stand beside me fully, eyes open to all the darkness and danger that comes with my name.

And I've never wanted her more.

17

CARMELA

I hear a commotion downstairs and venture out of my room to investigate. To my utter shock and delight, I see Sophia standing in the foyer, her signature mischievous grin plastered across her face.

"Surprise!" she exclaims, throwing her arms wide open.

I rush down the stairs, nearly tripping over my own feet in my excitement, and envelop her in a tight hug.

"What are you doing here?" I ask, still in disbelief.

"I couldn't let my best friend navigate married life alone, could I?" Sophia winks, her eyes sparkling with mirth.

I pull back from our embrace, tears of joy and relief welling up in my eyes. "Soph, you have no idea how much this means to me. I've missed you so much."

Sophia's expression softens, her brows knitting together in concern. "How are you doing, really? Your texts have been so... careful."

I take a deep breath, glancing toward the kitchen where I can hear the family. "It's been... complicated. But not in the way I expected."

"Complicated how?"

I bite my lip, trying to find the right words. "I think I'm falling for him, Soph. My arranged husband. How insane is that?"

Sophia's eyes widen, then a slow smile spreads across her face. "Not insane at all. Tell me everything."

"Wait—first, how long are you here for? Just a visit, or...?" I ask, suddenly realizing we haven't even discussed the logistics.

Sophia takes a deep breath, her smile turning more serious. "That's actually what I wanted to talk to you about. I'm not going back to LA, Carm. I'm staying here. In Philly."

My mouth falls open. "What? But your job, your apartment, your whole life is there!"

"Was there," she corrects. "I gave notice two weeks ago, sublet my apartment, and packed up everything that matters. It's all in a storage unit until I figure out where I'm living here."

"Sophia..." Tears spring to my eyes. "You did all that for me?"

"Of course I did." She squeezes my hands. "You're my best friend. You were forced to leave everything behind and start over in a strange city. I wasn't about to let you do that alone."

I pull her into a fierce hug, overwhelmed by her loyalty. "I don't deserve you, Soph."

"Nonsense," she scoffs, pulling back to look at me. "You deserve the world. And I'm going to make damn sure you get it, even if I have to take on the entire De Luca family myself."

I laugh through my tears. "You're insane, you know that?" I take Sophia's hand, excitement bubbling up.

"Speaking of the De Luca family, let me introduce you to them. Brace yourself—they're quite a bunch."

Sophia grins, squeezing my hand in reassurance. "Lead the way, darling. I'm ready for anything."

I guide her into the kitchen, where Silvo, Federico, and Isabella are gathered around the table. Federico and Isabella, caught in the middle of a lively debate, pause to take in the new arrival.

And then there's Silvo. His piercing blue eyes lock onto mine, a mixture of curiosity and possessiveness swirling in their depths. I feel a shiver run down my spine, but this time it's not from fear—it's anticipation.

"Everyone, this is Sophia, my best friend from back home," I announce, my voice steady and confident.

Isabella is the first to approach, enveloping Sophia in a warm hug. "I'm Isabella. Welcome to the madhouse. Any friend of Carmela's is a friend of ours."

Sophia returns the hug, her smile genuine. "Thank you, Isabella. It's a pleasure to meet you."

Fed nods, his eyes dropping down her body appraisingly. "I trust you'll be staying with us for a while, Sophia?"

"If it's not too much trouble," Sophia replies. "I couldn't bear the thought of Carmela navigating all this without her best friend."

I feel a surge of affection for my friend, grateful for her unwavering support.

It's Silvo's reaction that I'm most interested in. He rises from his seat, his movements fluid and deliberate. He extends a hand to Sophia, though his gaze keeps returning to mine.

"Sophia, it's a pleasure," he says. "I'm sure Carmela is thrilled to have you here."

I can't quite decipher the undercurrent of emotion in

his tone, but I refuse to let it unsettle me. Meeting his gaze head-on, I detect the question there—is this going to be a problem?

"I am," I confirm, my voice unwavering. "Sophia's presence here means the world to me."

Silvo's jaw tightens almost imperceptibly, but he quickly masks it with a charming smile. "Well, we're happy to have you, Sophia. Please, make yourself at home."

Fed stands, a charming grin spreading across his face, and pulls out a chair for her at the table. "Please, have a seat," he offers, his voice smooth as honey.

Sophia flashes him a dazzling smile. "Why, thank you, Federico. Such a gentleman."

I watch the exchange, amusement, and wariness swirling in my gut. The spark of interest in Sophia's eyes worries me, especially since Federico has a reputation as a notorious flirt.

As Sophia shifts in her seat, Federico leans in close. "So, tell me, Sophia. What brings a beautiful woman like yourself to our humble abode?"

"Well, aside from being Carmela's emotional support system, I couldn't pass up the opportunity to meet the infamous De Luca family."

Fed's grin widens. "Infamous, huh? I like the sound of that."

I clear my throat, shooting Fed a warning look. "Easy there. Sophia's here as my friend, not your latest conquest."

He holds up his hands in mock surrender, his expression one of feigned innocence. "Hey, I'm just being friendly. No harm in that, right?"

Sophia places a hand on my arm. "It's okay. I can handle a little harmless flirting."

I sigh, knowing that trying to control either of them is a

losing battle. "Fine. But remember, Fed, Sophia's off-limits."

My brother-in-law winks at me, his grin turning impish. "Duly noted, sis. I'll be on my best behavior."

Silvo, who has been observing the exchange with a calculating gaze, clears his throat. "Well, now that the introductions are out of the way, perhaps we can eat like a regular fucking family."

There's an edge to his tone, and I sense he's irritated by something. Maybe Fed's immediate interest in Sophia, or maybe simply the disruption to our routine. I catch his eye and see the tension there, the possessiveness that never quite leaves.

I lead Sophia up the grand staircase, our arms linked as we make our way to the guest room. The dinner had been a whirlwind of emotions, with Federico's relentless flirting and Silvo's brooding presence. I'm grateful for the momentary escape, the chance to catch my breath and reconnect with my best friend.

As we enter the guest room, Sophia flops down on the plush bed, a contented sigh escaping her lips. "Wow, Carmela. This place is something else."

I sit beside her, my fingers absently tracing the intricate embroidery on the duvet. "It's a lot to take in, isn't it?"

Sophia props herself up on her elbows, her eyes meeting mine with that knowing look that sees right through me. "Okay, now that we're alone—how are you really doing? And I want the truth this time."

I let out a shaky laugh. "Honestly? I don't even know anymore. Everything's changed so fast."

"Changed how?" She sits up fully, giving me her complete attention.

I take a deep breath, trying to untangle the knot of feelings in my chest. "Silvo... he's like a force of nature," I begin, my voice barely above a whisper. "When we're together, it's electric. The way he touches me, the way he looks at me... it's like nothing I've ever experienced before."

I feel a flush creep up my neck as memories flood my mind—the poker night, the car, this morning's kiss in the kitchen.

"But it's not just physical," I continue, my brows furrowing. "There are these moments when he lets his guard down. When he promises not to change who I am, when he looks at me like I'm the most important thing in his world."

Sophia nods, her expression shifting to understanding. "It sounds like you're falling for him."

I bite my lip, the truth of her words settling over me. "I think I already have. And it terrifies me, Soph. A few weeks ago, I hated the idea of this marriage. Now..." I trail off, unable to finish.

"Now you can't imagine your life without him," Sophia finishes gently.

I nod, a tear slipping down my cheek. "How did this happen? How did I go from resenting everything about this arrangement to actually wanting it?"

Sophia takes my hand, her touch a comforting anchor. "Oh, honey. Love doesn't follow rules or timelines. It just happens."

"But what if I lose myself in this?" I whisper, voicing my deepest fear. "What if I become just another mafia wife, existing only as an extension of him?"

"From what I saw downstairs, that man doesn't want to change you," Sophia says firmly. "The way he watched you during dinner—that's not a man who wants a docile wife. That's a man completely fascinated by your strength."

I manage a small smile. "He did say he doesn't want to change me."

"And do you believe him?"

I think about this morning, how he understood my fears without me having to explain. "Yeah. I think I do."

Sophia squeezes my hand. "Then maybe it's okay to let yourself fall. You don't have to have everything figured out right now."

I nod, wiping at my eyes. "When did you get so wise?"

"I've always been wise. You were just too stubborn to notice," she teases, making me laugh.

After a moment, a sudden idea sparks in my mind. "Hey, why don't we go out tomorrow night? Just the two of us, like old times."

Sophia's eyes light up, a grin spreading across her face. "Hell yes! I'm so down for a girls' night."

"It's settled then—tomorrow night we party." I grin at her, though a flutter of nervousness runs through me. Silvo won't love the idea of me going out without him. He's intensely protective. But he also said he doesn't want to change who I am, and going out with my best friend is part of who I've always been. He'll have to understand that.

18

SILVO

I check my watch again. 12:47 AM. Carmela and Sophia have been out for over five hours, and while I know girls' nights typically run late, the silence is eating at me. My calls go straight to voicemail, my texts are unanswered.

Club music is loud. She's probably having fun, lost in conversation with Sophia. Her phone's probably at the bottom of her purse.

But the rational explanations don't ease the knot tightening in my chest.

I search the house anyway, checking the library, her favorite sitting room, even the gardens—nothing. Each empty room confirms what I already know: she's still out.

I find one of the household staff in the hallway. "Have you seen Mrs. De Luca?"

The maid shifts nervously. "She and Miss Sophia left around seven, sir. I heard them mention a club—Inferno, I think?"

My jaw clenches. She'd mentioned wanting a girls' night out at breakfast, and I'd agreed—told her to have fun, even. But I'd expected her to at least check in, let me know she was okay.

"Thank you," I dismiss the maid.

I return to my study, the whiskey burning down my throat as I try to calm the protective instincts roaring through me. This morning, she'd asked me to be careful. The concern in her voice had touched something deep inside me. I thought we were finally building real trust.

But trust goes both ways, doesn't it? And right now, I'm sitting here imagining worst-case scenarios while she's out there, unreachable.

I pour another drink, the amber liquid catching the lamplight. Maybe I'm overreacting. Maybe this is exactly what it looks like—me being a possessive bastard who can't handle his wife having a life outside of him.

But what if something's wrong? What if she needs me and can't reach me because her phone died or—

I'm pacing the room when Fed saunters in, taking in my agitated state with one glance.

"Let me guess," he says, pouring himself a drink. "Carmela's still out, and you're losing your mind."

I shoot him a glare. "It's past midnight, Fed. She's not answering her phone."

Fed raises an eyebrow. "Did you tell her she had to be home by midnight? Give her a curfew?"

"No, but—"

"And girls' nights at clubs usually run until what, two or three in the morning?" Fed takes a casual sip of his drink. "Seems pretty normal to me."

"She's not answering," I growl, my frustration mounting.

"Club's probably loud as hell. Phone's in her purse. She's dancing, having fun with Sophia—you know, the friend she hasn't seen since moving across the country for you." Fed's tone is pointed but not cruel. "This is what normal people do, Silvo."

I stare into my whiskey glass. "I just... what if something happens to her? What if she's in danger and I'm not there?"

"That's fear talking, not logic." Fed leans forward. "You've got a security detail on her, right?"

I nod. "Tony's been tailing them at a distance."

"Then she's fine. She's just having fun with her friend. Something she probably hasn't done since being forced to move across the country." Fed's expression softens. "Look, I know you care about her. Hell, anyone with eyes can see you're falling for her. But if you want to keep her, you have to trust her. Really trust her, not just say you do."

I stare into my whiskey glass, seeing my distorted reflection. He's right. This isn't about Carmela betraying my trust—it's about my own fear of losing control, of losing her.

"So what do you suggest?" I ask grudgingly.

Fed grins. "Call Tony, verify she's safe. Then either you stay here and wait like a normal husband, or we go to Inferno. But not to drag her home—just to make sure she's okay. Have a drink, keep our distance unless there's actual trouble. Show her you respect her independence."

I consider it, then pull out my phone and dial Tony. He answers on the second ring.

"Boss?"

"Status report. Is Carmela safe?"

"Completely safe, boss. She and her friend are at Inferno, been there for a few hours. Dancing, drinking, having a good time. No problems, no unwanted attention. I've got eyes on them the whole time."

Relief floods through me, loosening the tension in my shoulders. “Any issues at all?”

“None. They’re having fun. Sophia’s keeping close to her, and they’ve stayed in the main room where it’s crowded and well-lit. Mrs. De Luca’s having a good time—lots of laughing, dancing. She’s safe.”

“Good. Keep watching. And Tony? If anything changes—”

“You’ll be the first call. I got this, boss.”

I hang up and turn to Fed. “She’s safe. Having fun.”

“See? Crisis averted.” Fed raises his glass. “Now you can either sit here and brood, or we can head over there. Not to control her, just to... be present. Maybe have a drink ourselves.”

I consider it. “And if she sees me there?”

“Then you smile, tell her you and I decided to grab a drink, and you’re glad she’s having fun. You keep your distance unless she needs you.” Fed’s expression turns serious. “This is the test, brother. Can you be the man who trusts his wife, or are you going to be the one who proves all her fears right?”

The words hit home. I remember this morning—the vulnerability in her eyes when she said she was scared of losing herself. My promise that I’d never let that happen.

“Okay,” I say finally. “We go. But we stay back unless there’s trouble.”

“Now you’re thinking straight,” Fed says with approval.

I grab my jacket and follow him to the door. This isn’t about dragging Carmela home or asserting dominance. This is about proving I meant what I said—that I trust her, that I won’t try to control her.

Even when every instinct screams at me to lock her away where she’s safe.

Climbing into my sports car, I turn over the engine, trying to calm the protective instincts still roaring through me. This is about her safety, I tell myself. And about proving I can give her the freedom she needs.

I grip the steering wheel as I weave through the city streets, Fed beside me watching the road.

"You good?" he asks.

"I will be once I see she's safe with my own eyes," I mutter.

"Just remember—we're there for a drink. Not a rescue mission. Not a confrontation." Fed's voice is firm. "You go in there acting like a possessive asshole, and you'll undo everything good that's happened between you two."

"I know," I say through gritted teeth. "I'll keep my distance. Unless there's a problem."

Fed nods, seemingly satisfied. "Good. Because Carmela's finally opening up to you. Don't fuck it up by proving you're exactly the controlling bastard she was afraid you'd be."

I take a sharp turn, the tires gripping the pavement. His words echo what I've been thinking all night.

"I'm not trying to control her. I'm trying to protect her. There's a difference."

"Is there? Because sometimes they look the same from the outside." Fed's voice is gentler now, not mocking. "You've fallen for her, Silvo. Hard. And that terrifies you because you can't control feelings. You can't strategize love."

I grip the wheel tighter, his words settling over me like a heavy blanket. He's right. I am scared. Scared that the woman I'm falling in love with will wake up one day and realize she deserves better than an arranged marriage to someone like me.

"So what do I do?" I ask quietly.

"You trust her. You let her have tonight with her friend. And when you see her in that club, you prove that you meant what you said about respecting who she is."

I nod slowly, the tension in my shoulders easing slightly. "Okay. We check that she's safe, have a drink, then we leave her alone unless she needs us."

"Good plan," Fed says with approval.

As we pull up outside Inferno, the bass thumping through the walls, I take a deep breath. Fed's right. This is a test—not of Carmela, but of me. Whether I can be the man worthy of her, or just another controlling bastard trying to cage a wild bird.

I'm about to find out which one I really am.

19

CARMELA

I take another sip of my drink, the bitter liquid burning my throat as I watch Sophia move her body to the pulsing beat on the dance floor. The flashing lights and pounding music assault my senses. We've been here for hours, and the excitement has worn off, replaced by a dull throb in my temples.

A sleazy guy slides up next to me at the bar, his eyes roaming over my body like I'm a piece of meat. "Hey, beautiful, can I buy you a drink?" he slurs, his breath reeking of alcohol.

I glare at him, disgust twisting in my gut. "No thanks," I snap, turning away from him. But he doesn't take the hint, his sweaty hand grabbing my arm.

"Come on, baby, don't be like that," he whines, trying to pull me toward him.

Anger flares through me, and I yank my arm out of his grasp. "Don't touch me," I hiss through gritted teeth. "I'm married."

The words come naturally now, not strange or forced as they might have weeks ago. Married. To Silvo. And the thought of anyone else touching me makes my skin crawl in a way that has nothing to do with duty and everything to do with desire.

I shake my head slightly. When did that happen? When did I start thinking of myself as truly his?

But I know the answer. It's been happening gradually—through every heated glance, every vulnerable conversation, every moment when he proves he sees me as more than just a trophy wife.

I down the rest of my drink, setting the glass on the bar with more force than necessary. Maybe coming here was about proving I still could—that I haven't completely lost myself to being Mrs. De Luca. But now that I'm here, surrounded by groping hands and leering stares, all I want is to be home with Silvo.

The realization should scare me, but it doesn't. Not anymore.

I scan the crowded club for Sophia, spotting her still lost in the music. I'll give her five more minutes, and then I'm dragging her out of here and going home to my husband. Where I want to be.

Sophia's eyes meet mine, and I mouth the word "Restroom."

I turn to head toward the restroom, pulling out my phone to finally check the messages I've been ignoring. Three missed calls from Silvo. Five texts. My stomach twists with guilt—I should have checked in, let him know I was okay.

But before I can read his messages, a large hand grabs my arm and yanks me backward.

I stumble, slamming against the rough brick wall near the club's back hallway. Panic surges through me as I look up into the leering face of a man I've never seen before. His eyes are glassy, and his breath reeks of cheap beer.

"I've been watching you all night, beautiful," he slurs, pressing his body against mine. I try to shove him away, but he's too strong, pinning me in place with his bulk.

"Get off me!" I shout, my voice drowned out by the pounding music. I struggle against his hold, twisting and clawing at his arms, but it's no use. No one can hear my cries for help over the din of the club.

Bile rises in my throat as I feel his hand sliding up my thigh, pushing the hem of my dress higher. His touch makes my skin crawl, and I squeeze my eyes shut, praying for this nightmare to end.

Suddenly, a dark figure looms behind my attacker, yanking him off me with brutal force. I gasp, my heart pounding as I recognize Silvo's enraged face.

His eyes blaze with fury as he slams the man against the wall, his forearm pressed against the drunk's throat. "You dare touch my wife?" Silvo snarls, his voice deadly.

The man sputters and chokes, his eyes wide with fear. But Silvo shows no mercy, his fist slamming into the man's face with a sickening crunch. Blood spurts from the man's nose as he crumples to the ground, whimpering pathetically.

I should be horrified by Silvo's violence, by the savagery in his eyes as he kicks the man in the ribs. But instead, relief washes over me, so strong it makes my knees weak.

Silvo saved me. He protected me when I needed him most. The violence that should repel me only makes me feel safer, more protected.

My beast of a husband turns to me, his chest heaving and his knuckles bloody. His eyes rake over my body, checking for injuries. "Are you alright?" he asks, his voice rough with emotion.

I nod, my throat too tight to speak. Silvo pulls me into his arms, crushing me against his solid chest. I cling to him, breathing in his familiar scent of sandalwood and musk.

"I've got you," he murmurs, his lips brushing my hair. "You're safe now."

Safe. In Silvo's arms, I finally feel safe. The adrenaline fades, leaving me shaky and exhausted. But there's something else too—a hunger that burns through my veins, intensified by the danger and his fierce protection.

I tilt my head back, meeting Silvo's intense gaze. The heat in his eyes matches my own, and I know he feels it too. This undeniable pull between us, this primal need.

"I'm sorry," I whisper. "I should have answered your calls. I should have—"

"We'll talk about it later," he says, his thumb stroking my cheek. "Right now, I need to get you home."

But there's no real anger in his voice anymore—just relief and that possessive heat that makes my core clench.

"I want to go home," I admit. "With you."

Something shifts in his expression—satisfaction mixed with tenderness. "Then let's go home, wife."

He keeps me tucked against his side as we make our way back through the club, and I realize I'm not fighting his protectiveness anymore. I'm leaning into it, accepting it, wanting it.

Maybe that's what was missing all night—him.

Silvo's gaze darkens, his eyes practically burning. I shiver, feeling a mix of excitement and apprehension as his lips brush my ear, his breath warm against my skin.

"You've been a very bad girl, baby." His voice is rough,

sending shivers down my spine. "Not answering your phone, making me worry."

My heart hammers in my chest as he threads his fingers through mine, his touch possessive. "I should teach you a lesson," he whispers. "Bend you over my knee and spank that beautiful ass of yours until it's nice and red."

I swallow hard, my breath coming in short gasps. The boldness of his words sends a rush of heat between my thighs. "Silvo—"

But he cuts me off, his lips claiming mine in a fierce kiss. I melt into him, my hands tangling in his hair as the kiss deepens. His tongue teases mine, tasting of mint and promise.

His hands roam over my body, igniting trails of fire everywhere they touch. "I'm going to take you home," he growls against my mouth. "And I'm going to fuck you until you can't remember anyone else's touch but mine."

A moan escapes my throat at his graphic words. The pulsing beat of the club seems to fade away, leaving only the two of us in our own world.

Silvo's hands slide down to cup my ass, pulling me tightly against his thick cock. "I'm going to start by ripping that pretty dress off you and tossing you over the bed." His thumbs stroke the sensitive skin just below the hem of my dress, making me squirm. "Then I'm going to spank you until your ass is burning and you're begging me to stop."

I whimper, my face flaming hot as my body betrays me, yearning for his touch. "Silvo, please..."

"Please, what, Carmela?" He nips at my ear, his hands continuing their torturous path. "Are you going to beg me to fuck you? To make you forget all about that piece of trash who touched you tonight?"

"Yes," I whisper, my face pressed against his neck. "Please, Silvo. Make me forget everything but you."

"As you wish, baby." He crushes his lips to mine in one last dizzying kiss before leading me out of the club and to his car.

I slide into the passenger seat of Silvo's car, my heart still pounding from our heated encounter in the club. Sophia is sitting in the back, chatting animatedly with Silvo's brother Fed. But as soon as Silvo climbs into the driver's side, Fed's eyes zero in on his bloody knuckles.

"Whoa, what happened to you?" Fed asks, his brow furrowing with concern. "You get in a fight or something?"

Silvo flexes his hand, wincing slightly. "Some asshole was getting handsy with Carmela. I had to teach him a lesson."

Fed's eyes widen, and he looks over at me, as if checking for himself that I'm okay. I give him a small nod, trying to reassure him that I'm fine. Physically, at least. Emotionally, I'm still processing everything.

"Damn, Silvo. You really did a number on him, huh?" Fed says, a hint of admiration in his voice. "Remind me never to piss you off."

Silvo just grunts, his jaw clenched tight. I can feel the tension radiating off him in waves, and I know he's still processing what happened.

Sophia reaches forward and squeezes my shoulder. "Are you okay, Carmela?"

I swallow hard, forcing a smile and glance back at her. "I'm fine, Soph. Thanks to Silvo." I glance over at him, meeting his intense gaze. "He saved me."

Something flickers in Silvo's eyes—possessiveness, relief, and something deeper. He reaches over and takes my hand, lacing our fingers together on the center console. "I'll always protect you. No matter what."

His words send a shiver down my spine. I know Silvo would do anything to keep me safe, and tonight proved it. The violence should disturb me, but instead it only makes me feel more connected to him, more certain that despite how this marriage started, it's becoming something real.

I squeeze his hand, my heart racing as I meet his heated gaze. "I know you will," I whisper, my voice barely audible over the hum of the car engine. "I trust you, Silvo."

And I mean it. Completely.

20

SILVO

Adrenaline still pumps through my veins as I lead Carmela back to our room. The violence from the club, the fear I felt when I saw that piece of shit put his hands on her—it all culminates in a possessive need that threatens to consume me.

I whirl around to face her, my jaw clenched tight.

"I'm going to clean that bastard's blood off my hands," I growl, my voice rough.

Carmela's eyes widen, but to my surprise, she reaches out and grabs my hand, stopping me in my tracks. "No, Silvo," she says. "Take me with your hands as they are—stained with that man's blood."

Her words catch me off guard, and I stare at her, stunned. The defiant glint in her eyes dares me to challenge her, and in that moment, I'm reminded of why I've been so drawn to her since Giovani's club in LA. Her unwavering spirit, her refusal to be cowed, speaks to me like nothing ever has.

Without a word, I pull her close, my blood-stained hands cupping her face as I kiss her. She responds with equal fervor, her body molding to mine as we lose ourselves in the heated embrace.

"Does it turn you on, seeing me like this? My hands covered in another man's blood?" I ask, my eyes searching hers.

"You know it does, Silvo," she says, her voice husky, sending a shiver down my spine. "You know the sight of your raw power sets my body on fire."

Her admission sends a rush of pride through me, and I grasp her hips, pulling her firmly against me. "You like it when I play rough, when I mark you as mine."

It's not a question, but she answers anyway. "I do. It makes me feel..." She trails off, biting her lip as her cheeks flush a pretty pink.

"Makes you feel what, baby?" I prompt, tilting her chin up, forcing her to meet my gaze.

She swallows. "It makes me feel alive. Protected. Like I'm exactly where I belong."

I bend my head and claim her mouth in a punishing kiss, my hands twisting in her hair to angle her head just so.

Up to now, I've kept my darker desires in check, wanting to ease Carmela into my world. But tonight, seeing her in danger, unleashed the beast within. That spark of defiance in her eyes—even after being attacked—dares me to push her; to show her exactly how much she means to me.

Yanking her around so her back is pressed to my chest, I unfasten the zipper down the side of her dress and strip her. My wife doesn't resist, helping as she steps out of it and then pulls her panties down eagerly, tossing them aside.

I bite her shoulder and unfasten her bra, yanking it

away. Once she's naked for me, I cup her tits and play with her pebbled nipples.

Carmela arches her back, moaning.

"Lie on the bed," I demand.

She does as she's told, lying down on her back and watching me. I open my nightstand and pull out a length of rope.

Her eyes widen. "What are you going to do with that?"

"Introduce you to a whole new world of pleasure," I state. Curiosity, apprehension, and a darker emotion flash across Carmela's face.

Uncoiling the rope, I let it dangle in front of her eyes. "Do you trust me?" I ask, my voice steady, belying the pounding of my heart. This is a moment of truth, a test of our connection.

She studies my face for a moment, her green eyes searching, and then she surprises me with a bold smile. "With my life, husband."

"Good," I murmur, my fingers already deftly working the rope, crafting intricate patterns against her creamy skin. "Because I'm about to show you how good it can be to submit."

This is a delicate process, one that requires focus and care. I start with Carmela's torso, wrapping the rope in intricate diamond patterns across her chest and around her waist. She watches me intently as I work, focused on creating beautiful rope lines that accentuate her curves.

I move down to her legs, gently bending her knees and binding her thighs to her calves so she's naturally spread for me.

The rope creeps steadily up toward her most sensitive areas, but I purposefully avoid them for now. I want her arousal to build, craving my eventual touch. Her breathing grows heavier in anticipation, skin flushing beneath the crisscrossing ropes.

I move upwards along her arms, restricting her movements. Her hands are bound palm to palm behind her back, secured but not uncomfortable. I check the ropes, ensuring they are properly tight and secure. Carmela tests the bindings.

The rope wraps her body like fine lingerie, emphasizing her beauty. She lies before me, vulnerable yet trusting, eyes bright with desire.

Leaning down, I press a soft kiss to her shoulder. "You look beautiful like this. Bound for me and only me."

I can't resist bending to capture one of her taut nipples between my teeth, biting down gently before soothing it with my tongue. She whines so prettily.

"You like that, don't you?" I murmur. "You like being tied up and played with."

"Yes... please, Silvo..." Carmela whimpers.

Hearing her say my name like that, her voice thick with need, sends a shot of lust straight to my groin. I trace my fingers down her stomach, watching her muscles clench with anticipation.

"Are you ready for more?" I ask, my tone dark and possessive.

She nods eagerly, her eyes fixed on me.

I take her response as permission to explore further, my fingers dipping lower, tracing lazy circles around her core.

She's wetter than she's ever been. "Look at this, Carmela," I whisper, my fingers gliding through her slickness. "You are so fucking wet."

A pretty red blush creeps up her neck, but her eyes remain locked on mine, daring me to continue. I chuckle darkly, my thumb pressing gently against her clit, relishing the small gasp that escapes her.

But I have other plans for now.

I position her like a doll on her knees for me, her shoulders resting against pillows on the mattress. Once she's settled, I grip her hips and bring my pelvis toward her ass, admiring the way her ass cheeks look framed in rope.

Taking a firm grip on one curved cheek, I squeeze.

Carmela whimpers, and I swat her playfully, the sound echoing in the room. The imprint of my hand stands out pink against her creamy skin, and I grow harder than I believed possible at the sight, knowing I put that mark there.

I pepper kisses down her spine, enjoying the taste of her skin, before pausing to nibble lightly on one side of her ass. Carmela mewls, pushing back against me, and I chuckle, the sound turning into a groan as I deliver a sharper smack, the sound filling the room.

Again and again, I alternate between torturing her with my tongue and biting her flesh before spanking her hard. Her skin grows pinker, marked by me. The sound of my palm connecting with her flesh becomes the cadence of our growing desire.

Carmela writhes before me, her hips pushing back to meet my hand, her bound arms straining. Her breath comes in sharp pants as each spank sends pleasure-pain through her body.

I feast on the sight of her like this—bound, writhing, and at my mercy. Every whimper, every squirm only fuels my desire, and I know I won't be able to hold back much longer. But I want her absolutely shattered, a boneless mess, before I finally claim her.

So, I continue my ruthless assault, enjoying the way her

moans fill the room, intermingled with the sharp sound of my palm meeting her flesh.

The sound is dark and full of promise as I watch her dance for me, bucking her hips against the bed. She's desperate, so close to the edge, and I want to savor every moment of her beautiful agony.

Reaching into my nightstand, I pull out a vibrator. As the low buzz fills the room, Carmela tries to look at me over her shoulder, but can't with the restraints. I run it gently up her calves, enjoying the way her breath catches as I trace lazy circles on her skin.

Then, slowly, deliberately, I drag the vibrating toy up her thighs, relishing her whimpers as it teases her wet, eager core. I pause, letting the toy hover just shy of where she wants it most, smiling at her frustrated whine.

She tries to buck her hips, seeking more friction. "Please, Silvo... I need... oh, God, please!"

"You need what, Carmela?" I ask.

"You know what I need," she bites out, her voice strained. "Don't stop, please don't stop!"

Teasingly, I run the vibrator along her slit, avoiding her clit. "You want to come, don't you, Carmela? Want to feel that sweet release?"

"Yes! Yes, please, I need to come," she begs.

"Not yet, beautiful. Not until I'm buried deep inside you."

"Please, Silvo... I can't take much more... please let me come."

My cock throbs at the desperate edge in her voice. "Not yet," I growl. "Not until I say so."

With that, I press the vibrator firmly against her clit, sending her close to the edge. Only to back off instantly, making her grunt.

Teasing is an art form. Knowing when to stop, when to start, and when to edge right up to the line.

I continue, building Carmela's anticipation with the vibrator, her needy whimpers spurring me on. I swipe the toy along her swollen folds, dipping it inside her.

"Please, Silvo..." she gasps. "I'm begging you... let me come."

The power I hold over her at this moment is heady. With a final swipe of the vibrator, I set it aside, instead delivering a sharp smack to her ass. The pink imprint of my hand stands out against her flushed skin, a mark of my possession.

My wife jerks at the contact, her body shuddering. "Please..." she whimpers.

I free my cock from the confines of my pants, lining myself up with her dripping wet core. Slowly, torturously, I rub the tip of my cock through her folds, not quite entering, but teasing her.

Carmela mewls, bucking her hips in an attempt to impale herself on my length. I hold her hips firmly, preventing her from getting what she craves. "Not yet. Be patient, wife."

Her cunt is hot and wet, her arousal coating my tip as I play with her. I groan, my control fraying, but I force myself to savor this moment just a little longer.

I tease my cockhead inside her, feeling her greedy muscles clench around me, begging me to fill her. But I pause, grinding my hips in tiny circles. She's so responsive, so damned perfect, and it takes every ounce of my self-control not to bury myself deep inside her right then and there.

"Silvo, please..." she pants, her body quaking as she

struggles against the restraints. "I need you. Please, just fuck me already!"

Hearing my wife beg for me, I know I won't be able to hold back much longer. I want to feel her heat enveloping me, taking all of me willingly.

I tease her with shallow thrusts, but it's too much for both of us. With a growl of possessive hunger, I slam into her, claiming every inch of her in one stroke.

Carmela's cry of pleasure is muffled by the pillow as her inner walls squeeze my cock in the most incredible way. Her release squirts from her cunt, drenching my cock and the sheets.

I grasp her hips, my fingers anchor into her soft flesh as I begin to move. Each thrust is a claim, a reminder that she's mine. Her body moves as best it can in the restraints, taking every stroke eagerly.

I bite back a groan as her inner muscles flutter around me, her second orgasm washing over her. Her body clenches and releases, again and again, milking my cock, threatening to push me over the edge. I've never felt anything like this, and I know I won't last much longer.

The desire to see her face is overwhelming. I want to watch the expressions cross her features as I take her, so I pull out.

I grasp the ropes binding her wrists behind her back and yank her up. Her eyes spark with surprise at the abrupt motion, but it only serves to fuel the fire burning between us. I reposition her, laying her down on her back.

The ropes bite into her skin, crisscrossing her breasts and marking her thighs, and her legs are spread wide, leaving her exposed and open to me.

I take a moment to admire her, my wife, laid out like a

feast. The flush on her chest, the heaving of her breasts, and the hunger in her eyes—it's all for me.

In one swift motion, I slide into her.

With each thrust, I feel the connection between us grow stronger, the tension and desire building like a storm. I can't get enough of the way she feels. Never get enough.

Leaning down, I capture her lips in a hungry kiss, our tongues tangling as passionately as our bodies. I want to consume her, and I know she wants the same. The kiss is fierce and demanding, a reflection of the raw need that's taken hold of us both.

"You like that, don't you?" I growl against her lips, my hips snapping forward. "You like being tied up and fucked by your husband."

Carmela whimpers into the kiss, her body arching to meet my thrusts. "Yes... yes, I do," she admits.

Pulling back, I look down at where our bodies are joined, watching as I slide in and out of her. "You're so fucking tight, Carmela. Your cunt grips me so perfectly. It's like you were made for me, designed to take my cock."

Her cheeks flush at my words, but her eyes smolder with desire. "I'm yours, Silvo. Only yours."

I thrust into her harder. "That's right, you're mine. And I plan to mark every inch of this beautiful body as mine."

My lips brush her ear as I whisper, "I'm going to fuck you until you can't remember your own name, until you're screaming mine."

"Yes... Silvo... oh, God, yes..."

My hands grasp her bound wrists, holding them above her head as I pound into her. "That's it, wife, take it. Take all of me."

Carmela bucks her hips against mine, meeting my hunger with her own. "Fuck... Silvo... I'm... so close..."

"Come for me, Carmela. Let me feel you fall apart around me."

Her inner walls clench tighter as her third orgasm rips through her. I continue my relentless assault, driving her through one climax and toward another.

I can feel my own release coiling in my balls, building with each stroke. "That's it, wife, let it wash over you. Come for your husband."

Her moans fill the room, her body trembling as she rides out the pleasure. "Carmela..." I groan, my voice rough as I reach my own peak. "Fuck!"

With a few more powerful thrusts, I spill myself into her, claiming her once more as mine. I collapse against her, my body shaking with the force of my release. For a long moment, I simply hold her bound body, enjoying the way she fits so perfectly against mine. Slowly, I roll off her and then reach out to undo the ropes binding her body, rubbing the marks left behind soothingly.

Carmela stretches languidly, a satisfied smile on her face. "That was..." she starts.

"Incredible," I finish for her, pressing a gentle kiss to her lips. "You're incredible."

She hums contentedly, snuggling into my arms. I pull her close, relishing the feel of her soft skin against mine. In this moment, everything else fades away—the responsibilities, the expectations, the weight of my role as head of the family. Right now, it's just us, Silvo and Carmela, husband and wife, lost in the aftermath of our passion.

I know there will be challenges ahead, obstacles we'll have to face. But as I hold Carmela in my arms, I feel a sense of certainty settle over me. Whatever comes our way, we'll handle it. Together.

21

CARMELA

Isabella and Sophia are by my side as we step into the bustling shopping mall. There's a ball being held tomorrow night, and Isabella suggested we all go and find new dresses for the occasion. After last night's intensity—the club, the rescue, the way Silvo claimed every part of me—today feels like a welcome return to something normal.

Isabella turns to me with a warm smile. "I'm so glad we could do this. After everything lately, we all needed a break."

I nod, feeling grateful for this moment of peace. "Me too. It's nice to just... be normal for a few hours."

Sophia links her arm with mine, a mischievous glint in her eye. "And what better way to spend that time than by spending your husband's money?"

I can't help but laugh at her boldness. "Sophia, you're terrible!"

As we weave in and out of stores, trying on dresses and shoes, I find myself opening up to Isabella in a way that feels natural now. We share stories, laugh freely, and for a while, I forget about the weight of my new world.

Isabella's eyes soften as she listens to me talk about adjusting to life in Philly. "You've adapted better than anyone expected. You're strong, and you have a fire in you that I admire."

I feel a lump form in my throat. "Thank you, Isabella. That means more to me than you know."

Sophia, sensing the emotional moment, breaks the tension with a playful nudge. "Okay, enough of the heavy stuff. Let's go find some lingerie that'll make Silvo's jaw drop!"

Isabella makes a sound like she's going to throw up. "That's my brother you're talking about."

Sophia chuckles. "Sorry, I forgot."

As we continue our shopping spree, I find myself genuinely enjoying myself.

We enter a high-end boutique, and Isabella immediately gravitates toward a stunning emerald green dress. She holds it up to her body, and I can't help but admire how it complements her olive skin and dark hair.

"Isabella, that dress is absolutely perfect for you," I encourage.

She smiles, a hint of shyness in her eyes. "You think so? I don't usually splurge on myself like this."

Sophia chimes in, "Girl, if you don't buy that dress, I will. And trust me, it won't look nearly as good on me."

As Isabella disappears into the fitting room, Sophia turns to me with a knowing look. "So, how's married life really treating you, Mrs. De Luca?"

I bite my lip, unable to stop the smile spreading across my face. "Honestly? Better than I ever imagined it could be."

"Oh my god, you're glowing. What happened to the Carmela who was ready to murder her arranged husband?"

I laugh softly. "She fell in love with him. Hard."

"I knew it!" Sophia squeals. "After what I saw at the club—the way he looked at you, the way he protected you —that man is head over heels."

My cheeks heat at the memory. "He is. And so am I. It's terrifying and amazing and completely unexpected."

"But?" Sophia prompts, sensing there's more.

"But this world..." I glance around to make sure no one's listening. "Last night reminded me how dangerous it is. That man at the club, he could have—" I shudder. "And Silvo, the violence he's capable of... I should be horrified, but instead..."

"Instead, it makes you feel safe," Sophia finishes, understanding in her eyes.

I nod. "Is that crazy?"

"In your world? Probably the sanest thing I've heard," she says, squeezing my hand. "You need someone strong to protect you. And from what I've seen, Silvo would burn down the world for you."

Isabella emerges from the fitting room, the emerald dress hugging her curves in all the right places. Sophia and I both let out appreciative whistles.

"Damn, Isabella, you look hot!" Sophia exclaims.

Isabella blushes. "You don't think it's too much?"

I shake my head. "Absolutely not. You're going to turn heads in that dress."

She nods decisively and heads back into the dressing room. Once out, she looks radiant as she hands her credit card to the cashier, a satisfied smile on her face.

As we exit the boutique, Sophia suggests grabbing a bite

to eat. "I'm starving," she declares. "Shopping takes a lot out of a girl."

We make our way to a chic little bistro, the aroma of freshly baked bread and savory dishes wafting through the air.

Our waiter approaches, a handsome young man with a charming smile. He takes our orders, his gaze lingering on Isabella for a moment longer than necessary. I raise an eyebrow, wondering if there might be a spark of attraction there.

Just as we're about to dig into our meals, a shadow falls over our table. I look up, my heart skipping a beat as I take in the sight of a tall, muscular man with piercing eyes and a dangerous aura.

"Well, well, well," he drawls. "If it isn't the infamous De Luca ladies."

Isabella tenses beside me, her eyes narrowing. "Maximo Moretti," she says, her tone icy. "To what do we owe the displeasure?"

I glance between them, immediately sensing the charged atmosphere. This must be one of the Morettis that Silvo has mentioned—their rivals.

Maximo smirks, his gaze drifting to me. "And you must be the new Mrs. De Luca," he says, his eyes raking over my form in a degrading way. "I must say, Silvo has excellent taste."

I bristle at his words. "I don't believe we've been introduced," I say coolly.

"My apologies," Maximo says, his tone anything but apologetic. "Maximo Moretti, at your service." He extends a hand, and I reluctantly shake it, feeling the strength in his grip and returning it with my own firm pressure.

Isabella clears her throat. "What do you want, Maximo?" she asks.

Maximo shrugs, a picture of nonchalance. "Just wanted to say hi," he says, his eyes flickering back to me before settling on Isabella with unmistakable heat. "And to remind you all that the Morettis are always watching."

Maximo's words send a chill down my spine, and I feel Sophia tense beside me. Isabella, however, remains unruffled, her gaze locked with Maximo's in a silent battle of wills.

"The Morettis may be watching," Isabella says, "but the De Luca women aren't easily intimidated. Don't forget that, Maximo."

"Oh, Isabella," he purrs, leaning in closer, "I could never forget you. Or how beautiful you look when you're angry."

The way he says it, with obvious desire beneath the threat, makes it clear that he's not just talking about family rivalry. There's an undercurrent of something that crackles between them like a live wire.

Isabella's cheeks flush, but she doesn't back down. "Watch yourself, Moretti. You're playing with fire."

Maximo's eyes glitter with amusement. "Maybe I like the heat," he murmurs, his gaze dropping purposefully to her cleavage.

I shift uncomfortably, feeling like an intruder in a private moment.

Sophia clears her throat pointedly, breaking the spell between them. "As much as I hate to interrupt this little... whatever this is," she says, waving her hand between Isabella and Maximo, "we're kind of in the middle of lunch. So, if you don't mind..."

Maximo straightens, his expression smoothing back

into one of cool indifference. "Of course," he says, nodding at Sophia and me. "Ladies, enjoy your meal."

He turns to leave, but not before throwing one last smoldering look at Isabella over his shoulder. "Until next time, *bella*."

Isabella watches him go, her expression unreadable.

I can practically feel the tension thrumming through her body, the unresolved heat between her and Maximo still hanging heavy in the air.

Sophia lets out a low whistle. "Damn, Isabella," she says, fanning herself dramatically. "I thought you two were going to start ripping each other's clothes off right here in the middle of the restaurant."

Isabella shoots her a withering look. "That man is insufferable," she mutters, picking up her fork and stabbing at her salad with a little more force than necessary.

"Was that Maximo Moretti?" I ask, recalling his name from the folder Silvo showed me.

Isabella takes a deep breath, her eyes flickering with a mix of anger and something else I can't quite place. "Yes," she begins, "the son of our biggest rivals. They've been a thorn in our family's side for generations."

I lean in, my curiosity piqued. "I've heard the name before. Back in LA, the Bianchi family knew to tread carefully around anything Moretti connected." I pause. "But I never knew the full history. What actually started it?"

"It goes back to our grandfathers," she explains. "They were once close friends, but a disagreement over territory turned them into bitter enemies. Since then, the De Lucas and the Morettis have been locked in a constant power struggle."

I absorb this information, filing it away. Silvo has mentioned the Morettis as enemies, but he's never told me the full story. "A friendship destroyed over business? That seems... tragic."

"Most wars start with something personal," Isabella says quietly. "Business is just the excuse we tell ourselves."

"It's hard to believe you're so ingrained in this world, yet it feels so distant at the same time," Sophia murmurs, shaking her head. "I can't imagine what it must be like for you, knowing all this and trying to navigate it."

I can't help but smile. "Trust me, Soph, it's not all it's cracked up to be. The glamour wears off when you're constantly aware of the danger."

Isabella nods in agreement. "It's a life we were born into," she says, her voice tinged with weariness. "But it's not one I would choose for myself, given the chance."

Sophia leans back in her chair, her eyes moving between us. "So what's it really like? Being married to Silvo?"

I feel my cheeks heat up at the mention of Silvo. "Intense," I admit honestly. "Silvo is passionate, possessive, fiercely protective. But he's also shown me a side of himself that I don't think many people get to see."

Isabella raises an eyebrow. "My brother, vulnerable? That's a first."

"He is with me," I say softly, surprised by my own defensiveness. "Beneath all that intensity, he's... he cares deeply. About family, about loyalty, about—" I stop myself before admitting too much.

"About you," Sophia finishes with a knowing smile.

I don't deny it.

Isabella reaches over and gives my hand a reassuring squeeze. "I can see that he's different with you. Softer, somehow. It's good for him."

I glance back toward where Maximo disappeared, then

at Isabella's flushed face. "And what about you and Maximo? That didn't look like a simple family rivalry."

Isabella's expression closes off immediately. "There's nothing between us. He's arrogant, insufferable, and everything I can't stand in a man."

"Everything you can't stop looking at, you mean," Sophia teases gently.

"Can we please change the subject?" Isabella pleads, her discomfort evident.

I catch Sophia's eye, and we both smile, but mercifully let it drop—for now. Whatever's brewing between Isabella and Maximo Moretti is clearly complicated, and pushing won't help.

Sophia clears her throat, breaking the moment. "Okay, enough heavy stuff," she declares, picking up her menu. "I don't know about you ladies, but I'm ready for some serious dessert action."

Isabella and I exchange amused glances, grateful for the change in subject. "Bring on the chocolate," I agree, feeling a sense of lightness wash over me.

As we peruse the dessert menu, laughing and joking, I realize how much I've grown to appreciate these women. Despite the challenges and complications of my new life, I know that with the support of my friends and new family, I can face anything that comes my way.

Even dangerous Moretti heirs who look at Isabella like they want to devour her—and maybe get devoured in return.

22

SILVO

I adjust my black velvet mask as I enter the grand ballroom, taking in the sea of disguised faces swirling around me. Laughter and chatter mingle with the lively music from the string quartet in the corner. I scan the crowd, searching for her.

And then I see her. Carmela. She is a vision in a shimmering emerald gown, her hair swept up elegantly, a glittering mask concealing her beautiful face. But I would know her anywhere. She is speaking with Isabella and Sophia, and I can't help but smile at the way she throws her head back and laughs.

I make my way through the throng of guests until I am standing before her. I bow and extend my hand. "May I have this dance, beautiful?"

She turns to me, her green eyes sparkling behind her mask. After a moment, she places her hand in mine. "You may."

I lead her onto the dance floor as a slow waltz begins to play. We move together so naturally, her body molding against mine like she was made to be in my arms. I drink in her subtle perfume, the smoothness of her skin, the way her dress shimmers under the chandelier light.

My hand presses firmly against the small of her back as we glide across the dance floor. She looks up at me, her eyes smoldering.

"You look stunning tonight," I murmur, my lips caressing her ear. "That dress... it's fucking beautiful, but it'll look so much better on our bedroom floor tonight."

Carmela shivers slightly in my arms. "You don't look so bad yourself," she replies. "Though I'm surprised you recognized me behind this mask."

I chuckle. "I'd know you anywhere, *bella*. The way you move, the sound of your laugh... you're unforgettable."

The music changes to a tango, and I spin her out before pulling her back against me, our bodies flush.

With each step, each turn, I'm drawn deeper into her spell. The realization hits me like a thunderbolt—I'm falling for my wife. This passionate woman who challenges me at every turn, who both infuriates and intoxicates me... I'm falling in love with her.

The thought takes my breath away. I never intended for this to happen. Our marriage was arranged, a business deal between families. I expected respect, obedience, maybe even desire. But love? That was never part of the plan.

Yet here I am, holding Carmela in my arms, my heart racing at her nearness. I need to tell her. She deserves to know the truth, to understand the depth of my feelings for her.

I lean in close, my lips brushing her ear. "Carmela, I..."

But before I can continue, a commotion at the entrance of the ballroom draws our attention. Raised voices, the sound of a scuffle. I instinctively pull Carmela closer, shielding her with my body.

The commotion at the ballroom entrance escalates, drawing the entire room's attention. I keep Carmela close, grabbing her hand and moving toward it to find out what is going on.

As we push through the crowd, I see my brother Fed locked in a scuffle with none other than Maximo Moretti, the young heir from our rival family.

What the hell is he doing here?

"What's going on here?" I demand.

Fed glances at me, his face flushed with anger. "This bastard was hitting on Isabella! I caught him trying to put his hands on her."

Maximo sneers, straightening his suit jacket. "I was being friendly, De Luca. No need to get your panties in a twist."

My blood boils at his disrespect. I step forward, getting in Maximo's face. "You have no business being here, Moretti. This is a private event."

Maximo smirks, his eyes flick to Carmela behind me. "I heard there was a party. Thought I'd come see what all the fuss was about. And I must say, your sister is looking particularly delectable tonight."

Fed lunges at him, but I hold him back. "Watch your mouth," I growl. "You're not welcome here. Leave now, before I make you regret ever setting foot in this ballroom."

Maximo holds up his hands in mock surrender. "Alright, alright. I can take a hint. But mark my words, De Luca, this isn't over. Your family won't be on top forever."

With that, he turns and stalks out of the ballroom, pushing past the shocked onlookers. I turn to Fed, my jaw tight. "What the hell was that about?"

Fed runs a hand through his hair, looking shaken. "I

saw him getting handsy with Isabella, and I lost it. You know how protective I am of her."

The Morettis have been a thorn in our side for years, but they've never been bold enough to crash one of our events before. Something's changed. And I have a feeling it's going to mean trouble for all of us.

I turn to Carmela, taking her hand in mine. "Are you alright, *bella*?"

She nods. "Are we in danger?"

I pull her close, pressing a kiss to her forehead. "I won't let anything happen to you. I promise. But we need to be careful. The Morettis are up to something, and we need to find out what it is before it's too late."

I watch as Isabella rolls her eyes at Fed, her annoyance palpable. "You were being an idiot, Fed," she scolds him. "I could have handled Maximo myself. He's harmless."

Fed scowls, clearly not convinced. "Harmless? The guy's a creep, Iz. I saw the way he was looking at you."

Isabella shakes her head. "He was just being friendly. You know how the Morettis are, especially Maximo. They love to push our buttons. But that doesn't mean he was a threat."

I place a hand on Fed's shoulder. "Isabella's right, Fed. Maximo may be an arrogant prick, but he's not stupid enough to try anything here. Not with all of us around."

Fed doesn't look happy about it, but he nods grudgingly. "Fine. But I don't like it. The Morettis are up to something, I can feel it."

I turn to Carmela, who has been watching the exchange. "Do you want to leave?" I ask her.

She shrugs, but I detect the tension in her shoulders. "I don't like all this talk of danger and rivalry. I thought we were here to have a good time."

I yank her against me, kissing her temple. "We are. And we will. I won't let anything ruin this night for us."

I turn back to Fed and Isabella, my expression serious. "We'll keep an eye out for any more trouble, but for now, let's try to enjoy the party. We're here to celebrate, not start a war."

They both nod, and I lead Carmela back onto the dance floor. As we sway to the music, I can't shake the feeling that something big is brewing. The Morettis have always been a problem, but crashing our event like this? It's a bold move, even for them.

I hold Carmela tighter, breathing in her scent. No matter what happens, I'll keep her safe. She's mine now, and I protect what's mine. Even if it means going to war with the Morettis, I'll do whatever it takes to keep my family out of harm's way.

23

CARMELA

I slip into the bedroom, sensing Silvo's tension as he removes his suit jacket. The events at the ball have left him on edge, his muscles coiled tight. I approach him from behind, trailing my fingers along the hard lines of his shoulders.

"You're so tense," I murmur, kissing the nape of his neck. "Let me help you relax."

Silvo stiffens, then gradually surrenders to my touch as I knead the knots in his back. A low groan escapes his lips, and I feel a surge of power at eliciting such a reaction from this powerful and formidable man.

Emboldened, I guide him to the edge of the bed and straddle his lap, my fingers undoing the buttons of his shirt. His eyes smolder with desire as I expose his chiseled chest, leaning in to trace my tongue along the intricate lines of his tattoos.

"Carmela," he rasps, his hands gripping my hips. "What are you doing?"

I capture his lips in a searing kiss. Our bodies meld together as Silvo kisses me back.

Sliding off him, I unbutton his pants and remove them with his boxers so he's sitting there in nothing. I trail kisses down his sculpted abdomen. Silvo's breath hitches as I take him into my mouth, his fingers tangling in my hair.

"*Dio mio,*" he groans, his head falling back.

I relish the taste of him, the power I hold over his pleasure. His hands grip my hair as I take him deep into my throat.

"Fuck, Carmela... you've no idea how good that feels."

I hum in response, savoring the taste of him, feeling his cock throb against my tongue. His praise fuels my confidence, and I moan softly, the vibration eliciting a curse from him.

"That's it, baby," he grits out. "Suck my cock."

His dirty talk sends a spike of desire straight to my core. I suck him harder, hollowing my cheeks, wanting to hear more. His hands tighten in my hair, guiding my movements as he thrusts into my throat.

"You like that, don't you?" he murmurs. "You like having me fuck your throat."

His words make me bolder, and I swirl my tongue, teasing the sensitive tip of his cock. His hips buck, and he groans, tightening his grip in my hair.

"God, you're going to be the death of me," he pants. "Keep going, baby. Take all of me."

I moan in response, the vibrations sending shudders through him. He's usually so in control, but right now, I have him at my mercy.

"Ah, fuck..." He yanks me off of him. "I'm close, so I want you to ride that dick like a good girl."

I stand and shed my dress and panties before he guides me to straddle his lap. Our eyes lock as I slowly sink down, taking him inside me.

A shudder ripples through my body as we connect. I feel full and wanted, a fire igniting in my belly as we begin to move together.

We set a rhythm, our breaths synchronizing as we move as one. His hands grip my hips, guiding me, but it's not about dominance this time. It's about us, and the pleasure we can give each other.

With each stroke, I feel a connection forming—a silent understanding that this is more than physical release. It's an unspoken language of touch and sensation that brings us closer.

Silvo's eyes remain locked on mine as we move together, his breath coming in sharp pants. The fire in my belly spreads, coiling until I'm riding him with abandon, chasing the pleasure building inside me.

"You feel so good," he whispers. "So fucking good."

His words spur me on, and I rock my hips faster, chasing the peak that's building inside me. He thrusts up to meet me, his grip on my hips becoming bruising.

Silvo pulls me closer, buried deep within me, and I gasp as he lightly spanks my asscheek.

"You're so beautiful like this," he purrs. "Taking my cock so perfectly."

His words send a shiver through me, and I feel my core clench around him.

"That's it, baby," he encourages, sucking one of my nipples into his mouth. "Feel how hard you make me."

His mouth trails kisses down my neck, and he nuzzles my pulse point, sucking.

The sensations are overwhelming, and I rock my hips faster, chasing the pleasure that's building. Silvo meets my movements, his hands gripping my ass.

"You like that, don't you?" he breathes. "You like being mine."

I whimper as he nibbles my earlobe, his tongue teasing the sensitive skin. His hands caress my ass, stroking and squeezing as I grind against him.

"Yes," I admit, my voice breathy. "I love being yours. Only yours."

His mouth curves into a satisfied smile, and I feel him thrust deep within me, his cock so hard. "That's it, baby," he urges, his voice thick with desire. "Ride my cock. Let me feel you come around me."

His words spur me on, and I rock my hips harder, chasing the peak that's building within. Silvo meets my movements, his hands sliding up my back to tangle in my hair. He pulls me down for a passionate kiss, his tongue dueling with mine.

Our kisses grow more intense, mirroring the rhythm of our bodies. My climax builds, coiling tighter and tighter, until suddenly, I shatter into a million pieces.

"Silvo!" I cry out, my body shaking as wave after wave washes over me.

He groans, and his thrusts become more erratic. With a final, deep thrust, he finds his release, his body shuddering against mine.

Collapsing against him, his arms wrap around me, holding me tight. We're both breathless, our hearts pounding.

This, I realize, is what it means to truly be intimate with someone. To bare your soul through the act of loving them. And in this moment, I feel a connection to Silvo that goes beyond our arranged marriage. A connection that is profound, and deep, and scary beyond measure.

24

SILVO

I pace back and forth in my study, the weight of the situation bearing down on me. The phone rings, shattering the tense silence.

"Yeah?" I answer.

"Boss, we got a problem." It's Paulie, one of my top lieutenants. His voice is laced with urgency.

"What is it?" I demand, my grip tightening on the receiver.

"It's the Morettis. They made a move on our shipment coming in from Miami. Two of our guys are down, and the merchandise is gone."

White-hot anger surges through me. "How do you know it was them?"

"They left their calling card, boss. Tommy and Rico were both shot execution-style—a single bullet to the back of the head. And they left Moretti family crests spray-painted on the warehouse walls. Big as day, can't miss 'em. They wanted us to know it was them."

My knuckles turn white as I grip the phone. That's Nico

Moretti's signature move—making sure everyone knows who struck the blow. "Details. Now."

Paulie launches into the report. "They hit the dock warehouse around midnight—killed Tommy and Rico, both with that distinctive Moretti MO. Took three hundred keys of product and torched the building. But before they torched it, they spray-painted those damn Moretti crests everywhere—on the walls, the loading bay doors, even on our delivery trucks. Local cops are all over it now, and our Miami capo, Lorenzo, is scrambling to contain the situation."

"Those arrogant bastards," I snarl. The Moretti family crest—a crowned lion—has been their symbol for generations. Leaving it at a crime scene is a blatant declaration of war.

"Lorenzo says the suppliers are spooked," Paulie continues. "Word's spreading fast that the Morettis are making a play for Miami. They're hitting our clubs next, boss. We need you down there."

My jaw clenches. This isn't just about one shipment. This is a coordinated attack on our entire Miami territory, and the Morettis are making damn sure everyone knows they're behind it.

"Tell Lorenzo I'll be there tomorrow," I say. "And Paulie? I want photos of those crests. Document everything. The Morettis want to make this personal? We'll give them personal."

When Paulie confirms and hangs up, I slam the phone down, my mind racing. The audacity of leaving their family crest—it's not just an attack, it's a taunt. Nico's telling me he's not afraid, that he's coming for everything we've built.

Miami is our gateway to the Caribbean and South American markets. If the Morettis establish a foothold there, they could choke off half our revenue stream. And those damn crests spray-painted everywhere? That's Nico making sure every criminal organization in Miami knows the De Lucas are weak, vulnerable.

I need to go personally—show our people we're not backing down, shore up our defenses, and send the Morettis a message that this aggression will be met with overwhelming force.

Grabbing my jacket, I stride into the living room where Carmela is reading.

"We have a situation," I say, my voice clipped. "The Morettis hit one of our shipments in Miami. Two men dead, product gone, and they left their family crest spray-painted all over the crime scene."

Her eyes widen, the book forgotten in her lap. "They wanted you to know it was them."

"Exactly." I run a hand through my hair. "It's a declaration of war. Nico's making a play for our Miami territory."

The resolve in her gaze steadies me. She's in this with me, no matter what. "What are you going to do?"

"I need to fly to Miami, handle this personally. Our operations there are under threat, and I need to stabilize the situation before we lose more ground."

Carmela stands, crossing to me. "How long will you be gone?"

"Three, maybe four days." I pull her close. "I need to meet with Lorenzo, assess the damage, and make sure the Morettis understand there will be consequences."

She nods, her jaw set with determination I've come to admire. "Then go. Do what needs to be done."

"I'm calling a meeting with my capos first," I tell her. "We need to strategize our response. Then I'll arrange the flight."

Carmela cups my face in her hands. "Just promise me you'll be careful. I need you to come back to me."

The vulnerability in her voice nearly breaks me. "Always," I vow.

Leaning down, I kiss her fiercely. "Stay here. I'll have extra security posted while I'm gone."

With one last lingering look, I turn and head out, my mind already plotting. The Morettis have awoken a beast, and they'll soon realize the grave mistake they've made.

I slide into the driver's seat of my sleek black Ferrari, the leather cool against my skin. Gripping the steering wheel, I take a deep breath, trying to channel the rage into focus.

As I navigate the busy streets of Philadelphia, my mind keeps returning to those spray-painted crests. The Morettis could have just taken the shipment and disappeared. Instead, they made it a spectacle—a public humiliation designed to make us look weak.

I pull up to our headquarters, a nondescript warehouse on the outskirts of the city. My men are already gathered inside, their faces grim. As I stride into the room, all eyes turn to me, waiting for direction.

"Gentlemen," I begin, my voice cutting through the tension. "The Morettis have made their move. They hit our Miami shipment, killed two of our men, and made off with three hundred keys of product." I pause, letting that sink in. "But that's not all. They left their family crest spray-painted all over the warehouse—on the walls, the doors, our trucks. They wanted everyone to know it was them."

Angry mutters ripple through the room. The disrespect of it—the sheer arrogance—has every man in here ready for blood.

"This is a declaration of war," I continue, my voice hard. "The Morettis think they can intimidate us, humiliate us publicly, but they've made a grave mistake. I'm flying to Miami today to personally oversee our response. We'll retaliate, and we'll do it in a way that leaves no doubt about our power."

I point to the map spread across the table. "Lorenzo reports they're making moves on our other Miami operations—our clubs, our distribution network, even approaching our suppliers. We need to shut this down before we lose the entire territory."

Sal, one of my most experienced soldiers, speaks up. "What do you need from us, boss?"

"Reinforce our positions here in Philly while I'm gone. Double security on all our key operations. The Morettis might try to hit us here while I'm distracted in Miami." I scan the room. "And I want to know how they got that shipment schedule. Someone talked, and I want to know who."

I turn to Leo, one of my most trusted men. "Leo, you're in charge of security at the house while I'm gone. My wife doesn't leave the property without an armed escort. Post men at every entrance, rotate shifts so no one gets complacent."

Leo straightens. "Understood, boss. The house will be locked down tight."

"Fed will coordinate operations here with our father," I continue, gesturing to my brother. "Any major decisions need approval from both of them. And remember—we're smart about this. No unnecessary risks. We hit them hard, but we do it cleanly."

As the meeting concludes, the men file out, their expressions determined. This is what the De Luca family does—we stand together, we protect our own, and we never back down.

I pull Fed aside as the room empties. "You're staying at the house with Carmela while I'm gone. Don't let her out of your sight."

Fed's usual playfulness evaporates. "You think they might make a move on her?"

"The Morettis left those crests as a message—they want me to know they can strike at will." My jaw tightens. "If they're bold enough to hit our Miami operation, they might be bold enough to go after my wife. I need you there, Fed. You and Leo."

"On my life, brother," Fed says solemnly. "Nothing will happen to her."

I grip his shoulder. "I'm counting on that."

Leaving the warehouse, I climb back into my car. My phone buzzes—Marco calling.

"I heard about Miami," Marco says when I answer. "You need legal cover for the trip?"

"No. This is personal, not business. But I need you to keep an eye on things here. If the cops start sniffing around those spray-painted crests, we need to make sure nothing leads back to our other operations."

"Already on it," Marco assures me. "And Silvo? Watch your back down there. The Morettis are playing dirty."

"When don't they?" I mutter before hanging up.

As I pull into our driveway, I see Carmela waiting for me on the front steps. Her face shows concern, but there's a steely determination in her eyes that matches my own.

I approach her, cupping her face in my hands. "I'll be gone three, maybe four days."

She nods, leaning into my touch. "Just... come back to me."

In that moment, I realize just how much she's come to mean to me. This isn't just about protecting my family's interests anymore. It's about protecting her, us, what we've built together.

I pull her close, inhaling the scent of her hair. "Always," I whisper, allowing myself this moment of vulnerability before the storm that's about to break.

I pull back from our embrace just enough to capture her lips with mine. The kiss is desperate, heated, and filled with everything I can't put into words. My hands slide into her hair as I deepen the kiss, tasting her, memorizing every sensation.

My chest aches with the thought of leaving her. These past months, she's become more than just my arranged wife. She's my anchor, my fire, my everything. The way she matches my intensity, challenges me, drives me wild. I never expected to find this with her.

Her fingers dig into my shoulders as she presses closer. I groan into her mouth, backing her against the wall of the house. I need to feel her, to brand this moment into my memory before I leave for Miami.

"You're mine to come back to," I whisper against her lips.

My mind races with all the dangers waiting in Miami. The Morettis won't stop at just one shipment. They'll keep pushing, testing our limits. And here I am, leaving Carmela behind when all I want is to stay and protect her myself.

But I have no choice. I'm the head of the De Luca family. This is my responsibility, my burden to bear. I have to handle this personally, show strength, or we'll appear weak to our enemies.

I break the kiss, resting my forehead against hers. Her breath comes in short pants, matching my own ragged breathing. Those fierce green eyes lock onto mine, full of understanding and something deeper that makes my heart clench.

"Fed's staying here with you," I murmur, stroking her cheek. "Leo and the security team will be posted around the property. No one gets near you without going through them first."

But it's not the same as being here myself. Not the same as holding her in my arms, knowing she's safe. The thought of being apart, even for a few days, feels like physical pain.

I capture her lips again, pouring all my conflicted emotions into the kiss. Her soft moan nearly breaks my resolve to leave.

I force myself to pull back, my breathing ragged. The look in her eyes nearly undoes me. Our arranged marriage has become something real, something vital, and now I have to leave her.

"I'll call you every day," I promise, running my thumb across her lower lip. "This won't take long."

Carmela nods, her fingers digging into my shoulders. "Make them pay, Silvo."

Her bloodthirsty response makes me smirk despite everything. She understands this life—my life—better than I ever expected.

My phone buzzes—my driver is waiting with the car. It's time.

Upstairs, I grab my bag, which Carmela packed for me, taking one last look at our bedroom—the bed we share, the life we're building together.

As we descend the stairs, I feel her strength beside me. In just a few months, she's become not just my wife but my partner in every sense. Whatever happens in Miami, I know I'm coming back to her.

At the door, Fed appears, his expression serious for once. "I've got her, Silvo. Go handle business."

I nod, then turn to Carmela one last time. "Stay inside. Stay safe."

"Just come home," she whispers.

With one final lingering look, I force myself out the door and into the waiting car. Miami awaits, and with it, a reckoning the Morettis won't soon forget.

25

CARMELA

The estate feels too large, too empty without Silvo. Three days since he left for Miami, and the walls seem to close in despite the mansion's vastness. I wander through the garden, trailing my fingers along the rose bushes I've been trying to maintain—though they're nothing compared to Giulia's expert touch.

"Careful of the thorns." Fed appears behind me, his footsteps silent on the stone path. "You'll ruin those pretty hands."

I roll my eyes. "I'm not made of glass."

"No, you're made of fire." Fed grins, so much like Silvo yet so different. "Has my brother called?"

"This morning." I don't mention how my heart races every time the phone rings, how I strain to hear any hint of danger in Silvo's voice. "He says it'll be another day or two."

A maid approaches us, carrying a small package on a silver tray. "This just arrived for you, Mrs. De Luca."

I take the unmarked brown parcel, feeling its lightweight in my hands. "No return address?"

"No, ma'am. It was hand-delivered to the gate."

Something cold slithers down my spine as the maid retreats. Fed frowns, stepping closer.

"Let me open it."

"I can handle a package, Federico." I tear through the brown paper, revealing a plain white envelope inside.

The moment I slide my finger under the flap, several photographs spill onto the stone path. I freeze, my blood turning to ice.

They're photos of Silvo and me. Leaving restaurants. Standing on our balcony. Even one through our bedroom window makes my stomach clench.

"What the fuck?" Fed snatches up the photos, his playful demeanor vanishing.

My hands shake as I pull out a typed note from the envelope:

The De Luca's prized possession. How easy it would be to take you. Your husband can't protect you forever. The Morettis send their regards.

Fed's face hardens as he reads over my shoulder. "We need to call Silvo."

"No." The word escapes before I can stop it. "He has enough to worry about."

"Carmela—"

"They want to frighten me." I crumple the note in my fist, anger replacing fear. "I won't give them the satisfaction. I'm not sitting around waiting to be the victim in someone else's war," I say, gathering the scattered photos. "Let them come. I'll be ready."

Fed studies me with newfound respect. "What are you planning?"

"Knowledge is power, and I'm tired of being powerless."

I march back toward the house with purpose. "The Morettis want to play games? I'll learn every rule before they make their next move."

I head straight for Silvo's office, a room I've barely entered since arriving. The heavy oak door swings open to reveal leather-bound books, filing cabinets, and a massive mahogany desk.

"Carmela, you shouldn't be in here," Fed warns, following close behind.

I ignore him, sliding into Silvo's chair. "Your brother married a Bianchi. I grew up in this world, too." My fingers trail over the sleek laptop on the desk. "The password. What would Silvo use?"

Fed hesitates, then sighs. "Try Carmela0522."

The screen unlocks. My wedding date. Something warm flutters in my chest before I push it aside.

"Now leave me alone."

"You know Silvo will—"

"What Silvo doesn't know won't hurt him." I fix Fed with the same glare that kept my own brothers in line. "Unless you plan to tell him?"

Fed raises his hands in surrender. "Your funeral," he mutters, backing out of the office.

Once alone, I dive into the De Luca database. Files upon files on every family in the country. I click on *Moretti* and begin scrolling through decades of intelligence. Names, businesses, territories, weaknesses. I jot notes, memorize faces, and map connections.

Nico Moretti, the head of the family. His son Maximo—the man Isabella can't seem to stop arguing with whenever they cross paths. I study their operations, their patterns, searching for anything I can use. I'm not just some prize to be threatened or protected. I'm Carmela Bianchi De Luca, and I refuse to be a pawn in anyone's game.

Hours pass as I build my own dossier. The Moretti family wants war? I'll learn exactly who I'm fighting.

The clock on Silvo's desk shows 2 AM when I hear the door creak open. I freeze, my fingers hovering over the keyboard.

"Carmela?" Isabella's voice is soft with surprise. "Fed woke me. He said something happened—are you alright?"

I glance up to see her in her pajamas.

"The Morettis sent me a message today." I gesture to the photos and threatening note spread across the desk.

Isabella steps forward, picking up one of the photos. Her face hardens. "They're watching your house."

"They're watching me." I tap the screen where Maximo Moretti's file is open. "And I'm tired of being a target without knowing my enemy."

I brace for a lecture, for her to tell me to leave this to the men, to remind me I'm overstepping my bounds as a new wife. Instead, Isabella slides into the chair beside me.

"The intelligence on the Moretti daughter is in a separate folder." She reaches across me, her fingers flying over the keyboard. "Valeria. She's studying business at Wharton. If they're targeting you, we should know everything about their family, too."

I stare at her, caught off guard by her willing participation. "You're helping me?"

Isabella gives me a small smile, tucking a strand of dark hair behind her ear. "You're a De Luca now. We protect our own."

"But Silvo—"

"My brother is a brilliant strategist, but he has blind

spots." She pulls up another file. "He sees you as something to protect rather than an ally. Men in our world often miss that women can be weapons too."

The tension in my shoulders releases as I realize I've found an unexpected ally. "My family taught me that from birth."

"Then between your Bianchi instincts and my De Luca knowledge, we'll be ready for whatever the Morettis are planning." Isabella squeezes my hand. "Family protects family. Even new members of the family."

For the first time since moving to Philadelphia, I feel like I might belong here.

Isabella pulls up a folder on Maximo Moretti, her fingers hesitating over the keyboard for a moment.

"There's something I haven't told anyone." Her voice drops to barely above a whisper. "Not even Silvo or Fed."

I lean closer, noticing the sudden tension in her shoulders. "What is it?"

"Maximo's been sending me messages." Isabella reaches into her pocket and pulls out her phone. "For weeks now."

My breath catches. "Messages? Like the one I received today?"

"Different, but just as unsettling." She scrolls through her phone and hands it to me. "See for yourself."

I scan through dozens of texts from an unknown number. Some are cryptic quotes about family loyalty and revenge. Others are disturbingly intimate comments about her daily routine, what she wore to dinner, and places she'd visited.

"Jesus, Isabella. How long has this been going on?"

"Since before your wedding." She takes the phone back,

her face pale in the blue light of the computer screen. "At first, I thought it was just someone trying to scare me. Then when we ran into him at that bistro the other day..."

"He confirmed it?" My mind races back to lunch, to the charged moment between them.

She nods. "He leaned in close, said he enjoyed our *conversations,* and looked forward to seeing me in person more often. The way he said it..." She shudders. "It wasn't just family rivalry, Carmela. It was something darker."

I feel sick. "This isn't just about territory or business deals."

"No." Isabella pulls up another file—an old newspaper clipping showing a younger Antonio De Luca standing over what appears to be a Moretti family member. "Our families have history. Blood history."

"And now they're targeting us. The women." My fingers curl into fists. "Making it personal."

"I think it always was." Isabella's eyes meet mine. "And Maximo seems determined to settle old scores—through us."

I lean back in Silvo's chair, the weight of this revelation settling over me. For weeks, I've been a pawn in a game I didn't understand—moved around the board by men playing with lives like they're expendable. But sitting here at 2 AM, surrounded by decades of intelligence, with Isabella as my ally, something crystallizes inside me.

I'm done being a target. Done waiting for men to protect me, or threaten me, or decide my fate.

The Moretti family wants war? They'll get it—but not the war they're expecting. By the time Silvo returns from Miami, I'll know their operations better than they know ours. Every weakness, every vulnerability, every secret they've buried.

"Let's keep digging," I tell Isabella, pulling up another file. "I want to know everything."

She nods, a fierce smile crossing her face as she settles in beside me. "Welcome to the family business, Carmela."

For the first time since my forced marriage, those words don't feel like a cage—they feel like armor.

26

SILVO

The Miami heat clings to my skin as I step out of the air-conditioned restaurant. Lorenzo, my Miami capo, follows a step behind, his normally jovial face grim.

"You're sure about this information?" I loosen my tie, the weight of what he's just told me settling like concrete in my gut.

"I verified it myself." Lorenzo's voice drops. "After the warehouse hit, the Morettis didn't stop. They hit two of our clubs last night—Velvet Room and Crimson. Same execution-style kills, same spray-painted crests everywhere."

I scan the busy street, suddenly aware of how exposed we are. "Let's continue this conversation somewhere private."

Thirty minutes later, we're in a secured warehouse by the docks. Maps and surveillance photos cover the table. Each red X marks a De Luca business or operation that's been targeted in the past four days since I arrived in Miami.

There are too many Xs.

Lorenzo spreads out crime scene photos. "Look at this

—every single location has those crowned lion crests spray-painted in the exact same style. Same paint brand, same technique. It's definitely coordinated."

"This isn't random." I trace my finger along the pattern. "They hit the warehouse to announce their presence, then immediately started systematic strikes on our clubs and distribution points."

Carlos, Lorenzo's second-in-command, points to a timeline. "They're accelerating too. The warehouse was four days ago. Then they waited—let us scramble. Now they're hitting two, three locations a night."

"Professional," I admit grudgingly. "Hit hard, let us spread resources thin, then strike where we're weakest."

"It gets worse," Lorenzo says, sliding over witness statements. "Three different people reported seeing what they believed were Moretti men leaving the scenes. And we found this at the Velvet Room." He holds up an evidence bag containing a gold cufflink embossed with the Moretti family crest.

I examine it closely. It's genuine—I've seen Nico wear similar ones at formal events. "They're not even trying to hide it."

"Why would they?" Carlos asks. "They want everyone in Miami to know the De Lucas can't protect their own territory."

"It's about more than Miami," I realize, looking at the bigger picture. "If word spreads that we're weak here, our suppliers across the entire South will start questioning whether we can protect their interests."

"Some already are," Lorenzo admits. "The Morettis have been making offers—better terms, better protection. If we can't stop these attacks within the week..."

"They'll flip," I finish grimly. "And we'll lose our entire southern operation."

Carlos leans forward. "We need to hit back. The Moretti operations in Miami Beach—we know where they are. We could—"

I hold up a hand, considering. "Not yet. I need to understand their full strategy first." Something about this feels off, too obvious, but I can't put my finger on what's bothering me.

I'm about to voice my concerns when a faint noise catches my attention. The warehouse suddenly feels wrong—too quiet, the usual dock sounds muted.

"Everyone down!" I shout, diving behind a stack of crates as the windows explode inward.

Gunfire erupts, shattering the fluorescent lights and sending plaster raining from the ceiling. Lorenzo drops immediately, but Carlos hesitates—just long enough to catch a bullet in his shoulder.

"Fuck!" Carlos screams, clutching his wound.

I unholster my gun and return fire toward the windows, providing cover as Lorenzo drags Carlos behind a metal container.

"Back exit," I bark, keeping low as bullets ping off concrete around us.

We navigate the maze of shipping containers as the gunfire grows more intense. I count at least five shooters. Maybe more.

"How did they find us?" Lorenzo pants as we reach the back door.

The answer hits me like ice water. "Someone told them."

I push the door open a crack and peer out. Two men with automatic weapons wait by a black SUV—I catch a glimpse of crowned lion tattoos on their forearms. Moretti soldiers.

"Shit." I close the door quietly. "We're surrounded."

My mind races as blood pounds in my ears. The information about our meeting was limited to just a handful of people—Lorenzo's inner circle and his security team.

"The boat," Carlos groans, gesturing toward the loading dock through a grimy window. "My boat is still tied up at pier seven."

It's our only chance. I lead the way through the warehouse, keeping to the shadows. When we reach the water's edge, I see it—a small speedboat bobbing in the choppy water.

"Go," I order, laying down cover fire as Lorenzo helps Carlos onto the boat.

The engine roars to life just as the gunmen spot us. I dive onto the deck as bullets spray the water around us. Lorenzo guns the throttle, and we lurch away from the dock.

Only when Miami's skyline shrinks behind us do I allow myself to breathe. Blood soaks through my sleeve—I've been grazed, but nothing serious. Carlos is worse off; his shoulder is bleeding heavily, and his face is pale with shock.

"Who knew we were meeting?" I demand, pressing a rag against my wound.

Lorenzo shakes his head, his hands white-knuckled on the wheel. "Just us three, my security detail, and whoever you told back in Philly."

I didn't tell anyone except Fed—and he wouldn't betray me.

"Carlos," I say, watching his face carefully through the pain. "Who did you tell about this meeting?"

His eyes widen, confusion mixing with agony. "Just...

just my driver and Luca. Luca Vega. He was supposed to secure the warehouse before we arrived."

"Luca Vega," I repeat, the name tasting bitter. "Where is he now?"

"He called in sick this morning," Carlos gasps, his face going even paler. "Said he had food poisoning."

Lorenzo curses viciously. "That son of a bitch. I've had him in my crew for three years. Three fucking years."

I pull out my phone and manage to dial Fed despite the wind and spray. "We have a leak in Miami. Luca Vega—find out everything about him. Bank accounts, family connections, and who he's been meeting with. I want answers within the hour."

The boat cuts through the waves as I process what just happened. The Morettis knew exactly where we'd be, exactly when we'd be vulnerable. Their spray-painted crests, their obvious displays of power, the cufflink left behind—it all screams of their arrogance.

But something still nags at me. Something I can't quite identify.

From now on, I can only trust blood—Carmela, Fed, Isabella, and my parents. Everyone else is a suspect until proven otherwise.

I SLAM the penthouse door behind me, the blood on my sleeve already drying to a rusty brown. The Miami skyline glitters through floor-to-ceiling windows, but I barely notice it. My hands shake as I peel off my jacket, wincing as the fabric pulls against the graze wound.

"Fuck," I mutter, tossing the ruined jacket onto the marble counter.

The ambush replays in my mind—the shattered windows, Carlos taking a bullet, the realization that someone in Lorenzo's crew betrayed us. But worse than any of that is the distance between Carmela and me. With the Morettis making coordinated moves, she's vulnerable in Philadelphia.

I grab my secure phone and dial her number, pacing the penthouse floor. Each ring stretches into eternity.

"Silvo?" Her voice finally comes through, instantly loosening the vise around my chest.

"Hey." I exhale, dropping onto the leather sofa. "You okay?"

"I should be asking you that. Fed told me there was trouble."

I run a hand through my hair. "Nothing I couldn't handle."

"Liar." Her tone softens. "Are you hurt?"

"Just a scratch."

Silence stretches between us. I picture her biting her lower lip, the way she does when she's worried but trying not to show it.

"Carmela," I say her name like a prayer. "I need you to stay inside. Don't go anywhere without Fed or the security team."

"About that..." She hesitates. "There's something you should know."

My body tenses. "What happened?"

"The Morettis sent a package. Photos of us, with a threatening note."

My fingers tighten around the phone. "What did it say?"

"That you can't protect me forever." Her voice remains

steady, stronger than I expected. "Isabella and I have been doing some research together on the Morettis."

The rage builds inside me, hot and violent. They're threatening my wife while I'm stuck in Miami, dealing with their attacks.

"I'm coming home." I stand, already planning the fastest route back.

"No," Carmela says firmly. "You need to finish what you started there. I'm safe. Fed is here, Leo has the house locked down, and I'm not alone."

Her pragmatism grounds me, pulls me back from the edge.

"I miss you, Carmela." The admission falls from my lips before I can stop it. This vulnerability isn't something I'm used to showing, but with her, the walls I've spent a lifetime building seem to crumble.

"I miss you too." Her voice softens, all the fire and defiance momentarily replaced with something tender. "The house feels empty without you stomping around and glowering at everyone."

Despite everything, I find myself smiling. "Is that what I do?"

"Among other things." There's a smile in her voice, too.

The line falls quiet for a moment, but it's not uncomfortable. It's the kind of silence that happens when words aren't necessary, when something deeper connects us.

"How's Fed treating you?" I ask. "He's not driving you crazy, is he?"

"He tries," she says with a soft laugh. "But Isabella keeps him in line. Your sister's been... amazing. I didn't expect to find an ally in her."

I chuckle, picturing my baby sister managing both Fed and Carmela. "She's tougher than she looks."

"I'm learning that." Carmela pauses. "Silvo, the research Isabella and I are doing—it's helping us understand the Morettis' patterns, their operations. We're building a dossier."

Pride swells in my chest at how quickly she's adapted to thinking strategically. "Smart woman. That's my girl."

"This separation—" Her voice wavers slightly. "It might be exactly what the Morettis wanted. To divide us, make us vulnerable."

"I had the same thought," I admit, glancing at the bloodstained jacket. "But we've got a leak here in Miami—someone in Lorenzo's crew fed the Morettis information about our meeting location. I need to root them out before I can come home."

"A traitor," she breathes. "Be careful, Silvo. If they're that deep in your operation..."

"I will be. Two days, maximum, then I'm coming home to you."

"Just be safe," she whispers. "I've barely gotten used to being your wife. I'm not ready to be your widow."

Something shifts between us in that moment—something profound. What started as an arrangement, a business transaction between families, has become so much more. The fierce, beautiful woman who fought me at every turn has become essential to me.

"Nothing could keep me from coming back to you," I promise. "Not the Morettis, not anyone."

27

CARMELA

The light from Silvo's desk lamp casts long shadows across the scattered papers as I dig deeper into the Moretti files. Isabella left an hour ago to get some sleep, but I can't stop now. There's something here—something beyond the business rivalry and territory disputes.

I pull open another drawer and find a weathered leather portfolio tied with a string. Inside, yellowed newspaper clippings and photographs spill onto the desk. One black and white photo catches my eye—two young men in suits, arms around each other's shoulders, grinning at the camera.

I flip it over. Written in faded ink.

Salvatore De Luca + Vincenzo Moretti, 1952.

"Grandfathers," I whisper, tracing their faces. They look like brothers, not enemies.

The next photo shows the same two men with a

striking woman between them. Her eyes—sharp, intelligent—remind me of Silvo's. On the back:

Salvatore, Maria, + Vincenzo.

I spread out more documents, piecing together fragments of history. Letters between Salvatore and Vincenzo hint at a deep friendship turned bitter. Court records show business partnerships dissolved in acrimony. But it's a water-damaged diary page that makes my breath catch.

> MAY 15, 1953: MARIA CHOSE SALVATORE TODAY. VINCENZO WILL NEVER FORGIVE THIS BETRAYAL. BLOOD HAS BEEN SPILLED. THERE CAN BE NO RECONCILIATION.

"Holy shit." I slump back in the chair.

This wasn't just business. This was love and betrayal—the most primal of wounds. Maria chose Salvatore De Luca over Vincenzo Moretti, and decades later, their grandchildren are still killing each other.

I find a wedding announcement: Salvatore and Maria De Luca. The bride's full name stops my heart: Maria Rossetti Moretti.

"She was already married to him," I breathe, the pieces clicking into place. "She left Vincenzo for Salvatore."

I trace a family tree penciled on thick parchment. Salvatore and Maria had Antonio, who had Silvo. Vincenzo Moretti remarried and had a son, who fathered Nico Moretti.

This isn't about territory or profit margins. This is about vengeance, spanning three generations.

I'm still digesting this revelation when my phone vibrates on the desk. Silvo's name flashes on the screen.

"Hey," I answer, trying to sound casual despite the late hour and my racing thoughts.

"What are you still doing up?" His voice is rough, tired, but warm. "It's almost three in the morning there."

"I could ask you the same thing." I glance at the scattered papers, photos, and clippings. "How's Miami?"

"Wrapping up. I'll be home tomorrow afternoon."

I take a deep breath, eyes still fixed on the weathered photos and yellowed papers spread across Silvo's desk.

"Silvo, I found something. About why the Morettis hate us so much."

He pauses before answering. "Tell me."

"It's not just about territory or business. It's personal. It's about a woman." I trace the edge of the old photograph with my fingertip. "Your great-grandfather, Salvatore, and Vincenzo Moretti were best friends. Like brothers. There are photos of them together, laughing, arms around each other."

"That can't be right," Silvo says, his voice tight with disbelief.

"It is. And there was a woman, Maria. She was married to Vincenzo Moretti, but she left him for your grandfather." I shuffle through the papers. "I found a diary entry that says 'Maria chose Salvatore today. Vincenzo will never forgive this betrayal. Blood has been spilled.'"

The line goes silent for so long that I think we've been disconnected.

"Silvo?"

"I'm here." His voice is rough. "Are you sure about this?"

"Her full name was Maria Rossetti Moretti. She left Vincenzo for Salvatore. Three generations later, we're still paying for it." I push my hair back from my face. "This doesn't feel like a business rivalry, Silvo. This is a blood vendetta. The Morettis believe your family stole something precious from them."

"So all of this—the attacks, the threats—it's revenge for something that happened over seventy years ago?"

"Old wounds run deep in families like ours." I look down at the wedding announcement in my hand. "And now I'm a De Luca too. Just another target in their revenge fantasy."

"I'll protect you, Carmela. Always." Silvo's voice deepens with conviction. "No one will touch what's mine."

Heat flares through me at his possessiveness. When did I start craving his protection instead of resenting it?

"I know." I gather the documents, carefully returning them to the portfolio. "I just wish you were here."

"Do you miss me, wife?" There's a smile in his voice.

"Don't let it go to your head." But my body aches for him, the emptiness of our bed these past nights a constant reminder of his absence.

"Because I miss you," he continues, his voice dropping lower. "I think about you every fucking minute I'm away."

My breath catches. "Silvo..."

"Show me." His tone shifts, commanding now. "Get on video. I want to see you."

I hesitate, glancing at the office door. "I'm still in your office."

"Then go to our bedroom. Now."

The authority in his voice sends a shiver down my spine. I gather my phone and hurry down the darkened hallway to our suite.

Once inside, I lock the door and switch to video. Silvo's face appears on screen, tired but hungry, his jawline dark with stubble.

"There you are," he says, eyes devouring me. "Take off your clothes."

"Demanding even from Miami," I tease, but my fingers are already working the buttons of my blouse.

"You love it." His voice grows rough as I reveal my lace bra. "Keep going."

I slip the blouse from my shoulders, then stand to shimmy out of my pants. His eyes darken as I stand before him in just my underwear.

"Everything," he commands.

I unhook my bra slowly, letting it fall away. His sharp intake of breath makes me bold. I hook my thumbs in my panties and slide them down my legs.

"Beautiful," he growls. "Touch yourself for me. Show me how wet you are."

I lie back on our bed, propping the phone where he can see me. My hand slides between my thighs, finding the slick heat there.

"I am wet," I admit, circling my fingers. "I've been wet since I heard your voice."

"That's it," Silvo says, his breathing growing heavier. "Play with your cunt. Make yourself feel good while I watch."

"This isn't fair," I breathe, my fingers working between my thighs. "I want to see you too."

Silvo's eyes darken on screen. "You want to see my cock, *amore?*"

"Yes," I admit, heat rushing to my cheeks. "Show me what I'm missing."

He growls low in his throat and shifts position. The camera angle changes as he props his phone somewhere, then leans back. I watch, mesmerized, as he unbuckles his belt and unzips his pants. When he pulls his thick, hard cock free and wraps his hand around it, a moan escapes my lips.

"Fuck, Silvo."

"This is what you do to me," he says, stroking himself slowly. "Hard as steel thinking about your tight pussy."

I spread my legs wider, giving him a better view. "I wish it were you touching me instead of my fingers."

"Tell me how wet you are," he demands, his hand moving faster.

"Soaking," I whimper, circling my clit. "I'm dripping down my thighs thinking about your cock inside me."

"That's it, *bella*. Show me how you play with your cunt when I'm not there to fill it."

I slide two fingers inside myself, gasping at the sensation. "God, Silvo, I need you."

"You'll have me tomorrow," he promises, his rhythm increasing. "I'm going to fuck you until you can't walk."

"Yes," I moan, rocking against my hand. "I want your cum inside me. I want you to mark me."

"You're mine," he growls, his muscled abs tensing as he strokes himself harder. "Say it."

"I'm yours," I gasp, my body tightening as pleasure builds. "Only yours, Silvo."

"Touch your tits," he commands. "Pinch your nipples like I would."

I follow his command, cupping my breasts and pinching my nipples between my fingers. The sharp pleasure makes me arch off the bed.

"That's my girl," Silvo growls, his hand moving faster on his cock. "Show me how close you are."

My fingers circle my clit faster as I watch him stroke himself on screen. The sight of his powerful body, tense with need, drives me wild. I slide two fingers deep inside, wishing it were him filling me instead.

"I'm close," I pant, my hips bucking against my hand. "Silvo, I'm so close."

"Wait for me," he commands, his jaw clenched and muscles taut. "We come together."

I whimper, trembling on the edge. "Hurry, please. I can't—"

"Look at me," he demands. "Keep your eyes on me."

Our gazes lock through the screen, the connection electric despite the miles between us. His rhythm becomes erratic, his breathing harsh.

"Now, Carmela. Come for me now."

The orgasm crashes through me, my back arching off the bed as I cry out his name. Through half-lidded eyes, I watch Silvo's release, his powerful body shuddering as white ropes of cum paint his stomach.

"Fuck," he groans, stroking himself through the aftershocks. "That should've been inside you."

I'm still trembling when he speaks again, his voice raw with promise.

"Tomorrow night, I'm breeding you properly," he vows, eyes dark with possession. "All fucking night long, Carmela."

My breath catches at the hunger in his voice.

"We're locking the door," he continues, "and forgetting about this war, about everything except each other. I'm going to fuck you until you can't walk, until neither of us can move anymore."

I press my thighs together, aftershocks of pleasure pulsing through me at his words.

"Promise?" I whisper.

"Count on it," he growls. "Be ready for me, wife."

28

CARMELA

Morning light streams through the windows as I sit cross-legged on the floor of Silvo's office, surrounded by stacks of files. My back aches from hours hunched over documents, but the pain fades when another puzzle piece clicks into place. The names and dates blur together in a web of connections that grows more intricate with each file I examine.

I haven't slept since my phone call with Silvo at three in the morning. After our... intimate conversation, I tried to rest, but my mind wouldn't stop spinning. The discovery of Maria and Vincenzo's tragic history opened a floodgate of questions, and I needed answers.

So I came back to the office. Made coffee. And kept digging.

The leather portfolio sits open beside me, those haunting photographs of Salvatore and Vincenzo as young friends a constant reminder of how deeply personal this war truly is. But now I'm looking beyond the emotional core to the tactical implications.

A soft knock interrupts my concentration. Isabella peeks around the door, two steaming mugs in hand.

"I figured you'd still be at it," she says, settling onto the floor beside me and handing me a cup. "Couldn't sleep either after what you told me last night about Maria."

I wrap my hands around the warm mug, grateful for both the caffeine and the company. "I can't stop thinking about it. A woman's choice seventy years ago, and we're still bleeding for it."

Isabella nods, scanning the documents spread around us. "Did you find anything else?"

"Actually, yes." I pull up the laptop and show her the timeline I've been constructing. "After I understood the Maria connection, I started looking at the attacks differently. Not just as random strikes, but as something more deliberate."

I bring up a digital map where I've marked each attack with a red pin, then overlay it with another map—one showing locations significant to Salvatore and Maria's relationship.

"Oh my God," Isabella breathes, leaning closer. "They match."

"Exactly." I point to each location in sequence. "The warehouse in Miami where they first attacked? That's where Salvatore had his first legitimate shipping business—the one he started to prove to Maria he could provide for her. The restaurant they hit in South Philly? Salvatore proposed to Maria there."

Isabella traces the pattern with her finger. "The club on Market Street—that was Salvatore's first real estate investment after they married."

"And here," I tap another pin, "the jewelry store they

torched last week. Salvatore bought Maria's engagement ring there."

Isabella sits back, processing. "They're not just attacking us. They're systematically destroying every place that represents Salvatore and Maria's love story."

"Erasing history," I murmur. "Or reclaiming it. Showing that nothing Salvatore built with Maria can last."

"This is psychotic," Isabella says, but there's a hint of sad understanding in her voice. "Vincenzo must have been destroyed when she left him."

I pull out the diary entry again, reading it aloud. "'Blood has been spilled. There can be no reconciliation.' Someone died the day Maria chose Salvatore. I think it was Vincenzo's brother."

Isabella's eyes widen. "How do you know?"

"This." I show her an obituary from 1953. "Giuseppe Moretti died May 15th in a 'tragic accident.' But the coroner's report—which someone filed incorrectly in the De Luca archives—shows he was shot. Execution style."

"Salvatore killed Vincenzo's brother?"

"Or had him killed," I say grimly. "The diary entry mentions blood being spilled the same day Maria chose Salvatore. It's not a coincidence."

Isabella runs her hands through her hair. "So Vincenzo lost the woman he loved *and* his brother on the same day. No wonder the Morettis can't let this go."

I nod, feeling an unexpected pang of sympathy for a man I never knew. "Nico's continuing what his grandfather started—making sure the De Lucas feel the same loss the Morettis did."

We sit in heavy silence, the weight of three generations of grief pressing down on us.

"There's more," I finally say, pulling myself back to the present. "I found something that doesn't fit the pattern."

I spread out financial records across the floor. "These attacks are expensive. The weapons, the manpower, the coordination—we're talking millions of dollars in operational costs."

Isabella frowns. "The Morettis have resources, but not unlimited ones. Not for a war of attrition like this."

"Exactly." I point to a series of shell company transactions. "Someone's been funneling money to offshore accounts that trace back to... I'm not sure yet. The paper trail gets murky. But there are payments coming from sources outside both our families."

"A third party?" Isabella leans forward, her analytical mind engaging. "Who would benefit from our families destroying each other?"

Before I can answer, my phone buzzes. A text from Silvo.

Landing in 2 hours. Miss you.

My heart does a little flip despite the serious conversation.

Miss you too. Found something important.
Hurry home.

"He's landing soon," I tell Isabella, gathering the financial documents. "We should get all this organized for him."

"Wait." Isabella grabs my wrist, her expression troubled. "Before Silvo gets back, promise me you won't tell him about the messages from Maximo."

My stomach tightens at her tone. "Isabella, he should know."

There's an odd flash in her eyes, making me wonder if

she's told me the whole story. Silvo will want to know about this fixation. Emotional investments cloud judgment. We could use that."

Isabella shakes her head. "I don't want to be bait, Carmela."

"I'm not suggesting that." I squeeze her hand. "But we need to tell Silvo about this. He should know the Morettis are targeting both of us specifically."

She nods reluctantly. "After you show him everything else you've found."

I return to the financial documents, my earlier discovery nagging at me. "Help me with these shell companies. There's something here I'm missing."

For the next hour, we trace money trails through dummy corporations and offshore accounts. Isabella's knowledge of the family's legitimate businesses helps identify which transactions are normal and which are suspicious.

"There," Isabella points to a series of wire transfers. "These don't match any known Moretti business activity. The amounts are too irregular, and the timing..."

"Corresponds with the attacks," I finish, excitement building. "Someone's paying for these operations, and it's not coming from Moretti accounts."

"Could it be the Russians?" Isabella suggests. "Funding the attacks to weaken both families?"

"Maybe." I make notes on my pad. "Or someone else entirely. A third player we haven't identified yet."

The sound of a car door slamming outside makes us both jump. I check the security feed—it's just Fed returning from an errand.

"Speaking of Fed," Isabella says with a knowing smile,

"I saw him with Sophia in the hallway last night. They looked pretty cozy."

I can't help but grin. "I noticed that too. Your brother's smitten."

"About time," Isabella laughs. "He's been alone too long. Sophia's good for him—keeps him grounded."

"Like Silvo's good for me," I say softly, surprising myself with the admission.

Isabella's expression softens. "You really have fallen for him, haven't you? My grumpy, overprotective brother."

"Completely." I look down at my wedding ring, remembering how much I'd resented it at first. "I fought it so hard, but somewhere along the way..."

"You realized he's worth fighting for instead of against," Isabella finishes.

"Exactly."

We continue working in comfortable silence, organizing evidence and building a comprehensive brief for Silvo. By the time we're done, the sun has climbed higher in the sky, and my exhaustion is catching up with me.

"You should rest before Silvo gets here," Isabella suggests, noting the dark circles under my eyes.

"Can't." I gulp more coffee. "Too much adrenaline. Besides, I want to be sharp when I show him all of this."

Isabella stands, stretching. "Then at least eat something. You're no good to anyone if you pass out from exhaustion."

She's right, of course. We head to the kitchen, where Sophia is making breakfast, Fed leaning against the counter watching her with obvious appreciation.

"Morning, sleepyheads," Sophia greets us cheerfully. "I'm making pancakes. Who wants some?"

"Me," I say, sliding onto a barstool. "I'm starving."

Fed pours me orange juice. "My brother texted. Says he's landing soon and that you found something important?"

"Very important," I confirm. "We've been up all night piecing it together."

"Should I be worried?" Fed's casual tone doesn't match the sharpness in his eyes.

"Yes," I answer honestly. "But not in the way you think."

Sophia sets a plate of pancakes in front of me, and I dig in gratefully. The normalcy of this moment—breakfast with friends and family—feels surreal given everything swirling around us.

My phone buzzes again. This time it's a call.

"Silvo?"

"I just landed," his voice comes through, rough with exhaustion. "I'll be home in forty minutes. Whatever you found, we'll handle it together."

"Together," I echo, warmth spreading through my chest at the word. "Drive safe."

"Always."

When I hang up, I find three pairs of eyes watching me with various degrees of amusement.

"What?" I ask defensively.

"Nothing," Sophia says innocently. "Just nice to see you so happy. Remember when you wanted to murder him?"

"I still do sometimes," I mutter, but I'm smiling. "He's infuriating."

"But he's your infuriating husband," Isabella adds with a grin.

Fed pushes off the counter. "Alright, lovebirds and love-adjacent people, I'm going to make sure the house is secure before Silvo gets here. He'll want to dive straight into whatever intel you've gathered."

"Good idea," I say, finishing my pancakes and draining my juice. "Isabella and I will get everything set up in the office."

As Fed heads out, Sophia begins clearing plates. "You know, Carmela, when you first got here, I never thought I'd see you like this."

"Like what?"

"Happy. Settled. Like you belong." She smiles warmly. "It's good to see."

Her words touch something deep inside me. She's right—I do belong here now. This house, this family, this life I initially resented has become mine in ways I never expected.

"Thanks, Soph," I say, hugging her. "For coming here with me. For staying. I couldn't do this without you."

"Please," she waves me off. "Like I'd let you face the mafia alone. Besides, the view isn't bad." Her eyes drift toward where Fed disappeared.

Isabella and I exchange knowing glances.

"Come on," I tell Isabella. "Let's make sure everything's perfect for Silvo's arrival. I want to hit him with all of this at once—show him what his wife is capable of."

Isabella grins. "He's going to lose his mind when he sees what you've put together."

We return to the office, making final adjustments to the presentation. I arrange the photos in order of importance, stack the financial documents by category, and ensure the maps are clearly labeled.

By the time we're finished, the office looks like a professional intelligence briefing room. Every surface covered with evidence, every connection clearly marked. This is more than just research—it's a complete breakdown of our enemy's strategy, psychology, and vulnerabilities.

"You've really outdone yourself," Isabella says, surveying our work with obvious pride.

"We did this together," I remind her.

"True. But you're the one who saw the bigger picture. Who connected the emotional history to the tactical reality?" She squeezes my shoulder. "Silvo's lucky to have you."

The sound of a car engine makes my heart leap. I rush to the window and see Silvo's black sedan pulling into the driveway.

"He's here," I breathe, suddenly nervous.

Isabella heads for the door. "I'll give you two some privacy. But call me when you're ready to discuss next steps."

"Thank you, Isabella. For everything."

She pauses at the doorway, looking back with a soft smile. "That's what sisters do."

Then she's gone, and I hear the front door opening, Silvo's deep voice greeting Fed in the foyer. My pulse races as his footsteps approach.

This is it. Time to show my husband exactly what I've become.

29

SILVO

The moment I step through the front door of our home, I sense something different. The air feels charged, as if the house itself breathes with a new energy. I drop my bag in the foyer, my body aching from the flight and the bullet graze on my shoulder, pulling with each movement.

"Welcome home," Carmela's voice comes from the doorway to my office.

I turn, and the sight of her stops me cold. She's leaning against the doorframe, arms crossed, wearing a simple black dress that hugs her curves. But it's not what she's wearing—it's how she's standing. There's a confidence in her posture that wasn't there four days ago.

"You look different," I say, crossing to her.

She doesn't move to meet me halfway as she might have before. Instead, she waits, watching me approach with those intelligent green eyes that have seen too little sleep.

"I've been busy while you were gone." A slight smile plays at her lips. "Your security protocols need updating.

Isabella and I found three blind spots in the east wing camera coverage."

I raise an eyebrow. "You've been analyzing my security systems?"

"Among other things." She turns and walks into my office, expecting me to follow.

When I enter, I'm struck by the transformation. Papers are spread across my desk in organized piles—surveillance photos, financial documents, tactical analyses. My laptop displays a detailed map of Moretti holdings across the Northeast, color-coded and annotated with notes in Carmela's neat handwriting. But it's the weathered leather portfolio sitting open that draws my eye—the one she told me about on the phone last night.

"You've expanded on what you found," I observe, picking up her analysis of the attack pattern. She's mapped every Moretti strike against locations significant to Salvatore and Maria's relationship—their first restaurant, the church where they married, even the hotel where they spent their honeymoon.

"After we talked last night, I couldn't sleep." Carmela traces the route on the map. "Once I understood the Maria and Vincenzo connection, everything else fell into place. The Morettis aren't just attacking us—they're erasing your family's history with her. Symbolically destroying everything Salvatore built with the woman Vincenzo loved."

I stare at the meticulous work spread before me. In four days, she and Isabella have compiled intelligence that would take my men weeks to gather. "This is incredible, Carmela. The tactical insight here—"

"Is personal, not just strategic," she interrupts softly. She picks up the photograph of Salvatore and Vincenzo as young men, arms around each other. "They were brothers in everything but blood. And Maria destroyed that. The Morettis see every De Luca as a reminder of that betrayal."

The weight of seventy years of hatred suddenly makes terrible sense. This isn't about territory or power—it's about a wound that never healed.

"You've uncovered the heart of it," I say, genuine admiration in my voice. "My father, my grandfather—none of them understood why the hatred ran so deep. They just knew it did."

She meets my eyes, unflinching. "I'm a De Luca now. If they're coming for this family, they're coming for me, too. I needed to understand why."

I groan, my body responding to this new side of her before my brain can catch up. "Fuck, you're so sexy like this."

Her eyes flash at my words—part defiance, part something else. I've come to recognize the subtle shifts in her expressions. The slight parting of her lips. The way her chest rises and falls more rapidly. And there it is—that telltale sign of desire as her thighs clench together unconsciously.

"Is that all you have to say?" Carmela challenges, but her voice has dropped an octave lower. "I spend days building actionable intelligence, and you just want to—"

"Fuck you on this desk?" I move around it, closing the distance between us in three long strides. "Yes. Absolutely yes."

The papers on the desk flutter as I approach, but I couldn't care less about strategy right now.

"You want more words?" I grab her waist, pulling her against me roughly. "How about this—seeing you take charge, stepping into this life without fear, uncovering secrets my own family never understood—it drives me fucking crazy."

Her hands press against my chest, not pushing me away but feeling the thundering heartbeat beneath my shirt. "I'm not afraid of who you are anymore," she whispers. "Maybe I'm more afraid of who I'm becoming."

That confession breaks something loose inside me. I crash my mouth against hers, kissing her roughly, desperately.

She responds immediately, her fingers tangling in my hair, pulling just hard enough to send sparks down my spine. I lift her onto the desk, shoving papers aside, not giving a damn about the hours of work scattered across the floor.

Carmela wraps her legs around my waist, pulling me closer, matching my passion with her own. Her teeth nip at my bottom lip—a challenge, a claim. I groan into her mouth, my hands sliding down her back to grip her ass, pressing her against my hardness.

"I missed you," she breathes against my lips, the confession seemingly torn from her unwillingly.

I kiss her harder in response, unable to form words for what I'm feeling. This isn't just lust—it's something deeper, more dangerous. Something I never expected from our arranged marriage.

I tear down the zipper of her dress, the sound echoing through the office. As the fabric falls away, revealing her black lace bra and matching panties, my cock throbs painfully against my pants.

"Look at you," I growl, tracing my finger along the curve of her breast. "So fucking perfect."

Carmela shivers under my touch, her nipples hardening beneath the thin lace. I unsnap her bra with practiced ease, letting it fall to the floor among the scattered papers.

"I made you a promise on our wedding night," I remind her, my voice dropping to a dangerous whisper. "And I always keep my promises."

Her breath catches as I press my lips to her ear. "I'm going to breed you properly, Carmela. Fill you up until my seed takes root."

Instead of the resistance I half-expected, she moans, her hips bucking against mine. But then she presses a hand to my chest, pushing me back just enough to create space between us.

"Not so fast," she purrs, her fingers trailing down to my belt. "My turn first."

The defiance in her eyes makes my cock twitch as she slowly unbuckles my belt, the metal clinking as she pulls it free. She takes her time with my zipper, dragging it down tooth by tooth while maintaining eye contact.

"You think you're in charge here?" I challenge, though I make no move to stop her.

Her smile is wicked as she slips her hand inside my pants, wrapping her fingers around my length. "Right now? Yes."

She strokes me, her grip firm but teasing—too slow to give real satisfaction. I groan, fighting the urge to thrust into her hand.

"You're playing with fire," I warn, my voice strained.

"Good thing I've always liked getting burned." She squeezes me harder, her thumb circling the sensitive tip.

I grab her wrist, stopping her movements. "Enough games."

I grip Carmela's waist firmly and lift her off the desk in one fluid motion. Her eyes widen in surprise as I settle myself onto the polished wood surface, knocking a few more papers to the floor.

"Come here," I growl, my voice thick with need. "I want your sweet pussy on my face while you suck my cock."

A flush spreads across her chest, rising to her cheeks. "Demanding as always," she says, but the hunger in her eyes betrays her desire.

"Always," I agree, reaching for her. "Now get that gorgeous ass up here and put that smart mouth to better use."

Carmela climbs onto the desk, her movements graceful despite her trembling thighs. She straddles my chest, facing away from me, and I grab her hips, pulling her core closer to my mouth.

"Fuck, you're already dripping for me," I groan as I see her slick folds mere inches from my face.

She wraps her hand around my length, her touch sending electricity through my body. "You're not exactly patient yourself," she teases, lowering her head to run her tongue along the underside of my cock.

The moment her warm mouth envelops me, I pull her hips down and bury my face between her thighs. She tastes like honey and sin, sweet and addictive on my tongue. I devour her, circling her clit with precision while she takes me deeper into her throat.

Carmela moans around my cock, the vibrations nearly pushing me over the edge. I slide two fingers inside her, curling them to hit that spot that makes her thighs quiver. Her rhythm falters as pleasure overtakes her, but she doubles her efforts, hollowing her cheeks and working me with her hand and mouth in tandem.

Heat builds at the base of my spine, my release

approaching fast. I pull away from her center, slapping her ass hard enough to leave a pink handprint.

"I'm going to come if you're not careful. Get on my cock now. I want to finish in that sweet pussy."

Carmela moans, the sound vibrating through her body as she releases my cock from her mouth. Her eyes flash with determination as she swivels around, turning on the desk until she's straddling me. Her pussy hovers just above my throbbing length, so close I can feel her heat radiating against my skin.

"Fuck, you're beautiful," I growl, watching her position herself above me.

She smirks, lowering her hips just enough to brush her slick folds against the head of my cock. The contact sends electricity shooting up my spine, making me grit my teeth to maintain control.

"Look how wet you make me," she purrs, sliding her pussy up and down my length, coating me in her arousal. Each stroke of her warm center against my hardness is exquisite torture.

I grip the edge of the desk, knuckles turning white. "Sit on it," I command, my voice rough with need.

Carmela raises an eyebrow, continuing her teasing movements. "I don't think so." She leans forward, placing her hands on my chest. "I'm the one in control right now."

Something primal snaps inside me at her challenge. I've endured hell in Miami, been shot at and betrayed, and all I've thought about is getting back to her. My patience shatters.

"You think so?" I growl, reaching up to grip her hips firmly, my fingers digging into her soft flesh. I position my cock directly beneath her entrance, the tip pressing against her slick opening. “Sit down like a good girl and take what you’ve been begging for.”

Her eyes widen, pupils dilating with desire at my dominance. For a moment, we’re locked in a battle of wills, neither willing to surrender.

Then Carmela sinks down on my cock in one swift motion, taking me to the hilt. We groan in unison, the sound echoing through my office as our bodies finally join. She’s tight and hot around me, her walls clenching with delicious pressure.

“Fuck,” I hiss through clenched teeth, my fingers tightening on her hips.

“Silvo,” she moans, her head falling back as she adjusts to the fullness of me inside her.

Carmela begins to move, slowly at first, rising and falling on my cock with deliberate, teasing strokes. Each time she sinks down, she rolls her hips, taking me deeper.

“Fuck, you feel so good around me,” I growl, watching her perfect tits bounce with each movement. “Your pussy was made for my cock.”

She smiles wickedly, slowing her pace even more. “Is that right? Maybe I should stop then...” She lifts herself until only the tip of me remains inside her.

I grip her hips tighter, forcing her back down. “Don’t you fucking dare.”

“Or what?” she challenges, clenching her walls around me.

“Or I’ll bend you over this desk and fuck you until you can’t remember your own name.”

She leans forward, her hair falling around us like a curtain. “Promises, promises.”

I thrust upward suddenly, making her gasp. “I never make promises I don’t keep.”

Carmela picks up her pace, riding me harder, her hands braced against my chest. "You want to fill me up, Silvo? Want to put a baby in me?"

Her words send fire through my veins. "Going to breed this pretty pussy. Make you swell with my child."

"Then fuck me like you mean it," she demands, grinding down harder.

I grab her ass, helping her movements, feeling myself getting closer. "Touch yourself. Let me see you come on my cock."

Her fingers find her clit, circling it as she continues to ride me. Her walls start to flutter around me, and I know she's close.

"Not yet," I command, stilling her hips. "Not until I say."

She whimpers in frustration but obeys, her body trembling with restraint. I hold her there, both of us on the edge, savoring the exquisite torture.

When I can't take it anymore, I thrust up hard. "Now. Come for me now."

Carmela crashes her lips against mine as her orgasm hits. I swallow her cries, my tongue tangling with hers as I pump into her once, twice more before exploding inside her, filling her with pulse after pulse of hot seed.

As she shudders around me, our bodies locked together in perfect sync, I hold her close. Her lips are still against mine, her breathing ragged, and I'm still emptying myself deep inside her.

Something shifts in my chest—not the realization that I love her, I've known that for weeks now. But something deeper. A certainty that settles into my bones.

I break the kiss to look at her face—flushed, eyes half-closed in pleasure, lips swollen from my kisses. My wife.

The mother of my future children. My partner in this dangerous world.

I want this forever.

Not just the passion or the connection, but everything. I want to watch her grow round with our child. Want to see her hair turn gray beside mine. Want decades of mornings waking up next to her, decades of nights falling asleep with her in my arms.

I pull her closer, burying my face in her neck as I continue to pulse inside her, my body giving her everything I have. My fingers tangle in her hair, gripping perhaps too tightly, but I need this anchor.

"Mine," I whisper against her skin. Not a claim of ownership—a vow of belonging. "Forever mine."

Her walls flutter around me, milking every last drop. "Forever yours," she whispers back, and I know she understands what I can't quite put into words yet.

I kiss her again, trying to show her what I'm feeling. This wasn't supposed to happen. We were an arrangement, a business transaction. I never planned to fall in love with my arranged wife.

But I did. And now I want everything—not just tonight, but every night for the rest of our lives.

30

SILVO

The basement air hangs thick with anticipation as I descend the stairs. Lorenzo waits at the bottom, arms folded across his chest. He made the trip up from Miami specifically for this.

"Where is he?" My voice echoes against the concrete walls.

Lorenzo nods toward the steel door at the end of the hallway. "Secured. Paulie's with him."

I roll up my sleeves methodically, one after the other. "How much did he resist?"

"Enough to earn the split lip he's sporting." Lorenzo falls into step beside me. "Fed tracked him down in Atlantic City. A one-way ticket to Argentina was already purchased."

My jaw tightens. Argentina—where organized crime figures disappear when they need to lay low. Luca knew exactly what he was doing.

The door creaks open to reveal Luca Vega strapped to a metal chair, blood trickling from his mouth. His eyes widen when he sees me, then Lorenzo behind me.

"Boss, there's been a misunderstanding—"

My fist connects with his jaw before he can finish. The crack reverberates through the room.

"Three months ago." I pull out the photograph Carmela found—Luca standing with a man outside the Sapphire Club. "You and this man. We've identified him as Alexei Tartarov's nephew, Dimitri."

I circle him slowly, letting the silence build. "Funny, because when Carlos told you about our meeting location, you called in sick. Food poisoning, wasn't it?"

Luca's face goes pale. "I was sick—"

"Bullshit." I slam the photo down on a metal tray beside him. "You fed our location to someone. The question is who—and why."

"They have my family," Luca blurts out, his voice cracking. "My mother, my sister—they're in Moscow. Tartarov's people grabbed them six months ago."

I exchange a glance with Lorenzo. This is new information.

"Tartarov?" I lean against the wall, reassessing. "Not the Morettis?"

Luca shakes his head frantically. "The Russians. They approached me last year when I was visiting family in Spain. Showed me photos of my mother and sister. Said if I didn't cooperate, they'd kill them both."

I grab his throat, forcing him to meet my eyes. "And you believed them?"

"I saw the photos, boss. They had them. My mother's apartment, my sister's work—they knew everything." Tears stream down his face. "What would you have done?"

The question hits harder than I expect. I think of Carmela, of how far I'd go to protect her. Of the choices I'd make if someone threatened her life.

I release him, my mind racing. If Luca's telling the truth,

then Tartarov's operation is far more sophisticated than we realized. Infiltrating our organization by leveraging family —it's exactly what I'd do.

"What information did you give them?" I demand.

"Schedules. Meeting locations. Shipment routes." Luca's words tumble out faster now. "But I swear, they told me they were Moretti associates. They wore crests, used the lion symbols, and spoke Italian."

I circle behind him, processing this. "Well they weren't."

"I know that now," he chokes out. "They played me."

Lorenzo steps forward, his face hard. "Why should we believe you?"

"Because I'm telling you everything!" Luca's voice rises in desperation. "Tartarov has people in both families. Not just ours—the Morettis too. He's been feeding intelligence to both sides, making each family think the other is behind the attacks."

The pieces start falling into place. The spray-painted crests. The obviously planted evidence—that Moretti cuff-link at the crime scene. The attacks that seemed too perfect, too calculated to be genuine Moretti operations.

"How many others?" I ask quietly. "How many people in my organization are compromised?"

"I don't know," Luca admits. "Tartarov compartmentalized everything. I only knew my part—feeding information about Miami operations and Lorenzo's schedule. But he mentioned having assets in Philadelphia, New York, even inside the Moretti organization."

I pull out my phone and text Fed:

Need you in the basement. Now.

"The Morettis," I say slowly, the full picture emerging. "They think we've been attacking them."

As the words leave my mouth, I can't shake the feeling that their vendetta against us runs deeper than mere business. It's personal for them, fueled by the grudge intertwined with Carmela's evidence. All those pieces she amassed pointed to a methodical assault on our reputation. The tension between our families has escalated to a boiling point—this isn't just about territory; it's about revenge. And now, with Tartarov lurking in the shadows, I realize he's the wild card we haven't figured out yet—using their personal grudge to his advantage. He's playing us against each other, and if we don't act fast, both our families could face annihilation.

"Yes," Luca confirms. "That's exactly what Tartarov wants. While you two destroy each other, he moves in and takes over both territories. He's been playing this game for at least a year, maybe longer."

Lorenzo curses viciously in Italian. "That manipulative bastard."

Fed appears at the door moments later, taking in the scene with sharp eyes. "What's going on?"

"Luca just confirmed what Carmela suspected," I tell him. "The attacks aren't Moretti operations. They're Tartarov's false flag—designed to reignite our war while he expands into our territories."

Fed's expression hardens. "Son of a bitch."

I turn back to Luca, studying his face for any sign of deception. "These people holding your family—where are they?"

"I don't know exactly. Moscow somewhere. They send me photos every week to prove they're still alive." His voice breaks. "Please, boss. I know I fucked up. But I was trying to protect them."

I study him for a long moment. Part of me wants to put a bullet in his head for the betrayal—nine good men died because of the information he leaked. Lorenzo nearly died. Carlos took a bullet in the shoulder. I took one myself.

But another part—the part that loves Carmela, that understands what it means to protect family—sees the impossible position he was in.

"Tell me about the communication methods," I say. "How does Tartarov contact you?"

"Encrypted messages through a burner app," Luca says quickly, eager to cooperate now. "Different phone each time. He has me destroy them after every communication."

"But you kept records," I guess, seeing it in his eyes.

He nods. "Screenshots. Backed up to a cloud account. I knew I might need proof someday that I was coerced."

Smart. Stupid for betraying us, but smart for covering his ass.

"Lorenzo," I say finally. "Contact our people in Moscow. Find Luca's family. I want them extracted within forty-eight hours."

Luca's head snaps up, hope flooding his face. "You mean—"

"I mean, we're going to get your family out of Tartarov's reach," I interrupt. "But you're going to earn it. You're going to tell us everything you know about his operation. Every contact, every meeting, every piece of intelligence you passed along. Names, dates, locations—all of it."

"Yes," Luca says quickly. "Anything. I'll tell you everything."

"And then," I continue, my voice dropping to a deadly

calm, "you're going to help us feed false information back to Tartarov. Make him think his infiltration is still working."

Fed catches on immediately. "A double agent."

"Exactly." I cross my arms, looking down at Luca. "You're going to help us destroy the man who's been using you. Give us access to those encrypted communications. Every message he sends, we'll see. Every order he gives, we'll know about in advance."

"I will," Luca promises, fresh tears streaming down his face. "I swear on my mother's life, I'll do whatever it takes to make this right."

I nod to Paulie to release him from the chair. Luca slumps forward, rubbing his wrists where the restraints bit into his skin.

"Fed, get him cleaned up and into a secure room upstairs. I want a full debrief—everything he knows about Tartarov's operation, organizational structure, communication methods, everyone he's met or heard mentioned." I turn to Lorenzo. "And get our Moscow contacts moving on his family. I want confirmation they're located before we trust anything else he tells us."

"On it, boss," Lorenzo says, already pulling out his phone.

As they lead Luca out, Fed lingers behind, closing the door. "You believe him?"

"About being coerced? Yes." I lean against the concrete wall, my shoulder throbbing. "About wanting to make it right? We'll see. But right now, he's our best source of intelligence on Tartarov's operation."

"And if he's lying?" Fed's voice is flat, tactical.

"Then he joins the other traitors in unmarked graves." I push off the wall, heading for the stairs. "But my gut says he's telling the truth. Tartarov's playing a much bigger game than we realized—and he's damn good at it."

Fed follows me up. "We need to tell the Morettis."

"I know." I pause on the landing. "But not until we have everything confirmed. Luca's testimony, his family's extraction, the financial trail Carmela found. We go to Nico with irrefutable proof, or we don't go at all."

"How long will that take?"

"Forty-eight hours, maybe seventy-two." I resume climbing. "Tell Marco to start preparing a legal brief—something that shows the pattern of false flag operations. We need documentation that even Nico's most suspicious capo can't dismiss."

"You really think this will work? That we can convince them we've been played?"

I reach the top of the stairs, pausing before opening the door. "It has to work, Fed. Because if it doesn't, if we can't unite against Tartarov..." I don't need to finish the sentence.

We both know what happens if we fail. More bloodshed. More bodies. The complete destruction of both families, while Tartarov picks up the pieces.

"Get started on the debrief," I tell him. "I want everything documented—video recorded, transcribed, cross-referenced with our existing intelligence. Nothing left to chance."

Fed nods and heads down the hallway toward the secure rooms. I stand there for a moment, the weight of everything pressing down on me. Nine men dead. Both families infiltrated. A Russian puppet master pulling strings we didn't even know existed.

I pull out my phone and open the security app, checking the feeds throughout the house. I find Carmela in my office, still analyzing intelligence reports, determination etched across her beautiful face. My heart aches at the sight of her.

She's hunched over the laptop, her hair falling forward as she types notes, completely absorbed in her work. Even exhausted, even after being awake for over twenty-four hours, she pushes forward. For me. For us. For the family she didn't choose but has claimed as her own.

I zoom in slightly on the feed, watching as she reaches for her coffee mug, takes a sip, then makes a face—probably gone cold hours ago. She sets it aside and continues working, her fingers flying across the keyboard.

This woman. This incredible, fierce, brilliant woman.

For the first time in my life, I have something truly precious to lose. Not just territory or power or legacy—but her. The thought of Tartarov's men getting anywhere near Carmela makes my blood run cold.

I close the app and head toward my office, my resolve hardening with each step. Whatever it takes—whatever alliance I need to forge, whatever enemy I need to destroy—I'll protect her. Protect what we've built.

Because Carmela isn't just my wife anymore. She's my entire world.

And I'll burn everything to the ground before I let anyone take her from me.

31

CARMELA

I slip out of Silvo's office while he's still debriefing with Fed and Lorenzo about Luca's confession. The tension is unbearable, and I need air. I need to feel like something other than a tactical analyst in a war I didn't choose.

I hover in the doorway, waiting for a break in the conversation. "I'm going shopping," I announce.

The room goes quiet. Silvo's eyes snap to mine, and I already know what's coming.

"No."

"Silvo—"

"I said no, Carmela." He sets down the folder in his hands, giving me his full attention now, which somehow feels worse than being ignored. "We have a confirmed leak. Tartarov's men are still out there. You think now is the time to browse boutiques?"

"I've been staring at surveillance photos and financial records for three days straight," I say, keeping my voice level despite the frustration rising in my chest. "I need two hours. That's all."

"The answer is no."

Fed clears his throat quietly and finds something fascinating to study on the ceiling. Lorenzo suddenly becomes very interested in his coffee.

I step fully into the room, closing the door behind me. "Silvo. I understand the threat. I've been living inside it with you every single day. But if I don't get out of this house for a few hours I'm going to lose my mind, and that helps no one." I hold his gaze. "I'm not asking to go alone. I'm not asking to cross the city. Rittenhouse Square. Two hours. I'll have bodyguards with me."

His jaw tightens. "Tony and Paulie aren't enough. Not right now."

"Then send more." I cross my arms. "Or better yet, send Federico with me."

Silvo looks at his brother, who immediately holds up both hands.

"Don't look at me," Fed says. "She makes a compelling argument."

Silvo's eyes return to mine. I can see him wrestling with it—the practical need to keep me contained, warring with the understanding that keeping me locked inside these walls indefinitely isn't sustainable either.

"Two hours," he finally says, his voice tight with reluctance. "Fed goes with you. Tony and Paulie on the doors. You stay in Rittenhouse Square, you don't deviate from the route, and if Federico says it's time to leave, you leave. No arguments."

"No arguments," I agree.

"I mean it, Carmela."

"So do I." I cross to him, pressing a quick kiss to his jaw. "Thank you."

He catches my wrist before I can pull away, his grip

firm. "Two hours," he repeats, his eyes serious. "Then you're back here."

"Two hours," I confirm.

He releases me, but I feel his eyes on my back all the way to the door.

Federico falls into step beside me in the foyer, shrugging on his jacket with a grin. "You know he's going to track your phone the entire time."

"I know," I say, grabbing my purse. "I'm counting on it."

Tony and Paulie are already waiting by the car, armed and alert. We drive to Rittenhouse Square in relative silence. When we arrive at the boutique, Federico takes a position just inside the entrance while Tony and Paulie cover the doors—visible enough to deter trouble, but far enough to give me space to breathe.

After twenty minutes of browsing, Fed appears at my elbow, nodding toward the window. "Everything seems calm. Tony and Paulie have the doors covered." He pauses, the picture of innocence. "There's a boutique across the street I wouldn't mind checking out."

I glance up from the rack I've been browsing, raising an eyebrow. "A boutique"

"What? I have impeccable taste." He straightens his jacket pointedly.

I laugh despite myself. "Go. I won't tell Silvo."

He grins and disappears through the door, leaving me to the quiet pleasure of browsing alone for the first time in weeks. I run my fingers over a silky emerald dress, admiring how the fabric catches the light. Isabella recommended this place for their exclusive European imports, and I needed the distraction from our family's escalating situation. For a few precious minutes, I let myself simply exist—no surveillance photos, no threat assessments, no war.

"That shade would complement your eyes perfectly."

The voice behind me is unfamiliar. I turn to find a striking dark-haired girl about my age examining the same rack. Something about her seems oddly familiar—the confident posture, those intelligent dark eyes.

"You think so?" I ask, holding the dress against me.

"Absolutely. Green on green creates depth." She smiles, extending her hand. "I'm Valeria."

My breath catches. Valeria Moretti. The daughter of our enemy. I've seen her in the surveillance photos, but they didn't capture her warmth.

From the corner of my eye, I see Tony stiffen near the entrance. I give him a subtle look—*it's fine*—and he reluctantly stays put, though his hand hovers near his weapon.

"Carmela," I reply, hesitating before taking her hand. I don't add my last name. She doesn't either.

A tall blonde joins us, her blue eyes widening slightly as she looks between us. "Val, I found those shoes you—" She stops abruptly.

"This is my friend Adele," Valeria says. "Adele, this is Carmela. She has impeccable taste in formalwear."

Adele's expression betrays nothing, but I recognize her too—the girl in the photos with Nico Moretti. The tension in the air could be cut with a knife.

"That's quite a statement piece," I nod toward a sapphire jumpsuit Adele's holding. "Bold choice."

"Life's too short for boring clothes," Adele replies with unexpected warmth.

The three of us stand there, enemies by association but drawn together by something I can't quite name. Fashion becomes our neutral territory.

"Are you new to Philadelphia?" Valeria asks, expertly shifting through a rack of cocktail dresses.

"Relatively. I'm from Los Angeles originally."

"West Coast girl! What brought you to our humble city?" Valeria's eyes sparkle with genuine interest.

"Marriage," I answer truthfully.

"Ah, love conquers distance," Valeria smiles. "Philadelphia has hidden treasures if you know where to look. The art museum is spectacular."

"I've been meaning to visit," I say, surprised by how easily conversation flows between us. "I paint a little myself."

"Really? So do I!" Valeria's face lights up. "Oils or acrylics?"

"Watercolors, actually," I admit. "There's something about the way they blend that feels... unpredictable. Like life."

Valeria nods earnestly. "I've never mastered watercolors. They require a willingness to surrender control."

Something in her words strikes me. Surrender control. Isn't that exactly what I've been fighting against since my arranged marriage?

Adele runs her fingers over a silk scarf. "Val's being modest. Her studio at home is filled with incredible pieces."

"You should see them sometime," Valeria offers casually, then checks herself. "If circumstances were different."

The unspoken truth hangs between us. Our families. The blood feud. The current war.

"This is ridiculous, isn't it?" Valeria suddenly says, her voice dropping. "Three women who clearly have things in common, standing here pretending we don't know who each other is."

I freeze, unsure how to respond.

Adele sighs. "Val..."

"No, I'm tired of it, Adele." Valeria's dark eyes meet

mine directly. "My grandfather's grudge shouldn't dictate my life. This war is destroying both our families, and for what? Ancient history?"

"You know about Maria and Salvatore?" I ask cautiously.

"Of course. My father made sure I understood exactly why we're supposed to hate your family." Valeria shakes her head. "But I don't. I can't. It's all so... senseless."

Adele touches Valeria's arm gently. "We've talked about it for months. None of us asked for this war."

I study these two women—one born into the same world as me, one drawn into it—and see the same frustration I feel reflected in their eyes. There's something captivating about their refusal to blindly accept the hatred they've inherited.

"Sometimes I think the men are too invested in vengeance to see what it costs," I admit.

Valeria nods. "Exactly. They could be building something instead of destroying everything."

"My father wasn't always this way," Valeria says unexpectedly, her fingers tracing the embroidery on a nearby blouse. "Before all this escalated, he used to paint with me on Sundays. Just us, in the sunroom, jazz playing softly."

Something shifts in her expression—a softness I hadn't expected from a Moretti.

"He raised us alone after our mother left," she continues. "I was only two. Max was five. Dad would make terrible pancakes every Saturday morning—burned edges, gooey centers—but we ate every bite because he tried so hard."

I watch Valeria's face as she speaks, the way her eyes drift somewhere distant, somewhere tender. This isn't the cold-blooded monster I've constructed in my mind from surveillance photos and threat assessments. This is a father who made bad pancakes.

"He used to read to me every night until I was twelve," Valeria says, smiling at the memory. "Even when he came home exhausted, suit rumpled, shoulders heavy with whatever burdens he carried. He never missed a night."

Adele watches me carefully, gauging my reaction. I struggle to reconcile this image with the man orchestrating attacks against my new family.

"Sometimes I'd find him in his study, staring at old photographs," Valeria adds, her voice quieter now. "Not plotting violence—just lonely. Just a man who didn't know how to stop fighting because fighting was all he had left."

The emerald dress feels heavier in my hands. I've never considered that Nico Moretti might be capable of tenderness, of loneliness. That behind the vendetta might be a man as trapped by history as the rest of us.

I stand there struck by the humanity in Valeria's stories. We're supposed to be bitter enemies—De Luca versus Moretti—yet here we are, discussing fashion and painting techniques like old friends.

"We should go," Adele says softly, checking her phone. "Your father will be wondering where we are."

Valeria nods but hesitates. "Carmela, before we leave..." She pulls out her phone, hesitation flickering across her face. "Would you... Would you consider exchanging numbers? Just in case things get worse between our families."

I blink, surprised by the boldness of her request. The urge to tell her everything rises sharply in my chest—that it's already worse, that the attacks tearing our families apart aren't coming from where either of us thinks, that a Russian with deep pockets and deeper ambitions is pulling strings while we point guns at each other. But I can't. Not without Silvo's blessing. Not here, not yet.

"I know it sounds crazy," she continues, "but maybe we could work together somehow. Behind the scenes. If the men lose their heads completely, perhaps we could talk them down together."

Adele watches our exchange with cautious eyes. "Val's right. Sometimes a different perspective can defuse situations before they explode."

I think about Silvo, about the fury in his eyes when he speaks of the Morettis. About the bodies already piling up in this vendetta. Bodies that didn't have to fall. I pull out my phone and nod. "Let me give you my number."

"Women have always been the secret peacekeepers," Valeria adds quietly. "While men wage war, we rebuild what they destroy."

A knot forms in my stomach—not just guilt about keeping this from Silvo, but something more urgent. This girl standing in front of me, sharing stories about her lonely father and Sunday painting sessions, has no idea her family is being manipulated just as much as mine.

"Let's hope we never need to use these," I say, slipping my phone back into my purse. Though I already suspect we will, and sooner than either of us would like.

"Hope for peace, plan for war," Valeria replies with a sad smile. "That's what my father always says."

As they turn to leave, guilt crawls up my spine—but it's a different guilt than I expected. Not just the guilt of going behind Silvo's back. The guilt of looking this girl in the eye and staying silent about something that could get her family killed.

32

SILVO

The phone vibrates against my desk. My father's name flashes on the screen.

"We're back from Sicily. We need a meeting in an hour."

My father doesn't waste words. Despite being retired, he still steps in when shit goes south. I hang up and rub my temples, exhaustion seeping into my bones. The situation has spiraled beyond containment. Five of our distribution centers were hit in the last week alone. Two more soldiers in the morgue.

I find Carmela in the bedroom, applying lipstick with careful precision.

"Family meeting in one hour. My parents are back."

Her eyes meet mine in the mirror. Something flickers across her face—hesitation? Guilt? It's gone before I can place it.

An hour later, my parents arrive home. My mother sweeps into the study first, kissing cheeks before settling into her high-backed chair near the window. My father follows, his stride purposeful as he takes his position behind the massive oak desk, shoulders squared like a general preparing for battle.

The tension in the study sits thick as cigar smoke. My brother Fed leans against the fireplace, face drawn. Isabella perches beside Marco Rossi on the leather sofa.

"Tell me what I've missed," my father says, his sharp eyes sweeping the room.

Fed and I exchange a glance.

"The attacks on our operations," I begin. "They're not what we thought, Father. We believed it was the Morettis behind everything—and that's exactly what someone wanted us to think."

My father's eyes narrow. "Explain."

I spread the surveillance photos across his desk. "Alexei Tartarov. His syndicate has been systematically hitting both our operations and the Morettis', making each side believe the other is responsible. While we've been tearing each other apart, he's been quietly moving into the vacuum we created."

My father picks up the photos one by one, his expression darkening. "The Russian," he says slowly.

"The shell casings don't match Moretti weapons," Fed adds. "Russian-made, exclusively. We have surveillance footage placing Tartarov's men at three separate attack sites—two on our properties, one on the Morettis'."

My father sets the photos down. "We've been played."

"Yes," I confirm.

A heavy silence fills the room. My father rises from his desk and moves to the window, hands clasped behind his back. When he turns, the anger in his eyes is cold and controlled—far more dangerous than heat.

"And the Morettis? Do they know?"

"Not yet," I say. "But they will."

My father returns to his desk. "So what are we dealing with?"

"Tartarov's goal is to dismantle both families," I say. "He wants Philadelphia for himself, and the simplest way to get it is to let us destroy each other first."

My father draws a deep breath. "I'm proposing a temporary ceasefire. An opportunity to meet with Nico Moretti and discuss terms that might end this blood feud once and for all."

I clench my jaw, the muscles in my neck tightening. "A ceasefire? After everything they've done?" The idea feels like surrender—like weakness. "They'll see it as an opportunity to finish what they started."

My father levels his gaze at me. "Sometimes the greatest strength is knowing when not to fight."

"With respect, this isn't just business anymore." I stand, unable to contain my restless energy. "This is a blood vendetta three generations in the making. Nico Moretti won't stop until we're all dead or broken."

Carmela clears her throat. All eyes turn to her.

"I think we should consider it," she says quietly.

I stare at her, surprised. "You can't be serious."

She meets my gaze without flinching. "War isn't sustainable, Silvo. We've lost men. They've lost men. At some point, someone has to break the cycle."

There's something in her eyes—a certainty I haven't seen before. Like she knows something I don't.

"Ever since I learned about Maria and Salvatore, I've been thinking." Carmela leans forward. "This vendetta started with love. Maybe it can end the same way—with understanding instead of bullets."

My mother speaks for the first time, her voice quiet but carrying unexpected weight. "I've buried too many of this family already." Her eyes find mine, then Fed's. "Cousins, nephews, friends who were like family. I won't bury my own children over a grudge that began before any of you were born."

The raw emotion in her voice silences the room. My mother rarely speaks at these meetings, content to let my father handle business. But when she does, we listen.

"Giulia—" my father starts.

"No, Antonio." She stands, moving to the center of the room. "I've held my tongue for decades while this family bled for pride. But I'm done watching the people I love march toward their graves." Her gaze sweeps across all of us. "If there's even a chance to end this, we take it."

The room falls silent. My father draws a deep breath.

"Fresh perspectives are valuable in old conflicts," he says, nodding at Carmela.

Fed pushes off from the fireplace. "I hate to admit it, but Carmela might be onto something. We can't keep losing people."

I run a hand through my hair, frustration warring with exhaustion. My wife watches me, those green eyes seeing right through my anger to the fear underneath.

"One meeting," I finally concede. "Neutral ground, full security. We hear them out, but I'm making no promises."

Carmela's hand finds mine again, her thumb tracing circles on my skin. "It's a start."

Looking at her, I see a future beyond endless retaliation —a possibility, however faint, of peace that might let us live without constantly looking over our shoulders. For her, for our future children, perhaps it's worth the risk.

"Fine," I say to my father. "Set it up."

The meeting concludes with my father promising to reach out through neutral channels. Everyone filters out of the study, the weight of our decision hanging heavy in the air. I linger, watching Carmela exchange quiet words with Isabella before she turns to me, ready to leave.

Back in our wing of the house, she kicks off her heels and curls into the corner of our sofa. I pour us both a drink —scotch for me, red wine for her.

"You're not convinced this is the right move," she says, accepting the glass.

I settle beside her, the leather creaking beneath my weight. "It's not about being right. It's about survival."

"Then why do you look like you're marching to your execution?" Carmela's voice softens as she shifts closer. "Talk to me, Silvo."

I take a long swallow of scotch, letting the burn settle in my chest. "The Morettis can't be trusted. This could be an elaborate setup. Maybe Nico is working with Alexei."

"Or it could be a genuine opportunity to end decades of bloodshed."

"That's naïve, Carmela." The words come out harsher than intended. "Men like Nico Moretti don't suddenly discover peace and forgiveness. Something else is at play here."

She studies me over the rim of her glass. "So what's your alternative? More deaths? More retaliation for something the Moretti family didn't even do?"

The question hangs between us. My phone buzzes in my pocket, rescuing me from answering.

My jaw clenches as I read it. "Nico Moretti has agreed to meet," I tell Carmela, setting down my glass. "Neutral ground. Tomorrow night."

"That's good news, isn't it?"

"There's a condition." I meet her eyes. "He'll only meet with my father and me. Alone."

Carmela's face pales as the implications sink in. "Alone? No protection?"

I shake my head, tension coiling in my gut. "Just me and my father facing the man who's made it his life's mission to destroy our family."

"It's a trap." Her voice trembles, fear creeping in around the edges of her words.

The same thought has been cycling through my mind since reading Marco's message. "Possibly. Probably." I drain the rest of my scotch. "But refusing looks like weakness or fear. Either way, we lose standing."

Carmela sets her wine glass on the side table and rises from her spot on the sofa. My eyes follow her movements as she approaches, her expression a complex mixture of fear and determination. Without a word, she climbs onto my lap, her thighs bracketing mine as she wraps her arms around my neck.

The weight of her against me grounds me, pulling me back from the edge of my darkest thoughts.

"I just want us to live in peace, Silvo," she whispers, her forehead pressed against mine. "No more looking over our shoulders. No more midnight phone calls about dead soldiers. No more wondering if today might be our last day together."

Her vulnerability cuts through me, sharper than any blade. I slide my hands up her sides, over her shoulders, cupping her face between my palms. Her skin is warm beneath my touch, reminding me of everything I stand to lose.

"I want that too," I murmur, pressing my lips to hers in a kiss that starts gentle but quickly deepens with the urgency of our shared fear. When we break apart, I trail my fingers down her neck, over the curve of her breast, worshipping her with my hands. "But sometimes this world is not so simple. Peace comes with a price, and I'm not convinced Nico Moretti is willing to pay his share."

I cradle Carmela's face in my hands, struck by how much has changed between us. What began as a cold arrangement, a strategic alliance between families, has somehow transformed into something I never thought possible. Something I never thought I deserved.

"Whatever happens tomorrow," I whisper, my thumb tracing the curve of her cheekbone, "know that meeting you—being forced to marry you—was the best thing that ever happened to me."

Her eyes glisten with unshed tears. "Even though I fought you every step of the way?"

"Especially because you fought me." A smile tugs at my lips. "You never let me get away with anything. You challenged me, pushed me to be better."

Carmela's hands tighten on my shoulders. "Promise me you'll be careful tomorrow. Promise me you'll come home."

The fear in her voice tears at something deep inside me. I want to promise her the world, want to swear I'll return unharmed, but we both know better than to tempt fate with empty assurances.

Instead, I pull her closer, eliminating the space between us. "I promise I'll do everything in my power to end this war and come back to you."

Her fingers thread through my hair, her breath warm against my lips. "I need you, Silvo. Not just for protection, not just for the family name. I need you because..."

"Because?" The word catches in my throat.

"Because somewhere along the way, I fell in love with you."

The confession hits me with physical force. I search her

face for any sign of deception or manipulation, but find only raw vulnerability.

Our lips meet in a kiss unlike any we've shared before. Not driven by lust or anger or power, but by something purer. Something that feels dangerously like hope. It's tender and fierce at once, the sweetness of it almost unbearable.

When we finally part, the shadow of tomorrow's meeting still looms over us. But even with that darkness waiting on the horizon, something has shifted irrevocably between us. Something stronger than fear, more powerful than vendettas or family legacies.

Love—unexpected, unplanned, and unbreakable.

33

SILVO

The abandoned warehouse on the outskirts of Philadelphia feels like neutral ground in name only. I scan the cavernous space as we enter—concrete floors, metal beams overhead, and enough shadows to hide a small army. My father walks beside me, his stride confident despite his age. Fed follows two steps behind, carrying the briefcase containing everything we learned from Luca's interrogation.

"Remember," my father murmurs, "we're here to show them the truth, not provoke."

I nod, though every instinct screams this could still be a trap. The memory of Carmela's face this morning—her eyes wide with fear as she straightened my tie—keeps me moving forward. She believes this alliance can work. For her, I have to try.

A door opens at the far end of the warehouse. Two figures emerge from the darkness like apparitions. Nico Moretti walks with the casual confidence of a man who's never doubted his power. His salt-and-pepper hair and tailored suit can't disguise the predatory gleam in his eyes.

Beside him struts his son, Maximo—younger, cockier, with that distinctive Moretti arrogance etched into every line of his face.

For three generations, our families have circled each other like wolves. Three generations of blood and betrayal, all because Maria chose my grandfather over Vincenzo Moretti. The weight of that history fills the space between us, thick enough to choke on.

"Antonio." Nico's voice echoes in the empty warehouse. "It's been a long time."

My father's face remains impassive. "Not long enough, Nico."

Maximo's lips curl into a smirk as he looks me over. "The prodigal son. Heard you married a Bianchi girl." His eyes narrow. "Pretty little thing. Shame she tied herself to a family that won't last the month."

My fists clench instinctively. "Careful, Moretti."

"Enough," Nico cuts in, his gaze never leaving my father. "You called this meeting, Antonio. State your business."

I step forward before my father can respond. "We didn't attack your clubs last week."

Nico's expression doesn't change, but something shifts in his eyes. "Is that so?"

"And you didn't hit our distribution centers," I continue, my voice steady. "Neither of us has been making moves against the other—not for the past three weeks at least."

Maximo scoffs. "Bullshit. We lost two properties and five men to your crews—"

"Not our crews," Fed interrupts, setting the briefcase on an overturned crate between us. "Alexei Tartarov's."

The name hangs in the air like a grenade. Nico's jaw tightens almost imperceptibly.

"Explain," he says, his voice dangerously quiet.

I open the briefcase and pull out surveillance photos. "These are shell casings recovered from the attack on your jewelry store—the one you blamed us for." I slide them across the crate. "Russian-made. 7.62x39mm, exclusive to Eastern European suppliers."

Nico picks up one of the photos, examining it closely.

"And this," I continue, laying out another set of images, "is security footage from your club fire. Notice the tattoo on this man's neck?" I point to a distinctive red scorpion. "That's Dimitri Tartarov, Alexei's nephew. Same tattoo appears at three different attack sites—two on your properties, one on ours."

My father adds, "We captured one of our men who'd been feeding information to what he thought were Moretti associates. They were Russians, Nico. Wearing your family crests, speaking Italian, using your symbols to create a false trail."

Nico's expression remains carefully neutral, but his fingers tighten on the photo. "You're saying Tartarov has been impersonating my people?"

"And ours," I confirm. "We found evidence of Russian operatives dressed in De Luca colors hitting Moretti targets. Every attack is designed to reignite our war while Tartarov expands into territories we've left vulnerable."

Fed pulls out a map, spreading it across the crate. "Look at the pattern. They're creating a corridor here, along the eastern seaboard. Small operations, nothing that would attract immediate attention from either of us because we're too busy killing each other."

Maximo leans forward, studying the map with a professional eye I hadn't expected. "Son of a bitch."

"They've been playing us for months," I say, meeting Nico's gaze directly. "Maybe longer. While we've been destroying each other, Tartarov's been quietly building an empire in our blind spots."

Nico's fingers drum against the crate, the only sign of his agitation. "Why bring this to me? Why not just let us keep bleeding each other dry?"

"Because my wife asked me a question I couldn't answer," I admit. "She asked what my alternative was to endless retaliation. More deaths? More funerals?" I pause, letting the weight of it settle. "I didn't have a good answer, Nico. And I think you don't either."

Something shifts in Nico's expression—a crack in his armor.

"You think I want this for my children?" His voice grows quieter, almost pained. "For my Valeria? She's in college now—art school. Talented girl. The things she paints..." He trails off, shaking his head.

I notice how his shoulders drop slightly at the mention of his daughter's name. Maximo stiffens beside his father, clearly uncomfortable with this display of vulnerability.

"Every time she comes home," Nico continues, "I see how she looks at me. The questions in her eyes. The fear. My daughter shouldn't have to live looking over her shoulder, wondering if today's the day her father doesn't come home."

My father shifts his weight, and I see understanding cross his face. "My wife said the same thing last night. That she's buried too many sons of this family already."

"Three generations," Nico says, his voice rough. "Three generations of blood over a woman's choice made seventy years ago. And for what? So Alexei Tartarov can waltz in and take everything while we're distracted?"

The warehouse falls silent except for the distant drip of water from a leaky roof.

"We're all just empty vessels, aren't we?" Nico continues. "Filled with our fathers' hatreds, carrying out vendettas we inherited but didn't choose."

My father nods slowly. "My son has become the head of this family since I retired. Just as yours will after you, Nico. Will they still be fighting this same war fifty years from now? Will our grandchildren?"

"Some legacies can't be escaped, Antonio," Nico says, but there's less conviction in his voice now. "You know that better than most."

"Maybe not," I find myself saying. "But they can be rewritten."

I pull out another document from the briefcase. "This is a financial analysis my wife compiled. Tartarov's shell companies have been purchasing property along both our distribution routes. He's been preparing this takeover for over a year."

Nico examines the papers, his expression growing darker with each page. "Your wife did this?"

"Carmela's a Bianchi," Fed states. "She understands this world better than most men I know."

"A ceasefire," my father proposes after a long moment, his voice rough with decades of distrust. "Two weeks initially. No moves against each other's territories, personnel, or interests. We coordinate intelligence on Tartarov's operations and root out his people from both our organizations."

Nico's eyes narrow, calculating. "And then what, Antonio? We shake hands and forget seventy years of blood?"

"No," I interject. "Then we meet again. Discuss long-term arrangements. Real ones." I meet Maximo's skeptical glare. "Find a way to coexist that doesn't end with Tartarov picking over our bones."

Nico runs a hand through his salt-and-pepper hair, suddenly looking older than his years. "My capos won't like it. Some of them have been waiting decades for the chance to destroy the De Lucas."

"And mine will call us weak for even speaking to you," my father counters. "We've both got battle-hungry men who'd rather die fighting than admit they've been played."

Fed adds, "But those men are smart enough to understand strategy. When we show them this evidence, when they see how Tartarov has infiltrated both families..." He taps the photos. "Pride is one thing. Survival is another."

Maximo leans over the crate, studying the surveillance photos more carefully now. "These tattoos—I've seen them. Three months ago, outside one of our casinos in Atlantic City. We thought they were your men casing the place."

"Probably were Tartarov's," Fed confirms. "Playing both sides, gathering intelligence on our routines and vulnerabilities."

The weight of what we're proposing settles between us. Generations of hatred don't disappear with a handshake, but neither do they survive when a common enemy is actively destroying both families.

"Two weeks," Nico repeats, testing the words. "We share intelligence, coordinate security, and identify Tartarov's operatives in both organizations."

"Exactly," my father confirms.

Maximo shifts beside his father, visibly uncomfortable. "Dad, we should discuss this with the captains before—"

"No," Nico cuts him off sharply. "Too many hotheads on both sides who'd sabotage this before it begins. We keep this between us until we have something concrete to show them."

I understand his reasoning. Marco will want to analyze every angle. Lorenzo will resist working with Morettis on principle alone. But if we present them with irrefutable evidence and a unified plan, they'll fall in line.

"Agreed," my father says. "We keep this quiet until we can present a complete strategy."

"Two weeks," I confirm, stepping forward and extending my hand across the invisible boundary that has separated our families for generations.

Nico's eyes search mine for a long moment, looking for deception or weakness. Whatever he sees must satisfy him because he grasps my hand firmly.

"Two weeks," he echoes. "But if this is some elaborate De Luca trick—"

"It's not," my father interrupts. "We're not the enemy anymore, Nico. Tartarov is."

Nico nods slowly, releasing my hand. "Then let's make sure he regrets ever setting foot in Philadelphia."

As the Morettis turn to leave, Maximo pauses, looking back at us. "For what it's worth, De Luca... those financial reports your wife compiled? That's quality intelligence work."

It's the closest thing to a compliment I'll ever get from a Moretti. I nod in acknowledgment.

After they're gone, the three of us stand in the empty warehouse, the weight of what we've just done settling over us.

"That went better than expected," Fed says, closing the briefcase.

"Or worse," I counter. "Now we have to convince our own people that working with the Morettis is the only way to survive."

My father places a hand on my shoulder. "Your mother was right. Sometimes the hardest battles are the ones we fight against our own pride."

As we walk back to our car, I pull out my phone. A text from Carmela.

Please tell me you're okay.

I type back quickly.

On my way home. It worked. We have a truce.

Her response is immediate.

Thank God. I love you.

The words on the screen make my chest tighten. She said it last night for the first time—actually said the words out loud instead of just showing me through actions. And now, seeing them in text, they feel even more real.

I type back.

I love you too. See you soon.

Fed glances at my phone and grins. "Texting your wife like a lovesick teenager?"

"Shut up," I mutter, but I can't keep the smile off my face.

My father chuckles from the front seat. "Enjoy it while

it lasts, son. Once you have children, the romance gets complicated."

"Speaking from experience?" I ask.

"Your mother and I had our moments," he admits, his tone softening. "Still do, when she's not threatening to bury me in the garden for tracking mud through her kitchen."

The normalcy of the conversation—the casual family banter—feels surreal after what we just accomplished. We've taken the first step toward ending a three-generation blood feud. The road ahead will be treacherous, but for the first time in my life, I feel something I never expected when it comes to the Morettis.

Hope.

34

CARMELA

I stare at my reflection in the full-length mirror, smoothing down the crimson silk gown I've chosen for tonight. My fingers tremble slightly as I fasten diamond earrings that Silvo gifted me last month. The joint charity gala—a public demonstration of the tentative truce between the De Lucas and the Morettis—looms just over an hour away.

"A unified front for childhood cancer research," Silvo had explained. "Neutral ground, public setting."

I adjust the plunging neckline of my dress, wondering if the bold choice sends the right message. Strong but not provocative. Confident without being threatening.

"You look beautiful." Isabella appears in the doorway, already dressed in midnight blue. "Though you might want to breathe at some point."

I realize I've been holding my breath and force my lungs to expand. "I'm terrified I'll say the wrong thing. Or worse, Silvo and Nico will interpret some innocent comment as an insult."

"That's why Antonio insisted on rehearsing talking

points yesterday." Isabella crosses the room, adjusting one of my curls. "Stick to safe topics—the charity itself, the children we're helping, the venue."

My stomach knots as I apply another coat of lipstick. "This isn't just a party, Isabella. This is the first time in seventy years that Morettis and De Lucas will stand in the same room without weapons or pretense."

"Or the perfect opportunity for someone to sabotage everything." Isabella's reflection meets mine in the mirror, her eyes serious. "One wrong move, one misinterpreted glance..."

I nod, remembering my conversation with Valeria at the boutique. Behind our families' backs, we've been texting—small, cautious messages about our hopes for tonight. Her father knows nothing of our friendship, just as Silvo remains in the dark.

"If this works," I whisper, more to myself than Isabella, "maybe we can stop looking over our shoulders every day. Maybe our children won't inherit this blood feud."

Isabella squeezes my shoulder. "And if it doesn't work?"

I don't answer. We both know what failure means. More violence. More bloodshed. More funerals.

Isabella adjusts my necklace one final time. "I'll see you downstairs in thirty minutes." She slips out of the room, leaving me alone with my reflection.

The door opens again, and Silvo's gaze finds mine in the mirror. He wears a black tuxedo that accentuates his broad shoulders, his dark hair slicked back. The intensity in his blue eyes steals my breath.

"You're stunning," he says, crossing the room to stand behind me.

His hands rest on my shoulders, warm and steady

compared to my trembling fingers. "Are you nervous about tonight?" I ask.

Silvo's reflection shows a vulnerability I rarely glimpse. "More than I'd admit to anyone but you." His fingers trail down my bare arms. "Three generations of hatred don't disappear with a handshake and charity auction."

I turn to face him, resting my palms against his chest. "What are you most afraid of?"

His jaw tightens. "That this is all for nothing. That someone—Maximo, one of our capos, anyone—will throw a match onto this powder keg we've created."

"And if it works?" I whisper.

Silvo cups my face, his thumb tracing my lower lip. "If it works..." He swallows hard. "I think about children, Carmela. Our children. Growing up without learning to shoot before they can ride a bike. Without bodyguards at school."

My heart pounds at this confession. Six months ago, Silvo never would have shared such intimate hopes.

"I want that future," I admit. "With you."

His mouth claims mine with sudden urgency. His kiss deepens as his hands slide down to my waist, pulling me against him. I feel his hardness pressing against me through the silk of my dress.

"We don't have time," I murmur unconvincingly as his lips move to my neck.

"I need you," Silvo growls, hiking my dress up my thighs. "Right now."

I gasp as his fingers find me already wet, already aching for him. "The gala—"

"Can wait." His voice is rough with desire. "Nothing matters but this. But us."

I moan as Silvo spins me around, bending me over the

vanity. Our eyes lock in the mirror—his dark with hunger, mine wild with need. He yanks my dress up around my waist, tearing my lace panties with one swift motion.

"Look at how wet you are for me," he growls, sliding two fingers inside me. "Even when the world's falling apart around us, your body knows who it belongs to."

I gasp as his fingers curl against that sweet spot inside me. "Silvo, please—"

"Please what?" He unzips his pants, freeing his hard cock. "Tell me what you need, Carmela."

"Fuck me," I beg shamelessly. "Hard. Now."

He enters me with one brutal thrust that sends makeup bottles scattering across the vanity. I cry out, bracing myself against the cool marble as he grips my hips with bruising force.

"That's it," I pant, watching his face contort with pleasure in the mirror. "Make me feel you. Make me forget everything but this."

Silvo grabs a fistful of my hair, pulling my head back as he pounds into me relentlessly. "You like it rough, don't you? My perfect, filthy wife."

"Yes," I moan as he reaches around to rub circles against my clit. "Only for you. Only ever you."

His rhythm turns punishing, each thrust pushing me closer to the edge. My carefully applied makeup smears as sweat beads on my skin.

"Say it," he demands, slapping my ass hard enough to leave a handprint. "Tell me who you belong to."

"You," I cry out. "I'm yours, Silvo. All yours."

He flips me suddenly, lifting me onto the vanity and spreading my legs wide. When he enters me again, his eyes hold mine with unexpected tenderness.

"And I'm yours," he whispers against my lips, his movements no less powerful but somehow more reverent. "Completely."

I wrap my legs around his waist, pulling him deeper. The contrast of his tender words and savage thrusts pushes me toward the precipice.

"I'm close," I whimper, digging my nails into his shoulders through his tuxedo.

"Come for me, Carmela," Silvo commands, his cock hitting that perfect spot inside me with each thrust. "Let me feel that tight pussy squeeze my cock."

I arch my back as the pressure builds, my body tensing. "Oh god, Silvo—I'm—"

My orgasm crashes through me in violent waves. I cry out his name as my walls clench around him, my vision blurring at the edges. Silvo doesn't slow his pace, fucking me through the aftershocks, prolonging my pleasure until I'm trembling and incoherent.

"That's it," he growls, his eyes dark with lust as he watches me come apart. "You look so fucking beautiful when you come on my cock."

He pulls out suddenly, flipping me onto my stomach across the vanity. I gasp as he slams back into me, one hand gripping my hip while the other tangles in my hair.

"You want more?" His voice is rough against my ear. "You want me to fill this sweet pussy?"

"Yes," I moan, pushing back against him. "God, yes."

His thrusts grow harder, more urgent. "You want me to breed this pussy? Put my baby in you?"

The filthy words send an unexpected jolt of pleasure through me. "Fuck, Silvo—yes."

"Say it," he demands, slapping my ass hard. "Tell me what you want."

"Breed me," I beg shamelessly. "Fill me up. I want to feel your cum inside me."

He groans, his rhythm faltering as his control slips. "Fuck, Carmela. You want me to knock you up? Want everyone at that gala to see my cum leaking down your thighs?"

"Please," I whimper, another orgasm building. "Make me yours. Completely."

"You're already mine," he growls, thrusting so deep I see stars.

I feel him swell inside me as his movements grow erratic. "I'm going to come," he pants. "Taking it all, aren't you? My perfect fucking wife."

When he erupts inside me, hot and pulsing, it triggers my second climax. I cry out as pleasure overwhelms me, my body milking every drop from him.

We collapse against each other, both of us panting, sweat cooling on our skin. My legs still tremble from the force of my orgasms. I feel Silvo's breath hot against my neck as he slowly pulls out of me.

"Don't move," he commands, his voice softer now but still authoritative.

I watch in the mirror as he retrieves a new pair of panties from the drawer. His cum starts to trickle down my inner thigh, but he quickly catches it, sliding the lace back into place with surprising gentleness.

"There," he murmurs, adjusting the delicate fabric. "Keep it all in there. My cum inside you, right where it belongs."

The tone of his voice makes me shiver despite the filthiness of our state. My makeup is smeared, my carefully styled hair now wild around my flushed face. Silvo doesn't look much better—his slicked-back hair now disheveled, his tuxedo wrinkled where I grabbed him.

He turns me to face him, not caring about the mess we've made. "You're fucking perfect," he whispers, brushing a strand of hair from my cheek.

"We're going to be late," I say, but there's no urgency in my voice. I don't care about anything beyond this room, beyond this moment.

Silvo cups my face between his hands, his thumbs tracing my swollen lips. "Worth it."

He kisses me deeply, slowly, neither of us caring about my smeared lipstick or the lingering taste of sex. It's messy and primal and perfect.

When he pulls away, his eyes hold mine with an intensity that makes my heart stutter. Three days ago, I told him I loved him. Tonight, that love feels more fragile and precious than ever—one wrong move at this gala could destroy everything we've built.

35

CARMELA

Isabella helps me repair my makeup while I adjust my dress. In the hallway mirror, I catch Silvo's smug reflection as he straightens his tie, looking entirely too satisfied with himself.

Thirty minutes later, we arrive at the Bellevue Hotel ballroom. The moment we step inside, the air feels charged with electricity. Both families have shown up in full force, creating distinct territories within the gilded space. Chandeliers cast golden light across the room but fail to warm the cold stares exchanged between rival capos.

"Ready?" Silvo murmurs, his hand possessive at the small of my back.

I nod, feeling the weight of my soaked panties beneath my gown—a secret reminder of what happened before we left.

The Morettis stand near the bar, Nico's silver-gray head visible above the crowd. When he spots us, his expression remains carefully neutral. Maximo stands beside him, wearing hatred more openly than his designer suit.

"They're watching us like hawks," I whisper to Silvo as we make our way through the crowd.

"Let them," he replies. "Tonight is about appearances. We smile, we drink, we make small talk. Nothing more."

We pause to accept champagne flutes from a passing server. My gaze catches Valeria's across the room. She stands in a stunning midnight blue gown beside a blonde woman I recognize as Adele. Valeria offers me the smallest nod—so subtle no one else would notice.

Isabella and Fed approach, creating a buffer between us and the nearest Moretti associates. The room buzzes with conversation, yet everyone seems hyperaware of invisible boundaries. No one crosses the invisible line dividing the two families.

Antonio De Luca, Silvo's father, works the room with practiced ease, shaking hands and laughing as though this were any ordinary charity function. But I notice how his eyes constantly scan for threats, how his hand occasionally drifts toward where a weapon would normally be concealed.

"Your dress is exquisite," a woman comments as she passes, her eyes lingering a moment too long on my neck. I realize with a flush that one of Silvo's marks is visible despite Isabella's best efforts with concealer.

"Thank you," I reply, fingers unconsciously rising to cover the spot.

Silvo's grip tightens slightly at my waist. Across the room, Nico Moretti raises his glass in our direction—a gesture that could be read as either a respectful acknowledgment or a silent threat. The silver-gray threading through his dark hair catches the light, framing a face that's undeniably handsome.

He laughs at something someone says, and I find myself

studying the way his entire face transforms. When serious, he looks carved from stone—when he smiles, unexpected warmth radiates from him. It's disarming.

Nico's hand movements are precise and deliberate as he gestures while speaking. Nothing wasted, nothing without purpose. Despite being at least twenty years Silvo's senior, he carries himself with the same coiled energy—like a predator at rest but ever vigilant.

Something about his intensity reminds me so much of my husband. The way his gaze sweeps the room, cataloging threats, exits, and opportunities. The casual way he touches the arm of the man beside him—a gesture that looks friendly but clearly establishes dominance.

His eyes suddenly meet mine across the room. Unlike Maximo's open hostility, Nico's expression is unreadable, an assessment without judgment. For a heartbeat too long, we maintain eye contact, neither willing to look away first. The corner of his mouth twitches upward slightly—not quite a smile, more an acknowledgment.

I feel a strange flutter in my stomach. This man has been trying to destroy my husband's family for weeks, yet there's something magnetic about him. Something compelling that makes me understand how he commands loyalty.

I drift toward the bar for another drink when I notice Adele weaving through the crowd toward Nico Moretti. She passes so close to him it could be accidental, but something in her deliberate movements suggests otherwise. Nico's gaze follows her, his expression transforming in a way that makes my breath catch.

The hardness melts from his face. His eyes soften at the corners, and something private passes between them—a look that belongs in bedrooms, not ballrooms. He straightens almost imperceptibly when she approaches, like a man preparing himself. It's subtle, but unmistakable.

Adele says something to him while maintaining a respectable distance. Anyone watching would see nothing untoward, just a polite exchange. But I catch how his fingers twitch at his side, as though fighting the urge to reach for her. When she walks away, his eyes track her movements with naked hunger before his mask of indifference slides back into place.

The surveillance photos flash through my mind. This confirms everything.

A commotion across the room pulls my attention. Maximo Moretti has cornered Isabella near a marble column, his body language aggressive as he towers over her.

"You De Luca women think you're too good for everyone," Maximo sneers, loud enough for nearby guests to hear.

Isabella's spine straightens. "And you Moretti men think with the wrong head."

Guests around them fall silent, champagne glasses suspended midair.

"At least we have courage," Maximo steps closer, invading Isabella's space. "At least we don't pretend centuries of blood can disappear with one handshake and a charity ball."

"Is that what you call courage?" Isabella laughs, the sound brittle. "Coming to neutral ground to pick fights with women?"

Something dark and possessive flashes in Maximo's eyes. He reaches for Isabella's wrist, and she yanks it away, sending her champagne splashing across his custom suit.

"You'll regret that," he growls, but his gaze drops to her lips.

"I doubt it," Isabella retorts, color high on her cheeks.

The tension between them crackles with something beyond hatred—something primitive that makes me flush just witnessing it.

Fed appears at Isabella's side, positioning himself between them. Antonio and Nico approach from opposite sides of the room, their faces mirroring identical expressions of controlled fury.

I can't tear my eyes away from the electric tension between Isabella and Maximo. There's something familiar in the way they glare at each other—a reflection of how Silvo and I once circled one another, all teeth and claws hiding something deeper.

The realization hits me like a thunderbolt.

Behind their hostility, beneath the family names they carry like armor, Isabella and Maximo can barely contain their attraction. I see it in how Maximo's eyes linger on Isabella's lips even as he threatens her. I recognize it in Isabella's flushed cheeks and the way she stands her ground instead of retreating.

They're fighting the same magnetic pull that once existed between Silvo and me.

My mind races ahead, connecting pieces of a puzzle I hadn't known existed. What if this forbidden attraction could be channeled and legitimized? An utterly insane thought forms: what if Isabella and Maximo could enter an arranged marriage, just as Silvo and I did?

Our families are drowning in three generations of bloodshed. The ceasefire feels tenuous, fragile as spun glass. But marriage—marriage has weight. It carries tradition, expectation, and legitimacy.

I glance at Silvo, who's watching the confrontation with narrowed eyes, then to Nico Moretti, whose face reveals nothing. Both bosses look exhausted beneath their masks of strength. Neither truly wants more violence.

A second alliance, another binding tie between our families—it could be the reinforcement this peace needs. If Isabella and Maximo's hatred could transform into something else, as mine and Silvo's did...

I press my lips together, knowing how Isabella would react if I suggested it. She'd be furious, just as I was when my brother sold me to Silvo. But I've found something real with my husband, something that started as an obligation and blossomed into love.

Could the same transformation happen for Isabella and Maximo?

I watch Fed pull his sister away, but not before she throws one last heated glance over her shoulder at Maximo. His eyes track her movement across the room like a predator following prey.

Yes, there's something there worth exploring.

36

SILVO

The gala's tension follows us into the night. The cool Philadelphia air hits our faces, a welcome relief after hours of calculated smiles and veiled threats.

"I need to clear my head," I mutter, leading her away from the valet stand.

"Where are we going?"

"Just walk with me."

We stroll in silence, the city lights casting long shadows. My mind replays every interaction with the Morettis —Nico's calculating gaze, Maximo's confrontation with Isabella. But mostly I think about how Carmela looked tonight, commanding the room in that crimson dress like she was born to stand by my side.

"You were magnificent in there," I say, pulling her closer as we turn down a quieter street.

"So were you." Her eyes gleam in the streetlight. "The way you stared down Nico without flinching—"

I push her against the brick wall of the deserted alleyway, my mouth crushing against hers. She gasps, then melts into me, her fingers digging into my shoulders.

"Fuck, I've wanted to do that all night," I growl against her throat. "Watching you move through that room like you own it."

"Silvo—someone could see—"

"Let them." I hike her dress up, my fingers finding the lace of her thong. "You're soaking wet for me already."

Her head falls back against the brick. "Someone might walk by—"

"Then you better be quiet." I slide her panties to the side, stroking her slick heat. "Or not. Let everyone hear what I do to my wife."

Carmela moans as I drop to my knees, throwing her leg over my shoulder.

"Look at this pretty cunt," I murmur, licking slowly through her center. "All dressed up for a gala, but dripping for me in an alley."

"Silvo, please—"

"Please what?" I circle her clit with my thumb. "Please eat this pussy right here where anyone could see you coming on my face? Is that what my filthy wife wants?"

I plunge my tongue deep inside her, savoring her taste as she whimpers above me. Her fingers tangle in my hair, pulling hard enough to hurt. Good. I want that edge of pain.

"Silvo—fuck—this is insane," she pants, even as she grinds harder against my face.

I grip her ass, holding her in place. "Then I'd better make you come fast, shouldn't I?"

Her leg trembles against my shoulder as I suck her clit between my lips. I work two fingers inside her, curling them to hit that spot that makes her melt.

"That's it," I growl against her pussy. "Give it to me, Carmela."

She comes with a strangled cry, her body shaking

against the brick wall. Before she can catch her breath, I stand and spin her around, pressing her face against the rough surface.

"Hands on the wall."

She obeys instantly, arching her back to present her ass to me. I yank my belt open, freeing my cock that's been straining against my pants all fucking night.

I line myself up and thrust hard into her, burying myself to the hilt in one savage stroke.

"Fuck," I growl against her ear. "Can't get enough of you."

She moans as I pound into her, my hands gripping her hips hard enough to leave marks. I want to mark her. I want everyone to know she's mine.

"Silvo—God—" she gasps, trying to muffle her cries against her arm.

"Already had you before the gala," I growl, slamming deeper. "And I'll have you again when we get home. Can't stop thinking about filling you up."

Her pussy clenches around me at my words, and I know she loves this—loves being claimed by me in public where anyone could catch us.

"Want to put a baby in you," I confess, the words pouring out. "Want to see you growing round with my child."

She whimpers, pushing back against me.

"You like that idea?" I bite her neck. "My wife carrying my baby? Everyone seeing what I did to you?"

"Yes," she moans, trembling around me.

I reach around to rub her clit, determined to make her come again. "You're going to look so fucking beautiful pregnant. Tits swollen, belly round. Everyone will know you're mine."

I feel Carmela's walls tightening around me, her body trembling as she approaches the edge again. My fingers work her clit in tight, merciless circles as I continue driving into her against the brick wall.

"That's it," I growl against her ear, "Let go for me again."

Her back arches sharply, pressing her ass harder against my hips. "Silvo—I can't—it's too much—"

"You can and you will," I demand, thrusting deeper. "Give me another one. Now."

She shatters around me, her pussy clenching rhythmically on my cock as she muffles her scream against her arm. Her legs shake so violently I have to wrap my free arm around her waist to keep her upright.

"Look at you," I growl, my hips still pumping relentlessly. "Getting fucked in an alley where anyone could see. Coming all over my cock like the filthy girl you are."

Her whimper at my words sends fire through my veins.

"You're so fucking filthy," I hiss against her neck, biting down on the tender skin. "So fucking perfect."

My rhythm falters as the pressure builds at the base of my spine. I grip her hips hard enough to bruise, holding her exactly where I want her.

"Taking every inch of me," I groan, burying myself deep one final time. "Taking every drop."

I explode inside her, filling her with a load of my cum, grinding against her to push it as deep as possible. My vision blurs at the edges as pleasure wracks through my body.

I spin her around, still breathing hard, my hands cupping her flushed face. Her lips are swollen, eyes glazed with pleasure, hair falling wildly around her shoulders.

Even disheveled against a brick wall, she's the most beautiful thing I've ever seen.

I crush my mouth to hers. The kiss is different this time —not desperate or hungry, but something deeper. Something that still terrifies me, even though I've already admitted it to her.

When I finally pull back, her emerald eyes lock with mine.

"Carmela," I whisper, my thumbs stroking her cheekbones. "When you told me you loved meI didn't know if I deserved it."

She opens her mouth to protest, but I press my thumb gently against her lips.

"Let me finish." I swallow hard. "Tonight, watching you navigate that room full of our enemies with such grace and strength... I realized something."

Her breath catches, waiting.

"I don't love you because you're my wife or because our families needed this alliance." I press my forehead against hers. "I love you because you're the strongest, most fearless woman I've ever known. Because you challenge me. Because you make me want to be better than the man I was raised to be."

Her eyes shimmer with unshed tears. "Silvo..."

"I love you, Carmela," I say again, needing her to hear it, to feel it. "More every fucking day. And tonight, standing beside you in front of my family—I've never been more proud to call you mine."

She rises on her tiptoes, brushing her lips against mine. "I love you too. More than I thought possible." Her voice cracks. "You're not just my husband anymore. You're my home."

Something in my chest cracks wide open at her words. "Say that again."

"You're my home," she whispers. "The only place I feel safe. The only place I want to be."

I pull her against me, holding her like she's the only solid thing in my world. "This is what I was afraid of," I admit into her hair. "That I'd fall so completely that losing you would destroy me."

Her hand slides up to cup my cheek. "Then it's a good thing you're not losing me. Ever."

I capture her mouth in a kiss that's driven by the bone-deep certainty that this woman is mine and I am hers. Completely. Irrevocably.

When we break apart, I keep her face between my hands. "Whatever comes with Tartarov, with the Morettis, with this whole fucked-up situation—we face it together. You're my partner, my equal."

"Your heart," she whispers.

"My fucking soul," I confirm, the words flowing easily. "I'd burn this whole city down before I let anyone hurt you."

She presses her body against mine, and I feel her heartbeat matching my own rhythm. In this moment, the vendetta, the family obligations, the looming threats—they all feel distant. What's real is her skin against mine, the trust in her eyes, the love that binds us tighter than any arranged marriage ever could.

37

CARMELA

I pace the office floor, checking my watch for the fifth time in ten minutes. Silvo should have been back two hours ago. The call came just after lunch—one of our shipments from Atlantic City had been hit. Three men were wounded, and cargo was stolen.

My stomach twists into knots. We're barely a week into this fragile truce with the Morettis, coordinating our defenses against Tartarov. But someone hit us anyway—and they knew exactly when and where to strike.

The door flies open, and Silvo strides in with Fed close behind. His face is granite, jaw tight, but his eyes soften momentarily when they land on me.

"What happened?" I ask, not bothering with pleasantries.

Silvo throws his jacket onto the chair. "Ambush at the county line. Professional job. They knew exactly when the trucks would arrive and the route they'd take."

"Tartarov," I say, my heart sinking.

"Yeah." Fed pulls out his phone and shows me photos of shell casings. "Same Russian ammunition. Same red scorpion tattoos on two of the attackers we managed to corner." He swipes to another image. "But here's the problem—this route was only finalized and shared with our inner circle and the Morettis' coordination team two days ago."

My blood runs cold. "You think the leak is from the Morettis?"

"Or from us," Silvo says grimly, sinking into the chair behind his desk. "Someone on one of our teams is feeding Tartarov real-time intelligence about our coordinated operations."

I perch on the edge of the desk, the implications hitting me like a physical blow. "If we accuse the Morettis of having a leak—"

"The truce collapses," Fed finishes. "We're back to killing each other while Tartarov picks us apart."

"But if we don't tell them about this attack..." I trail off, imagining the scenario.

Silvo nods, his jaw tight. "Nico hears through the grapevine that we got hit and didn't inform him immediately. He thinks we're keeping secrets, doubting the alliance."

"Or worse," I add, my mind racing ahead, "Tartarov hits one of their operations next, and the Morettis think *we* did it to retaliate for this."

Fed looks between us. "So what's the play? We can't keep this quiet, but we also can't point fingers without proof of where the leak is."

Silvo runs a hand through his hair, frustration evident in every line of his body. "We need to tell Nico about this attack before rumors spread. But we need to do it carefully—present it as an issue we're solving together, not an accusation."

"Agreed," I say. "The leak could be anywhere. One of

our guys, one of theirs, or someone neither family has identified yet as compromised."

While Fed makes the call to Marco, I pull up my own phone, scrolling to a conversation I've kept hidden from Silvo. My heart pounds as I make a split-second decision. Valeria's last message from this morning stares back at me.

Dad's on edge. Says something feels wrong but can't put his finger on it. How are things on your end?

I'd responded vaguely, not wanting to alarm her before we knew more. Now I realize she might be our fastest path to Nico.

"There might be a faster way to get this information to Nico," I say quietly.

The room goes quiet. Silvo's eyes narrow. "What are you thinking?"

I take a deep breath, my heart hammering against my ribs. "I... I have a direct line to the Moretti family."

"What?" Silvo's voice drops dangerously low.

I pull up my messages, my thumb trembling slightly. "Valeria Moretti. We exchanged numbers after meeting at that boutique in Rittenhouse Square a few weeks ago."

Silvo's jaw tightens. "And you didn't think to mention this?"

"It started as just... two women trying to understand each other across enemy lines," I explain, standing my ground despite the guilt churning in my stomach. "Then it became a way to gauge the Morettis' temperature without official channels. I wasn't hiding it—I just hadn't found the right moment to tell you."

Fed whistles low. "Well, that's certainly convenient timing."

"It's more than convenient," Isabella adds, moving to stand beside me. "It's exactly what we need right now. An unofficial channel that won't trigger alarm bells on either side."

I face Silvo directly. "I know I should have told you sooner. But right now, people's lives are at stake. Both our families are being played, and this could be our fastest way to get Nico to understand what's happening before Tartarov drives another wedge between us."

Silvo stares at me for a long moment, his expression unreadable. Then he extends his hand. "Show me."

I unlock my phone and hand it to him. He scrolls through my conversations with Valeria—careful discussions about art and college life mixed with subtle references to our families' situations, hopes for peace, fears about the future.

"You've been talking about peace this whole time," he says, a note of surprise in his voice.

"We both want the same thing," I say quietly. "A future without looking over our shoulders. Without worrying about which one of us won't come home at night. Valeria understands that better than most—she lost her mother when she was two. She doesn't want to lose her father to this vendetta too."

Silvo hands my phone back, and something shifts in his expression. "Make the call."

I stare at him, stunned. "You're not mad?"

His jaw tightens, but his eyes hold understanding rather than rage. "I don't have the luxury of anger right now. This is bigger than us—bigger than our families' history." He reaches out, tucking a strand of hair behind my ear. "And honestly? I'm impressed. You saw an opportunity to build a bridge, and you took it. That's exactly the kind of thinking we need right now."

I'd prepared for shouting, for accusations of betrayal. His measured response catches me completely off guard.

"I was sure you'd..." I trail off, my prepared defenses suddenly unnecessary.

"Explode?" Silvo's mouth quirks into a half-smile. "Believe me, I want to. But you've proven something to me these past weeks, Carmela." He gestures at the evidence we've gathered. "You're thinking like a De Luca. Not just by name, but by choice. You saw a strategic advantage, and you cultivated it."

Fed clears his throat. "Much as I hate to interrupt this touching moment, we're running out of time. If the Tartarovs hit another Moretti property tonight—"

"I know," I say, already dialing Valeria's number. My heart pounds against my ribs as I put the phone on speaker. Three rings, then her voice fills the room.

"Carmela? Is everything okay?"

I take a deep breath. "No, it's not. We need to talk—all of us. The De Lucas and the Morettis. It's urgent."

A pause. "This sounds serious."

"It is. We were just hit—Atlantic City shipment. Three men were wounded. But here's the thing, Val—the attackers knew details that were only shared between our coordinated teams two days ago."

Valeria's sharp intake of breath is audible. "You think there's a leak."

"We know there's a leak. We just don't know which family it's in." I glance at Silvo, who nods encouragingly. "We need to meet tonight. Compare intelligence, figure out who's compromised before Tartarov uses this to destroy the truce."

Another pause, longer this time. When Valeria speaks

again, her voice is steady but urgent. "I'll talk to my father. He needs to hear this directly from you and Silvo."

Silvo leans closer to the phone. "This is Silvo De Luca. Can you get us the meeting?"

"I'll make it happen," Valeria promises. "Where and when?"

I look at Silvo, who mouths "The boathouse."

"The neutral property on the river," I tell her. "In two hours. Just your father, Maximo, you, and whoever else he trusts completely. We can't risk this information getting to whoever's feeding Tartarov."

"Understood. We'll be there." Valeria hesitates. "Carmela? Thank you. For trusting me with this."

"We're in this together now," I say softly. "All of us."

The line goes dead. I look up at Silvo, Isabella, and Fed, the weight of what we're about to do settling over us all.

Isabella squeezes my shoulder. "That took guts. Admitting to Silvo about Valeria, then using that connection to potentially save the alliance."

"It was the right call," Silvo says firmly. He pulls me into his arms, his chin resting on top of my head. "You see things the rest of us miss, Carmela. Connections, possibilities. It's why you're so valuable to this family—to me."

Fed grins, some of his usual lightness returning. "Plus, having a secret backchannel to the Morettis is pretty badass. Very spy novel."

"This isn't a game, Fed," I say, but I can't help the small smile.

"I know." His expression sobers. "But if this works—if we can identify the leak and plug it before Tartarov tears apart the alliance—we might actually have a shot at lasting peace."

Silvo releases me, his hand sliding down to lace his

fingers with mine. "Let's get ready. We have two hours to prepare a presentation that convinces Nico we're not trying to blame him while also making it clear we have a serious security problem."

As we gather the evidence and prepare for the meeting, I catch Silvo watching me with something like pride in his eyes.

For the first time since being forced into this marriage, I don't feel like an outsider trying to survive in his world. I feel like exactly what he called me—a De Luca by choice, not just by name.

38

SILVO

The boathouse stands dark against the moonlit river as we pull up, our headlights cutting through the mist. I kill the engine and check my watch. Ten minutes early.

"You're sure about this?" I ask Carmela, studying her profile in the dim light.

She nods, determination hardening her features. "If there's a leak, we need to find it before Tartarov uses it to destroy everything we've built."

Pride wells up in my chest. A week ago, she was attending her first gala with the Morettis. Now she's attending emergency strategy sessions like she's been in this life for years.

"Stay close to me," I tell her, tucking my gun into my waistband. "If anything feels off—"

"We leave," she finishes. "I know."

Headlights appear on the winding road behind us. The Morettis.

"Here we go," I mutter, stepping out of the car.

Two black SUVs pull up alongside us. Nico emerges

from the first vehicle, his face grim in the darkness. Maximo flanks him, and for once, he's not wearing his usual smirk. Behind them, Valeria slides out, her expression worried.

Nico's gaze finds Carmela immediately. "Mrs. De Luca. Your message through Valeria suggested urgency."

"We were hit this afternoon," I say without preamble. "Atlantic City shipment. Three men wounded, cargo stolen."

Nico's jaw tightens. "Tartarov?"

"Red scorpion tattoos confirmed." Fed steps forward with his tablet. "But here's the problem—this route was only finalized and shared with our joint coordination team two days ago."

Maximo's expression darkens. "You're saying there's a leak."

"In our organization, for sure," I confirm, meeting Nico's eyes. "Maybe yours, too."

The temperature in the air seems to drop ten degrees. This is the moment where the alliance could shatter—accusations, distrust, old hatreds resurfacing.

Nico runs a hand through his salt-and-pepper hair. "We had a similar incident yesterday. Warehouse in South Philly—only our joint security team knew about the shipment timing."

"Two attacks in two days," Carmela says quietly. "Both on operations that only coordinated teams knew about."

We move inside the boathouse. Unlike our first meeting here a week ago, there's no need for formal introductions or lengthy explanations. We're past that now. This is about the survival of an alliance we've all invested in.

"Someone close to both families is feeding Alexei information," Nico says, his voice deadly calm. "Someone who has access to our joint operations."

"Or multiple someones," I counter. "Tartarov's been planning this for months. He wouldn't rely on a single asset."

Isabella spreads out a timeline on the weathered table. "Every attack that's happened since we started coordinating—I've been tracking them. There's a pattern."

Valeria leans in, her analytical mind clearly engaged. "Show me."

For the next hour, the women work together, cross-referencing attack times with meeting schedules, comparing who had access to which pieces of information. Fed and Maximo, despite their mutual dislike, collaborate on security protocols and identifying weak points in our combined defenses.

Nico and I watch our families work together—De Lucas and Morettis moving in sync, thinking strategically as one unit rather than two opposing forces.

"Strange times," Nico murmurs, echoing his words from our first meeting.

"Strange indeed," I reply. "But effective."

Isabella taps a name on her laptop. "This man—Carlo Benedetti. He's been at every joint strategy meeting. Has access to both family communication systems. And look—" She pulls up financial records. "Three deposits from a Brighton Beach account in the last month."

"That's one of my men," Nico says, his voice going cold.

"And this one," Fed adds, pointing to another name on the screen. "Vincent Shaw. De Luca security. Same pattern—deposits, access, presence at every coordination meeting."

My jaw clenches. "Two leaks. One in each family."

"Tartarov's been playing both sides," Carmela says. "Making sure no matter what we do, he has eyes on it."

Nico meets my gaze across the table. "We handle this together. Simultaneously. No one tips off the other."

"Agreed," I nod. "Tomorrow night. We take them both at the same time."

Maximo looks at Fed. "Your men can handle Shaw?"

"Without breaking a sweat," Fed confirms. "You got Benedetti?"

"He'll regret the day he sold out the Moretti family," Maximo says darkly.

As the meeting concludes, there's a shift in the atmosphere. We're not just coordinating anymore—we're truly working as one unit. The boundaries between De Luca and Moretti operations are blurring.

Valeria hugs Carmela before leaving. "Thank you," she whispers. "For trusting me. For giving us this chance."

"We're in this together now," Carmela replies. "All of us."

The Morettis exit first, but this time there's no lingering suspicion, no checking over shoulders. Just a nod of mutual respect before their SUVs disappear into the night.

Fed and Isabella head to our car, giving Carmela and me a moment alone.

I turn to her, taking her hands in mine. "You were right. About Valeria, about building bridges, about all of it."

She squeezes my hands. "We were right. Together."

I pull her close, breathing in her scent. "Let's go home, *amore mio*. Tomorrow we will deal with the traitors. Tonight, I just want to hold my wife."

39

CARMELA

I slide into the corner booth at Café Artiste, a tiny French bistro exactly halfway between De Luca and Moretti territories. The neutral ground we've claimed as our own over the past week. Through the window, I spot Tony idling across the street in an unmarked sedan—my security detail keeping a respectful distance.

Valeria arrives first, her dark hair swept into a messy bun. She smiles when she sees me, though tension lines her eyes.

"Another attack on your family's shipment last night?" I ask as she sits.

She nods, wrapping her hands around her coffee cup. "Dad barely stopped Maximo from retaliating against your western warehouse. Old instincts die hard, even when you know better."

"Silvo traced the shell casings to the same Russian supplier," I say firmly. "Tartarov, same as always. Driving wedges wherever he can find them."

"I know. Dad knows." She sighs. "Knowing and feeling are two different things when it's your men taking the hits."

Adele arrives, sliding in beside Valeria with an apologetic smile for her lateness. Her blonde hair catches the sunlight, and I notice the subtle hickey at her neckline that she's tried to conceal with makeup. I file that away without comment.

"I brought the shipping manifests," Adele says, sliding a folder across the table. "Nico thought these might help Silvo identify which routes are being targeted next."

I take the folder, nodding my thanks. These meetings have become almost routine now—intelligence shared over coffee, two families learning the unfamiliar language of cooperation.

"How's Isabella?" Valeria asks, stirring sugar into her coffee.

"Still furious about your brother," I laugh softly. "But she helped analyze those surveillance photos from the waterfront. You'll find her notes in here too."

Our conversation flows easily now, unlike our first awkward meeting. We've developed a rhythm; these thrice-weekly meetings have become essential to maintaining the fragile peace between our families.

"The men are too stubborn to admit it," Valeria says, lowering her voice, "but this intelligence sharing is the only reason we've managed to identify Tartarov's patterns at all."

I nod. "Silvo would never say it, but he was impressed by your father's analysis of the supply chain vulnerabilities."

"And Dad actually acknowledged Federico's security protocols were solid," Adele adds.

What started as necessary communication has evolved into something more—genuine friendship forming across battle lines. These women understand my world in ways no one else can. We're all trying to survive in families built on violence while maintaining our humanity.

"My father still doesn't fully trust your father-in-law," Valeria admits over coffee. "Every time something goes wrong, his first instinct is to blame the De Lucas."

"Silvo's the same," I confess, tracing the rim of my cup with my fingertip. "Old habits die hard."

I glance over at Adele, noticing she's quieter than usual. She stirs her latte absently, her gaze unfocused. There are dark circles under her eyes that makeup can't quite conceal, and I catch how she flinches when a barista drops a mug behind the counter.

"How are you really doing?" I ask gently, leaning forward.

Adele's smile doesn't reach her eyes. "I'm fine. Everyone keeps asking that."

"Because we care," Valeria says, squeezing her friend's hand.

I observe the gesture between them, the unspoken language of friendship that reminds me of Sophia. As my gaze drifts past them toward the window, something catches my attention—a black sedan with tinted windows parked across the street. It wasn't there when we arrived. The hair on the back of my neck stands up.

Life with Silvo has taught me to recognize the warning signs. The car is positioned with a clear view of the café entrance, engine likely running, no visible driver. My pulse quickens as I process what I'm seeing.

"We need to leave," I say quietly but urgently. "Now."

I don't wait for questions. I throw cash on the table, grab my purse, and motion for them to follow me toward the kitchen. The staff knows me by now, and they don't protest as we push through the swinging doors and out the service entrance into the alley.

Just as the heavy door shuts behind us, I glimpse men entering through the front—their sleeves pushed up to reveal the distinctive red scorpion tattoos of Tartarov's crew.

My hands shake as I unlock my car and usher Valeria and Adele inside. I slide behind the wheel, start the engine, and pull away from the curb with controlled urgency, speed-dialing Silvo with my free hand.

"Tartarov just tried to grab us," I tell Silvo, my voice steadier than I feel. "All three of us."

My hands are still trembling slightly as I grip the wheel. I navigate through Philadelphia's back streets, taking a circuitous route to ensure we're not followed. In the rearview mirror, I check on Valeria and Adele, both pale but composed.

The response is immediate. Within an hour, both family patriarchs are in Silvo's office, the tension thick enough to cut.

I stand near the window, watching the men pace like caged predators. Silvo hasn't let go of my hand since I walked through the door, his fingers intertwined with mine so tightly it almost hurts.

"He's targeting the women now," Nico says, his face carved from stone. But his eyes betray him when they land on Adele, wrapped in a blanket on the sofa. The look is too intense, too personal for merely his daughter's friend.

I catch it, file it away. That look contains volumes—fear, possession, desperation. It's the same way Silvo looks at me when he thinks I'm in danger.

"This is escalation," Antonio observes. "Tartarov is testing our alliance. Seeing if we'll fracture under pressure."

"Then we don't give him the satisfaction," Silvo says firmly. He looks at me, and I see the fear he's trying to hide. "We need better security. For all of them."

What follows is a tense negotiation about protection details, safe houses, and protocols. Maximo and Fed clash over whose men should guard whom, their rivalry barely contained.

"My men are better trained for close protection," Fed insists, his normally playful demeanor replaced with cold professionalism.

Maximo scoffs. "Your men couldn't protect a goldfish. We'll handle Valeria and Adele's security."

"Good luck with that. You wouldn't know a threat if it punched you in the face" Fed snarls, stepping forward.

I exchange glances with Valeria across the room. We're both thinking the same thing: the men are playing right into Tartarov's hands.

"Enough!" Isabella snaps, silencing both men. "This isn't a competition. Alexei wants us fighting each other instead of him."

The room falls silent. I watch a flush creep up Federico's neck as he steps back, hands raised in surrender. Maximo's jaw tightens, but even he can't argue with Isabella's logic. I shoot her a grateful look across the room.

She's right. We've spent generations tearing each other apart while outsiders like Tartarov waited for the perfect moment to strike. I reach for Silvo's hand, squeezing it gently.

"Isabella makes a valid point," Nico says, his deep voice breaking the tense silence. His eyes meet Antonio's across the room—two patriarchs who've spent decades as enemies now forced into alliance.

Antonio nods slowly. "We need coordination, not competition."

What follows is surreal—De Lucas and Morettis huddled over maps of Philadelphia, marking territories, identifying vulnerabilities, assigning mixed security teams. I watch Silvo work alongside Nico, their movements mirroring each other in ways neither would care to admit.

"Each woman gets two guards—one De Luca, one Moretti," Silvo decides, looking to Nico for confirmation.

"Rotating shifts, different routes each day," Nico adds. "We share all intelligence directly, no filters."

The older capos shift uncomfortably in their seats. Lorenzo, Antonio's most loyal lieutenant, doesn't bother hiding his scowl. On the Moretti side, an older man with a jagged scar down his cheek mutters something under his breath that makes Maximo shoot him a warning glance.

Three generations of blood feud don't disappear in a day, no matter how great the external threat.

When the meeting finally concludes, the room empties slowly, both families careful not to turn their backs on each other—old habits die hard. Soon, only Silvo and I remain, the silence heavy after hours of strategic planning.

"Let's go to bed," Silvo says softly, exhaustion etched into every line of his face. "Tomorrow will be... complicated."

I nod, taking his hand as we climb the stairs to our bedroom.

I slip under the cool sheets beside Silvo, his body radiating heat as he pulls me against his chest. For several minutes, we lie in silence, his heartbeat steady beneath my ear. The events of the day hang between us—the near miss at the café, the tense strategy session, the uncomfortable alliance with people who were our sworn enemies mere weeks ago.

"I almost lost you today," he says against my hair. "If you hadn't noticed that car..."

"But I did," I reassure him, tracing my finger along the tattoo that winds across his collarbone.

"It's not enough." His arms tighten around me. "Tartarov is obsessed with destroying both families. He won't stop until we're all dead or broken."

I turn in his embrace, cupping his face between my palms. His stubble is rough against my skin, his eyes dark with worry and something fiercer.

"Then we make sure he fails. Together."

Silvo's mouth crashes against mine, his kiss brutal and desperate. I taste his fear, his rage—all the emotions he'd kept carefully controlled in front of the Morettis. I match his ferocity, digging my nails into his shoulders, reminding him I'm here, I'm alive, I'm his.

His hands are everywhere, tearing at my nightgown until the silk shreds beneath his fingers. I don't care. Material things can be replaced; this moment between us can't.

Silvo flips me onto my stomach, his body covering mine like a shield. His lips trace a burning path down my spine while his fingers dig possessively into my hips.

"I need all of you tonight," he growls, voice rough with desire. He strokes the curve of my ass, his intention clear. "Let me have this."

I nod, breathless with want. "Yes."

"I want you," I whisper against his ear, arching my back to press myself against him. "Every part of me is yours, Silvo."

His breath catches. I feel his hesitation melt into hunger as his hands grip my hips tighter.

"You're sure?" he asks, his voice gravelly with desire.

I nod, face flushed with want. "I'm sure."

Silvo reaches for the bedside drawer, extracting a small bottle. The snap of the cap opening sends a shiver through me—anticipation mixed with nervous energy.

"Relax," he murmurs, spreading warm oil across his fingers. "I'll take care of you."

The first gentle pressure makes me gasp. Silvo's free hand strokes my lower back in soothing circles.

"All of you is mine," he says, his voice possessive yet tender. "Every inch, every breath."

His fingers work slowly, carefully, stretching and preparing me with a patience I didn't know he possessed. The initial discomfort gives way to a strange, building pleasure that makes my thighs tremble.

"That's it," he encourages when I press back against his hand. "You're perfect."

When his other hand reaches around to stroke between my legs, I nearly collapse. The dual sensations—his finger inside me, his expert touch on my clit—send sparks shooting up my spine.

"Silvo," I moan, no longer caring how desperate I sound. "Please..."

He increases the pressure, the rhythm perfectly synchronized. My body responds with a will of its own, rocking between his hands as tension coils tighter in my core.

"Come for me," he commands, curling his finger just right while his other hand works relentless circles. "Let me feel you."

The orgasm crashes through me without warning, intense and all-consuming. I cry out his name as my body pulses around his finger, the pleasure almost too much to bear.

Behind me, Silvo's breathing turns ragged. "You're ready," he says, his voice a low growl that sends shivers across my skin.

I glance over my shoulder to see him slicking lubricant over his cock, his eyes locked on my body with primal hunger. His length glistens in the dim light as he strokes himself.

"I need this," he groans, positioning himself. "Need to claim every part of you."

The blunt pressure against my entrance makes me gasp. My fingers clutch at the sheets as he presses forward, stretching me in a way I've never experienced before.

"Fuck, you're tight," he hisses. "So perfect for me."

I bite my lip as he pushes deeper, the burn of the stretch giving way to an unfamiliar fullness that makes my nerves sing.

"That's it," Silvo says, gripping my hips hard enough to bruise. "Take all of me, Carmela."

"Silvo," I whimper as he sinks fully inside, my body trembling with the intensity.

"You like being filled like this?" His words are filthy against my ear as he begins to move. "Like being fucked in your tight little ass by your husband?"

"Yes," I admit, the word escaping on a moan as he establishes a rhythm that leaves me breathless.

"Tell me who you belong to," he demands, reaching around to stroke between my legs again. "Say it."

"You," I gasp, pushing back against him. "I'm yours, Silvo—all of me."

His thrusts grow more intense, each one sending shock-waves of pleasure-pain through my body. The initial discomfort has given way to something primal and consuming—an intensity I never knew possible.

"You take my cock so well," Silvo growls, his fingers digging into my hips, positioning me exactly how he wants me. "So fucking tight around me."

I push back against him, meeting his thrusts with my own desperate movements. The fullness is overwhelming, forbidden in a way that makes my core clench with need. When his hand slides around to stroke my clit again, I nearly collapse face-first into the mattress.

"Oh god, Silvo," I gasp, my body trembling as the dual sensations build. "Don't stop—please don't stop."

His rhythm becomes relentless, perfectly timed with the circles he's drawing between my legs. The pressure builds impossibly, a coiling tension that threatens to shatter me completely.

"That's it," he rasps against my ear. "Come with my cock in this perfect ass. Show me how much you love it."

The orgasm crashes through me without warning—more intense than anything I've experienced before. My body clenches around him as waves of pleasure radiate outward, making me cry out his name in a broken sob.

Silvo groans deeply, his thrusts becoming erratic. "Fuck, I'm going to fill you up," he growls, his fingers digging harder into my flesh. "Take it all, Carmela."

I feel the hot pulse of him coming inside me, claiming this final part of me as his own. His body tenses against mine as he empties himself with a guttural moan.

After a moment of shared breathlessness, he pulls me back against his chest, still inside me.

"Push it out," he whispers roughly against my ear. "Show me what I've done to you."

I obey, feeling both dirty and desired as I do what he

asks. Silvo watches with dark, possessive eyes, his breath catching at the sight.

"Beautiful," he murmurs, finally collapsing beside me on the bed, pulling me into his arms.

Silvo gently turns me to face him, his calloused fingers tracing the curve of my cheek with surprising tenderness. The fierceness from moments ago has melted into something softer, more vulnerable.

"When Tartarov tried to get you..." He draws a shaky breath. "When you called and said men were coming for you—I've never been more terrified in my life."

I press my palm against his racing heart. "I'm here. I'm safe."

"Because you're smart," he says, pride mixing with the fear in his voice. "You saw the danger and got yourself and the others out. But Carmela—" His arms tighten around me. "I can't always be there to protect you. And that fucking terrifies me."

"Then it's a good thing I can protect myself," I whisper, kissing him softly. "We protect each other now. That's what partners do."

He kisses me deeply, pouring all his fear and relief and love into the connection between us. When we break apart, his eyes hold mine with an intensity that steals my breath.

"I love you," he murmurs—not a confession, but a reminder. A vow renewed.

"I love you too," I breathe back. "Always."

He pulls me closer, his hand sliding possessively over my hip to rest on my stomach. "When this is over—when Tartarov is gone and our families are truly safe—I want to fill you with my children. I want to see you round and glowing, carrying the future we're building together."

My heart swells at his words, at the tenderness in his

touch. "I want that too," I admit. "A family of our own. A future without fear."

"We'll have it," he promises, his lips brushing my forehead. "I swear to you, we'll have it."

As I drift toward sleep in his arms, I allow myself to believe him. To imagine a world where our children grow up knowing only peace, where the names De Luca and Moretti mean alliance rather than war.

Tomorrow will bring new challenges, new dangers. But tonight, wrapped in Silvo's embrace, I let myself dream of the future we're fighting for.

40

SILVO

My phone rings at 3 AM. Paulie's name flashes across the screen.

"This better be important," I growl, careful not to wake Carmela beside me.

"Boss, our guy inside the Tartarov operation just made contact. Alexei himself is coming to the docks tomorrow night to oversee a major weapons shipment. Military-grade stuff—assault rifles, grenade launchers, even some experimental tech."

I sit upright, instantly alert. "You're certain it's Alexei, not one of his lieutenants?"

"Confirmed by two separate sources. One of Nico's guys validated it too—they got the same intel."

"Call Nico. Tell him I need a meeting in two hours. Neutral ground."

By sunrise, Nico Moretti and I sit across from each other at an abandoned warehouse office. Despite the early hour, he looks as immaculate as ever in his tailored suit. Our decades-old rivalry is temporarily suspended by a common enemy.

"My people confirmed it," Nico says, sliding surveillance photos across the table. "Alexei's flying in from Brighton Beach specifically for this shipment. He doesn't trust his captains with this one."

"He's never exposed himself like this before," I note, examining the photos. "Makes me wonder what's on that boat that's worth the risk."

Nico leans forward. "Whatever it is, it's our opportunity. Take out Alexei, and his organization crumbles. The power vacuum will tear them apart from within."

"We'll need both our crews," I say, pulling out a map of the docks. "My men here and here—yours covering these approaches. We'll need snipers on these three buildings."

Nico nods, adding his own annotations. "We should coordinate through a single command channel. Less chance of friendly fire."

For an hour, we plot positions, escape routes, and contingencies. Two families that spent generations trying to destroy each other, now working in lethal harmony.

"Federico will coordinate with Maximo on the tactical frequency," I say, marking the final positions.

Under the cover of darkness, I lead my men toward the docks. The briny scent of the harbor mingles with the metallic smell of weaponry as we move in practiced formation. Nico and his crew approach from the opposite direction, their shadows gliding between shipping containers like ghosts.

Through my earpiece, Fed confirms all teams are in position. "Snipers have eyes on the perimeter. No sign of Alexei yet, but the shipment's arrived."

"Copy that," I mutter, signaling my men to advance. "Maintain radio discipline from here on."

We've been planning this for days—the perfect ambush. Take out Alexei Tartarov and cripple his organization in one surgical strike.

The massive cargo ship looms ahead, a skeleton crew visible on deck. Too few men for a shipment this valuable. Something feels off.

"Visual on target," comes Maximo's voice through the comm. "East entrance, moving with four bodyguards."

"All teams hold positions," I command. "Wait for my signal."

I peer through my scope at the figure entering the warehouse. The build matches Alexei, but his movement seems wrong. Too casual for a man overseeing a critical shipment.

Suddenly, my instincts scream danger.

"It's a setup! Fall back!" I shout into my comm, but it's too late.

Blinding spotlights flash on from all directions, pinning us in their glare. Heavy gunfire erupts from positions we'd already cleared. They've been waiting for us.

"Ambush!" I yell, diving behind a concrete barrier as bullets pepper the ground where I stood.

Screams and curses fill the comms as men from both families take hits. Marco goes down three feet from me, clutching his shoulder. Lorenzo, my most experienced captain, collapses with a spray of blood from his chest.

Through the chaos, I spot Nico pinned down behind a forklift, two of his bodyguards already motionless beside him.

"They knew we were coming," Fed shouts, returning fire as he drags a wounded soldier to cover. "They've got mounted guns on the containers!"

The air fills with the deafening rattle of automatic weapons as Tartarov's men pour devastating fire into our position. We're caught in the open, outgunned and surrounded.

I spot a shooter with a laser sight tracking toward Nico's position. Without thinking, I sprint through the hail of bullets.

"Nico, down!" I bellow, launching myself across the open space.

The bullet meant for Nico's head tears through my shoulder instead. White-hot pain explodes through my body as I crash into him, both of us tumbling behind a stack of crates. Blood soaks my shirt, but adrenaline keeps the worst of the pain at bay.

"What the hell are you doing?" Nico gasps, eyes wide with shock.

"Saving your ungrateful ass," I grunt, pressing my hand against the wound. "Our families die if both of us don't make it out of here."

A grenade lands five feet away. I grab Nico's collar and heave us both behind a concrete pillar as the explosion rocks the warehouse, showering us with debris.

"Fed!" I shout into my comm. "Emergency extraction, now!"

"On it!" Fed's voice crackles through static.

Nico pulls out his sidearm and returns fire, covering us as we crawl toward the east exit. "My men are cut to pieces out there."

"So are mine," I say through gritted teeth. "But we're no good to them dead."

A black SUV crashes through the warehouse doors, Federico behind the wheel. Maximo provides covering fire from the passenger seat.

"Move!" I push Nico toward the vehicle, firing blindly behind us.

We dive into the backseat as bullets shatter the rear window. Fed floors it, tires screeching as we burst through a chain-link fence.

"Tartarov?" I demand, pressing a rag against my bleeding shoulder.

"Gone," Maximo spits. "Disappeared during the first volley."

Nico's eyes meet mine across the blood-smeared leather seat. "You took that bullet for me."

"Yeah, well, don't read too much into it," I mutter.

A ghost of a smile touches his lips. "Three generations of hatred, and you risked your life for mine."

"Our war ends with Tartarov," I say firmly. "Not with either of us in a body bag."

Nico extends his hand. I clasp it, feeling something shift between us—not friendship, not yet, but something more profound than mere alliance.

The SUV speeds through the night, tires screeching against wet pavement. Blood—mine and others'—stains the leather seats. No one speaks. The weight of our failure hangs heavy in the cramped space.

"Nine dead," Fed finally says, breaking the silence. "Four ours, five Morettis. Plus a dozen wounded."

I press my hand against my throbbing shoulder. Maximo had examined it during our escape, pouring vodka over the wound and wrapping it with a torn shirt. Just a graze, but deep enough to leave a new scar.

"He knew we were coming," I mutter, watching the city lights blur past my window. "Someone's feeding Tartarov information."

"Another leak," I mutter, watching the city lights blur

past my window. "Someone's feeding Tartarov information. Again."

Nico's face hardens in the dim light. "We rooted out our last one two months ago. I thought we were clean."

"So did I." The unspoken question hangs between us—how deep does this go? How many times can we purge our ranks before we run out of men we trust? This fragile alliance has nearly cost us everything tonight, and the enemy is apparently still inside both our walls.

"Third time someone's sold us out," I say grimly. "Tartarov has deep pockets and a long reach."

We pull up outside the estate, armed guards immediately surrounding the vehicle. Maximo climbs out first, scanning the perimeter before nodding to his father.

Nico pauses before exiting, his eyes meeting mine. "Why'd you do it, De Luca? Take that bullet?"

"Because Tartarov wins if either of us dies," I answer flatly.

"You sure that's the only reason?"

I don't answer. I'm not sure myself.

Nico nods almost imperceptibly, then disappears into the night surrounded by his men.

Twenty minutes later, we pull into my driveway. The house lights are on—Carmela's waiting. My body aches with each movement as I drag myself from the car.

"Get some rest," I tell Fed. "Tomorrow will be worse."

I find Carmela in our bedroom, pacing. When she sees me, the blood staining my shirt, she freezes.

"It's not as bad as it looks," I say.

She crosses the room in an instant, her fingers carefully peeling back the makeshift bandage. "You promised me you'd be careful."

"I was. That's why it's just a graze."

Her eyes search mine, finding the truth I can't hide. How close I came to not returning at all.

"We were ambushed," I admit. "Tartarov knew we were coming."

Carmela pulls me close, careful of my injury. Against her warmth, the shaking I've been suppressing finally breaks free.

Carmela's hands tremble as she inspects my wound. Her fingers, usually so steady, brush against my skin with a gentleness that almost breaks me. The fear in her eyes cuts deeper than any bullet could.

"I thought—" Her voice catches. "When Federico called, he just said there was an ambush. He didn't know if —" She can't finish the sentence.

I cup her face with my good hand, wiping away a tear with my thumb. "Hey, I'm right here."

"This time." Her voice hardens, but her eyes remain vulnerable. "What about next time? Or the time after that?" She presses her forehead against my chest, careful to avoid my injured shoulder. "I can't lose you, Silvo. I can't."

The words hang between us. Three months ago, they would have surprised me—an arranged wife caring whether I lived or died. Now, they're the most natural thing in the world.

"Look at me," I whisper.

When she raises her gaze to mine, I see everything I never knew I wanted—fear and love and fierce determination all mixed together. This woman, forced into my life against her will, has somehow become my reason to return home alive.

"You won't lose me," I promise, knowing it's a vow I might not be able to keep.

I lean down and capture her lips with mine. The kiss

starts gentle, almost hesitant, but quickly deepens into something desperate and hungry. She responds immediately, her body molding against mine as if trying to prove to herself I'm really here, whole and alive.

For one perfect moment, there are no rival families, no ambushes, no Tartarovs waiting to destroy everything we've built. Just Carmela and me, finding shelter in each other while the world burns around us.

41

CARMELA

My hands shake as I clean Silvo's wound. The bullet grazed his shoulder, leaving an angry red path across his skin. He winces when I apply the antiseptic, but doesn't pull away.

"Sorry," I whisper, trying to be gentler.

"Don't be. I've had worse." His voice is steady, but I can see the pain in his eyes—not just physical pain.

The house bustles with activity below us. After the ambush, both families agreed to consolidate forces at our estate after counting their losses and regrouping. The Morettis will arrive soon for an emergency council.

"Nine men," Silvo murmurs, staring at nothing. "Nine families that won't see their fathers, brothers, sons come home."

I say nothing as I begin wrapping his shoulder in gauze. What could I possibly say to make this better?

The bedroom door swings open, and Isabella appears, tablet in hand. "Security teams are in position," she reports, all business despite the late hour. "I've coordinated with

Valeria on the Moretti protocols. They'll be here in twenty minutes."

From the hallway behind her, I hear Sophia's laugh mixing with Federico's voice. Shortly after, they appear in the doorway.

"Someone's got to keep morale up around here," Fed says, his rakish grin not quite reaching his eyes. Sophia stands close beside him, her hand brushing his.

"Fed," Sophia chides, but there's affection in her tone. "Now's hardly the time for jokes."

"On the contrary," Fed counters, his smile faltering for just a moment. "After what we saw tonight? Now's exactly the time."

I notice how Sophia's fingers intertwine with his, how she leans slightly into his space. Their connection seems to have deepened tonight. Fed's usual charm is there, but beneath it, I see something raw. Sophia must see it too, because she squeezes his hand when she thinks no one's looking.

"The Tartarovs knew exactly where we'd be," Isabella says, redirecting us. "Every exit point, every sniper position."

Silvo nods grimly as I finish securing his bandage. "We have a leak. Maybe in both families."

The weight of his words settles over the room. Trust, already fragile between longtime enemies, now seems impossible.

"At least last night proved one thing," I say, finishing with Silvo's bandage. "The Tartarovs can't drive us apart anymore. Not after you took a bullet for Nico."

Fed flops into the armchair by the window. "Nothing brings enemies together like a common enemy trying to kill them both."

"Very philosophical, brother," Silvo says dryly.

"I have my moments." Fed winks at Sophia, who rolls her eyes but can't hide her smile.

Isabella checks her watch. "The Morettis will be here any minute. I need to arrange refreshments." She heads for the door.

"Need help?" Sophia offers.

"I've got it. You stay and take care of these hotheads." Isabella waves her hand dismissively and disappears down the hallway.

When her footsteps fade, I perch on the edge of the bed beside Silvo. The idea that's been forming in my mind since the charity gala suddenly feels urgent.

"I've been thinking," I start, my voice low. "About strengthening the alliance between our families."

"We're working on it," Silvo says, reaching for his shirt. "Last night was a disaster, but—"

"No, I mean something more permanent." I take a deep breath. "Something like what we have."

Fed raises an eyebrow. "An arranged marriage? Between who?"

"Isabella and Maximo."

The room goes silent. Then Silvo laughs—a short, sharp sound.

"You're crazy." He shakes his head. "They hate each other."

"Do they?" I challenge. "Or do they remind you of us? The way we were at first?"

Sophia sits up straighter. "Carmela might be onto something. I've seen how they look at each other when they think no one's watching."

"It's not going to happen," Silvo says firmly. "Isabella would never agree to it."

"We didn't exactly agree to our arrangement either," I remind him, touching his uninjured shoulder. "But look at us now."

Fed drums his fingers on the armrest. "Maximo is a loose cannon and a complete asshole. I don't want him anywhere near my sister."

Silvo shrugs. "It's not the worst idea I've ever heard. But Isabella's too stubborn to admit she feels anything for that Moretti punk."

"You've got to be kidding. Why the fuck would you even consider Isabella marrying that piece of shit?" Fed asks.

Silvo's jaw clenches. "Because Carmela has a good point. There's no better alliance than uniting our families through marriage." He tilts his head. "Alternatively we could always have you marry Valeria."

Fed pales and shakes his head. "No thank you. I'm not marrying a Moretti."

"I'm not saying it would happen right away," I press. "I'm saying we plant the seed. They're already drawn to each other—anyone with eyes can see that. The way she flushed when he grabbed her wrist at the gala? The way he watches her when she enters a room? It's already happening whether we acknowledge it or not."

Sophia nods. "The tension between them is practically visible."

"An alliance sealed with blood," Silvo muses, wincing as he pulls his shirt over his bandaged shoulder. "Our fathers might actually consider it, especially after tonight's bloodbath."

I feel a surge of hope. Maybe something good could come from all this horror. "It would unify our families permanently, just like us."

The door swings open, and Isabella reappears, her

expression tense. "They're here. The Morettis just pulled up —Nico, Maximo, and Valeria. Dad's in the study waiting."

My pulse quickens. Antonio rarely attends tactical meetings—meaning the stakes have escalated beyond what I even imagined. I touch Silvo's arm. "This is perfect timing. With Antonio here, we could—"

"Not now, Carmela," Silvo cuts me off, his voice gentle but firm. "Let's focus on the immediate threat first."

I bite my lip, frustrated. With both families under one roof, Antonio present, and emotions raw from shared loss, the timing couldn't be more perfect for proposing to bind our families together. But I see the determination in Silvo's eyes and the exhaustion lining his face.

"We'll talk about it later," he promises, squeezing my hand.

I nod, swallowing my disappointment. "Later."

As we follow Isabella downstairs, I can't help feeling we're missing a crucial opportunity. But I've learned when to push and when to trust my husband's judgment. After last night, with nine men dead and a traitor in our midst, I'll follow his lead.

42

SILVO

Three weeks of silence from Tartarov feels worse than daily gunfire. I pace my office, checking surveillance feeds for the tenth time today. Nine good men gone, and what? The Russians vanished like smoke.

"Anything?" Carmela asks from the doorway, her face drawn with the same tension we've all been carrying.

"Nothing." I slam my palm against the desk. "It's the waiting that kills you."

She crosses to me, resting her head against my chest. My shoulder's almost healed, but the memory of that night at the docks haunts me—how close I came to leaving her a widow. How close Nico came to death beside me.

"The meeting starts in twenty minutes," she reminds me.

I nod, kissing the top of her head. "Let's get this over with."

The conference room feels smaller with both families squeezed around the table. Nico sits opposite me, dark circles under his eyes matching mine. Tartarov's silence has been harder on our businesses than his attacks—shipments delayed, territories undermanned, everyone jumping at shadows.

"We can't keep operating like this," Fed says, spreading maps across the table. "We're bleeding money maintaining double security details."

"You think we don't know that?" Maximo snaps, leaning forward. "My men haven't had a day off in three weeks."

Isabella rolls her eyes. "Poor babies. Maybe they should learn to multitask like our crews."

"Rich coming from someone who's never worked a day in her life," Maximo retorts.

Isabella's cheeks flush. "You don't know the first thing about me."

"I know enough," he says, eyes sliding down her body.

"Enough," I interrupt, but the electricity between them is unmistakable—like watching Carmela and me months ago, hatred barely masking something else entirely.

A realization hits me like a thunderbolt. I glance at Carmela, who gives me a subtle nod—she's been right all along.

I clear my throat. "Nico, could I speak with you and my father privately?"

We step into the hallway, closing the door on the continuing tension.

"What is it?" Nico asks, guard still up despite weeks of alliance.

I take a calculated risk. "I have a proposition that could permanently unite our families."

My father clears his throat. "And you didn't think to run this proposition by me first?"

I clench my jaw. "Trust me."

His eyes narrow. "I'm listening."

"Maximo and Isabella. An arranged marriage—like mine with Carmela."

Nico's eyebrows shoot up, and a deep chuckle rumbles from his chest. It's the first genuine laugh I've heard from him since this mess began.

"Those two?" He shakes his head in disbelief. "They bicker like cats and dogs. Maximo can barely be in the same room with her without starting an argument. That's a cruel option, even by our standards."

"I agree, it's pretty farfetched, Silvo," my father states.

I lean against the wall, my shoulder still tender. "Carmela and I were the same way. She hated me when we married—thought I'd tricked her when we met at a club." I can't help the small smile that forms. "Now? She's the first person I want to see every morning and the last one I want to hold at night. What began as business became... everything."

Nico studies me, and there's a shift in his expression. I've never shared anything this personal with him before, and I can sense he's weighing my sincerity.

"Look at them in there," I continue, nodding toward the conference room. "That's not just hatred. That's chemistry masquerading as contempt. They're circling each other like wolves."

Through the glass panel, we can see Isabella gesturing animatedly while Maximo leans forward, his face intense as he argues back. Yet neither walks away.

Nico and my father follow my gaze, watching them for a long moment. "My boy needs someone who won't bow to his every whim. Someone with fire." He taps his fingers against his chin, considering. "And the alliance would be... substantial."

"Permanent," I correct. "Family."

He nods slowly. "It's a good idea, Silvo. But we can't force them. Let's run it by them together." He rubs his jaw thoughtfully. "See how they react when it's not just another order."

"Agreed," father says, and him and Nico exchange a nod before stepping back into the room.

The moment we enter the conference room, the arguing stops. Something in my expression must betray me because Carmela sits up straighter, a small smile playing at her lips.

"We have a proposal," Nico announces, his voice commanding immediate attention. "One that would cement our alliance permanently."

I scan the faces around the table, lingering on my sister. She's smart enough to sense what's coming.

"The De Lucas and the Morettis have been enemies too long," Nico continues. "We propose uniting our families through marriage—Isabella De Luca and my son, Maximo Moretti."

Isabella's jaw drops. "No freaking way." She stands abruptly, her chair scraping against the floor. "You can't be serious."

To my surprise, Maximo's expression shifts from shock to something like delight. A slow, predatory grin spreads across his face as he leans back in his chair, eyes roving over Isabella.

"I don't know," he drawls. "I think I could get used to having you in my bed every night, *bella*." His voice drops lower. "Imagine all the fun we could have... fighting and making up."

Isabella's cheeks flush crimson. "You're disgusting," she hisses, but I don't miss how her breath catches.

"That blush suggests otherwise," Maximo continues,

standing to approach her. "You've been watching me since day one. Don't think I haven't noticed."

"I'd rather marry a rattlesnake," Isabella retorts, but she doesn't back away as he steps closer.

"At least a rattlesnake warns you before it strikes," he murmurs. "I prefer to... surprise."

The tension between them crackles like a live wire. Isabella's blush deepens, and though her mouth opens for another retort, no words come out.

Isabella looks like she might actually strike Maximo, and I've seen my sister angry enough times to know she's not above it.

Nico steps forward, his hands raised in a placating gesture. "Isabella, please. This isn't just about two people. This is about two families." His voice softens, surprising me with its gentleness. "Think of what we could build together—real peace after three generations of bloodshed."

My father nods solemnly beside him. "The feud ends with us. Here. Now."

Isabella's eyes dart between them, then to Carmela, who gives her a sympathetic smile. My wife understands better than anyone what it means to be the bridge between families.

"So I'm supposed to take one for the team?" Isabella throws her hands up. "Be chained to him forever?" She glares at Maximo with such intensity I'm shocked he doesn't burst into flames.

Maximo, the smug bastard, seems to be enjoying every second of her discomfort. He leans against the conference table, muscled arms crossed over his chest.

"I don't mind being chained to you, *bella*," he purrs, eyes traveling down her body and back up again. "We could make it fun. I even have the cuffs already."

Isabella makes a strangled sound of outrage while Fed coughs to hide a laugh. I shoot my brother a warning look, but it's too late—Maximo caught it, and his grin only widens.

"And that concludes today's business," my father announces, tapping the table. "We'll reconvene tomorrow to finalize our strategy against Tartarov."

The tension lingers as everyone files out, murmuring in small groups. As expected, Isabella storms toward me, green eyes blazing.

"A word," she hisses, grabbing my arm and pulling me into the adjacent study.

The door slams behind us. "What the hell, Silvo? You couldn't warn me before offering me up like a sacrificial lamb?"

I lean against the desk, giving her space to vent. "We didn't decide anything. It's a suggestion that deserves serious consideration."

"Consideration?" She laughs bitterly. "You watched him humiliate me in there with those disgusting comments!"

"I saw a man who couldn't take his eyes off you," I counter. "The same way I looked at Carmela when we first met."

Isabella crosses her arms. "That's different."

"Is it?" I step closer. "Being a De Luca means considering sacrifices for the greater good of the family. Always has."

"So I'm supposed to sacrifice my happiness?"

"I married Carmela because our family needed strength and power from the Bianchi alliance. We needed to expand our reach in California." I soften my voice. "I resented it at first. Thought I'd be trapped in a loveless arrangement forever."

Isabella's anger falters. "And now?"

"Now I can't imagine my life without her." I take my sister's hands, feeling the same protectiveness I've had since she was born. "I found love in the last place I expected. You might too."

She stares at our joined hands. "And if I don't?"

"Then we'll find another way," I promise. "But at least think about it. For all of us."

Isabella's shoulders drop slightly, the fire in her eyes dimming to embers rather than flames. She tugs her hand away from mine, but gently now.

"I'll... think about it," she concedes, tucking a strand of hair behind her ear. "But I'm not promising anything, Silvo. That man is insufferable."

I bite back a smile. "So was I, according to Carmela."

"That's different. You were just brooding and controlling. Maximo is..." She waves her hand, searching for words.

"Cocky? Arrogant?"

Isabella rolls her eyes, but a reluctant smile tugs at her lips. "All of the above, and worse."

"Just consider it," I squeeze her shoulder. "For the family, yes, but for yourself too. Maybe there's more to him than meets the eye."

"Fine." She straightens her blouse. "I'll talk to him. Once. In public." She points a warning finger at me. "And if he makes one inappropriate comment, the deal's off."

As Isabella leaves, I remain in the study, staring out at the Philadelphia skyline. For the first time since bullets started flying at those docks, a wave of genuine optimism washes over me.

If we pull this off—if the Morettis and De Lucas truly become family—Philly will never be the same. Our combined territories would stretch from the Delaware River to the western suburbs. Our manpower would double. Our influence would reach into sectors neither family could touch alone.

Most importantly, Alexei Tartarov wouldn't stand a chance against a united front. The Russians might have resources, but they don't have what we're building here—blood ties, history, family bonds that run deeper than business.

Two of the oldest Italian families in Philadelphia united after three generations of bloodshed. The thought feels like something from a dream.

43

EPILOGUE

CARMELA

I stare at the calendar app on my phone for the fifth time today, counting the days since my last period. Six weeks. Six weeks and nothing.

The knowledge sits heavy in my stomach—or maybe that's morning sickness.

I haven't been able to look at eggs without gagging for days now.

From downstairs, Isabella's voice rises in another argument with Maximo.

Two months of engagement haven't softened their edges. If anything, wedding planning has given them even more to fight about.

"That's not where the seating chart goes, you insufferable man!" Isabella's voice carries up the stairwell.

"It's a piece of paper, *bella*. Does it matter where I put it?" Maximo's deep laugh follows.

"When it determines whether your uncle sits next to my aunt, whom he insulted at the engagement party, yes, it matters!"

I smile despite my nerves. For all their shouting about

flower arrangements and guest lists, I've caught them in the garden at night, her back against a tree, his hands tangled in her hair. They're fooling no one but themselves.

The pregnancy test burns a hole in my purse where I've kept it hidden for three days. I've been waiting for the perfect moment—when Silvo is occupied with business and the house staff are changing shifts. That moment is now.

I lock the bathroom door and unwrap the test with trembling fingers. Following the instructions, I set the timer on my phone for three minutes and place the test on the counter.

Three minutes feels like three hours. I pace the marble floor, my mind racing with possibilities. A baby. Our baby. Silvo's heir. A child born into this precarious peace we've built through blood and marriage.

The Tartarov threat has gone quiet—too quiet. Alexei hasn't made a move since the ambush, but Silvo and Nico remain vigilant. Our families operate in an uneasy alliance, strengthened by Isabella and Maximo's marriage but still fragile.

Is this the world I want to bring a child into?

The timer chimes softly. I freeze, suddenly afraid to look.

I force myself to take those three steps to the counter. My heart pounds in my chest as I reach for the test.

Two pink lines.

Positive.

I clutch the test to my chest as tears spring to my eyes. A child—our child—grows inside me. The joy crashes over me in waves, stealing my breath. This baby is the physical manifestation of what Silvo and I have built together, a love forged from arrangement and obligation into something fierce and real.

But fear follows close behind. Our world drips with danger. Just weeks ago, bullets flew and blood spilled. The Tartarov threat may have subsided, but for how long? The legacy of violence stretches back generations. What right do I have to bring an innocent life into this?

Yet hope burns brighter. This child could be something new—a De Luca born into peace rather than vendetta. A symbol of unity where there was once only division.

I find Silvo in his study, bent over maps and reports. When I enter, he looks up, concern immediately crossing his face.

"Sweetheart, what's wrong?"

I place the test on his desk. "I'm pregnant."

His eyes widen, darting between my face and the test. For a heartbeat, he's frozen, processing.

Then he stands so quickly his chair crashes backward. In two strides, he's around the desk, lifting me into his arms, spinning me in circles.

"A baby?" His voice cracks. "Our baby?"

I nod, tears streaming freely now.

He sets me down gently, his hands framing my face. "I never thought... I never imagined I could be this happy."

"You're not worried?" I whisper.

"Terrified," he admits, pressing his forehead to mine. "But it's you and me now. We'll protect our child together. And with the alliance between our families, we're in a safer position than we've been in years."

His lips find mine, soft and reverent. The kiss deepens, and I melt into him.

"I love you," he murmurs against my mouth. "Both of you."

He lifts me into his arms, carrying me to our bedroom. His touch is different tonight—tender, gentle, almost worshipful. Each caress, each kiss feels like a promise.

Silvo lays me gently on our bed, his eyes never leaving mine. The tenderness in his gaze makes my heart swell. His fingertips trace my face as if memorizing every curve and contour.

"My wife," he whispers, "the mother of my child."

I pull him down, claiming his mouth with mine. Our tongues dance as his hands slide beneath my blouse, caressing the sensitive skin of my stomach where our child grows.

"I need you," I breathe against his lips.

He undresses me slowly, reverently, pressing kisses to each newly exposed inch of skin. When I'm naked beneath him, he takes a moment to simply look at me, his eyes darkening with desire.

"You're so beautiful it hurts," he says, his voice rough.

I reach for him, unbuttoning his shirt, pushing it from his shoulders to reveal the tattooed expanse of his chest. My fingers trace the inked patterns as I've done countless times before, but tonight feels different—sacred somehow.

When he enters me, it's with exquisite care. I gasp, arching beneath him as he fills me completely. He moves slowly at first, his forehead pressed to mine, our breaths mingling.

"I love you," I whisper, clinging to his shoulders. "God, Silvo, I love you so much."

His pace increases, his powerful body moving against mine. One hand slides between us, his thumb finding that sensitive bundle of nerves, and I cry out.

"That's it," he murmurs. "Let me hear you, *amore mio*."

Pleasure builds inside me, wave upon wave. His thrusts

become more urgent, more desperate. I wrap my legs around his waist, drawing him deeper.

"You're mine," he growls. "Forever mine."

"Yes," I gasp. "Yours. Always yours."

My release crashes over me like a tidal wave. I call his name as my body pulses around him. He follows moments later, my name a prayer on his lips as he spills inside me.

We remain joined, our bodies slick with sweat, hearts pounding in tandem. His hand finds my stomach again, splaying protectively over our growing child.

I WAKE the next morning to find Silvo watching me, his eyes soft in the early light. His hand still rests protectively over my stomach, as if he's already guarding our child.

"Good morning," I whisper.

He places a gentle kiss on my forehead. "Morning, beautiful."

We lie together in comfortable silence, savoring this quiet moment of peace. Outside these walls, our world remains complicated—families once at war now cautiously allied, a Russian threat currently silent but not forgotten. But here, in the warmth of our bed, there is only us and the miracle growing inside me.

"What are you thinking about?" Silvo asks, his fingers tracing lazy circles on my skin.

"Everything. Nothing. How strange life is." I turn to face him fully. "At first, I hated you. Now I'm carrying your child and can't imagine my life without you."

His smile reaches his eyes, crinkling the corners. "From arrangement to love. Who would have thought?"

"I keep wondering when Alexei will make another move," I admit. "This silence makes me nervous."

Silvo's expression sobers. "The Tartarovs are calculating. They're watching, waiting. But we're ready for them—both families united now."

"Do you think our baby will ever know a world without all this?" I place my hand over his on my stomach.

"I'm going to make damn sure of it." His voice carries the weight of a vow. "This child will be born into something new, something better than what we had."

I believe him. Despite everything—the danger, the history, the blood that's been spilled—I believe in the future we're building together. Our families united, old vendettas buried, a new generation on the way.

"I love you, Silvo De Luca," I whisper, my voice thick with emotion. "With everything I am."

"And I love you, Carmela De Luca." He kisses me deeply, his lips promising a lifetime of tomorrows. "I love both of you."

ALSO BY BIANCA COLE

Beautiful Monsters Series

Stalk Me: A Dark Mafia Romance

Shatter Me: A Dark Mafia Romance

Chain Me: A Dark Captive Mafia Romance

Hunt Me: A Dark Mafia Romance

Once Upon a Villain

Pride: A Dark Arranged Marriage Romance

Hook: A Dark Forced Marriage Romance

Wicked: A Dark Forbidden Mafia Romance

Unhinged: A Dark Captive Cartel Romance

Beast: A Dark Billionaire Romance

Wolf: A Dark Primal Mafia Romance

The Syndicate Academy

Sinister Games: A Dark Forbidden Mafia Academy Romance

Cruel Bully: A Dark Mafia Academy Romance

Sinful Lessons: A Dark Forbidden Mafia Academy Romance

Twisted Games: A Dark Enemies to Lovers Forbidden Mafia Academy Romance

Chicago Mafia Dons

Cruel Savior: A Dark Forbidden Mafia Romance

Violent Leader: A Dark Enemies to Lovers Captive Mafia Romance

Evil Prince: A Dark Arranged Marriage Romance

Brutal Daddy: A Dark Captive Mafia Romance

Cruel Vows: A Dark Forced Marriage Mafia Romance

Dirty Secret: A Dark Enemies to Lovers Mafia Romance

Dark Crown: A Dark Arranged Marriage Romance

Boston Mafia Dons Series

Empire of Carnage: A Dark Captive Mafia Romance

Cruel Obsession: A Dark Mafia Arranged Marriage Romance

Savage Bidder: A Dark Captive Mafia Romance

Ruthless King: A Dark Forbidden Mafia Romance

Vicious Bond: A Dark Brother's Best Friend Mafia Romance

Wicked Captor: A Dark Captive Mafia Romance

New York Mafia DonsSeries

Her Irish Daddy: A Dark Mafia Romance

Her Russian Daddy: A Dark Mafia Romance

Her Italian Daddy: A Dark Mafia Romance

Her Cartel Daddy: A Dark Mafia Romance

Romano Mafia Brother's Series

Her Mafia Daddy: A Dark Daddy Romance

Her Mafia Boss: A Dark Romance

Her Mafia King: A Dark Romance

New York Brotherhood Series

Bought: A Dark Mafia Romance

Captured: A Dark Mafia Romance

Claimed: A Dark Mafia Romance

Bound: A Dark Mafia Romance

Taken: A Dark Mafia Romance

Forbidden Desires Series

Bryson: An Enemies to Lovers Office Romance

Logan: A First Time Professor And Student Romance

Ryder: An Enemies to Lovers Office Romance

Dr. Fox: A Forbidden Romance

Royally Mated Series

Her Faerie King: A Faerie Royalty Paranormal Romance

Her Alpha King: A Royal Wolf Shifter Paranormal Romance

Her Dragon King: A Dragon Shifter Paranormal Romance

Her Vampire King: A Dark Vampire Romance

DARKER PEN NAME

SELENA WINTERS

Did you know that I also release darker contemporary romance, particularly masked man romance and stalker romance under my other pen name, Selena Winters?

The Hollow's Hunt Series

Unmasking Darkness: A Dark Romance

Kindred Kings: A Dark MM Romance

Double Trouble: A Dark Romance

Blackwood Brothers

Haunted: A Dark Primal Romance

Doomed: A Dark Primal Romance

Cursed: A Dark Primal Romance

Stalked: A Dark Primal Romance

Carnival Series

Carnival Nightmare: A Dark Stalker Romance

Carnival Obsession: A Dark Stalker Romance

Carnival Monster: A Dark Serial Killer Romance

Carnival Stalker: A Dark Stalker Romance

Carnival Master: A Dark Romance

Carnival Mayhem: A Dark Romance

Carnival Shadows: A Dark Stalker Romance

Convicts Series

Stranded: A Dark Romance novella

Salvation: A Dark Stalker Romance

Carjacked: A Dark Hitchhiker Romance

Hunted: A Dark Romance

Imprisoned: A Dark Prison Romance

Valentines Duet

My Bloody Valentine: A Dark Serial Killer Romance

My Savage Valentine: A Dark Serial Killer Romance

Standalones

Game Over: A Dark Stalker Romance

Forbidden Harvest: A Dark Taboo Romance

Grave Intentions: A Dark Taboo Romance

Silent Stalker: A Dark Serial Killer Romance

Welcome to Carnage: A Dark Romance Novella

ABOUT THE AUTHOR

I love to write stories about over the top alpha bad boys who have heart beneath it all, fiery heroines, and happily-ever-after endings with heart and heat. My stories have twists and turns that will keep you flipping the pages and heat to set your Kindle on fire.

For as long as I can remember, I've been a sucker for a good romance story. I've always loved to read. Suddenly, I realized why not combine my love of two things, books and romance?

My love of writing has grown over the past four years, and I now publish exclusively on Amazon, weaving stories about dirty mafia bad boys and the women they fall head over heels for.

If you enjoyed this book, please follow me on Amazon, Bookbub, or any of the below social media platforms for alerts when more books are released.

Printed in Dunstable, United Kingdom

81531629R00190